If It All Fades Away

Myra King

Edited by
Robin Fuller

Woodland Harmony Publishing

Copyright © 2025 by Myra King

All rights reserved.

No part of this book may be reproduced in any form or by any electronic or mechanical means, including information storage and retrieval systems, without written permission from the author, except for the use of brief quotations in a book review.

ISBNs: 979-8-9941495-0-8 (paperback), 979-8-9941495-1-5 (ebook)

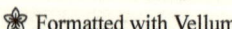 Formatted with Vellum

For Christine and Kyle

CONTENT WARNING

This book contains physical and verbal abuse, sexual content, bullying, underage drinking, and attempted assault, and is suitable for readers ages 16+.

Chapter 1

Personal Foul

Blair was used to being in the vice principal's office. She had been here many times before for getting into trouble. Girls in tears would report her, and just like clockwork, she would be summoned to receive her punishment. The boys, of course, kept it to themselves whenever they got into verbal altercations with her, too embarrassed to admit that a girl had bested them.

Today, however, she was here because she had told Mrs. Dakota to "go get some dick" instead of bothering Blair about why she didn't turn in last week's paper. The whole classroom laughed. It wouldn't have been so bad if she hadn't just gotten out of detention for skipping class.

Sitting slouched in a stiff chair, waiting for the vice principal to get off a phone call, Blair was mindlessly picking at a hangnail when the door to her right swung open, startling her. The entrance of a dark-haired boy washed away the library-like energy of the room. He was tall with broad shoulders, a backpack hanging off one shoulder. He paid her no attention as he approached the secretary's counter.

"Oh, you must be Andrew!" Mrs. Welsh chirped. "I've

got your class schedule right here, and..." She rose from her swivel chair. "I also have the AP Biology textbook you'll need."

Blair found herself slowly sitting up straight as the boy placed his backpack on the floor, slipping the thick textbook into its mouth. She tugged at the hem of her plaid skirt, suddenly feeling dry and itchy in her Catholic school uniform. Andrew was attractive—magnetic, even—and Blair wanted to get his attention, but wasn't sure how.

The secretary glanced at the wall clock as he stood up straight again. "Come on. I'll give you a quick tour of the building, and by that time, it should be lunch."

Mrs. Welsh started to make her way around the cubicle area. The boy turned slightly to make way for her.

"You stay right there." She pointed sternly at Blair near the door. "Mr. Davis is expecting you, so no funny business, you hear me?"

Blair glared up at her like an angry dog as Mrs. Welsh exited the room first. She realized she was still glaring as Andrew walked out. He finally looked at her with an almost indiscernible expression. Almost. Except Blair was pleased to see, somewhere in his eyes, a curiosity about what exactly she could have done and what type of person she must be, that she had to be warned to stay put.

A self-satisfied smirk crept across Blair's face as the door clicked shut. The room was suddenly cooler in temperature again, and just as tranquil as before the boy entered.

The vice principal's door finally opened.

"You can come in now, Blair."

She swallowed, her smirk melting away as she stood up and made her way to the door.

* * *

"Let's go through this again," Mr. Davis said. "She asked you why you didn't turn in your paper, and you said what, now?"

"I told her to 'go get some dick,'" Blair replied nonchalantly.

Mr. Davis leaned back in his chair and sighed, pinching the bridge of his nose. "How hard is it for you to just ... behave for once?"

Blair shrugged.

"I mean, you were *just* in here for detention, and now here you are again."

Silence.

"You know I could call your parents," Mr. Davis said in a low voice.

Blair's heart sank. "No... Please don't."

"I was technically supposed to call them after you punched Bentley Hudson in the face."

Two months prior, Blair had been in gym class playing basketball when Bentley Hudson snapped her exposed bra strap. Embarrassed and furious that he had penetrated her calm demeanor after weeks of little taunts, she had punched him in the jaw, knocking him to the floor.

Blair cried to Mr. Davis and begged him not to call her parents. He had never seen her like that and nervously agreed, too uncomfortable to ask the deeper questions. She would have to serve her three-day suspension outside of school, which she would do by going to the local library, instead of staying at home, where her parents would know.

"Please don't call them, Mr. Davis," Blair begged once more. "I promise I'll do my paper and turn it in. And I'll apologize to Mrs. Dakota."

"Okay," he said. "But consider this a stern warning." He pointed his finger at her.

"Yes, sir."

Chapter 2

Butterflies

Once outside of Mr. Davis's office, Blair heaved a sigh of relief.

Like butterflies in her stomach, a strange sensation compelled her to get to the lunchroom as quickly as possible. Arriving outside the cafeteria, she tossed her backpack onto a mountain of other backpacks and went down the hallway to the lunch line.

Just as she was advancing, she heard a familiar cackling behind her. She audibly groaned, then straightened her posture, readying herself.

"Hey, B3, I heard you were sucking Mr. Davis again to get off. Heh, get it? *Get off?*"

Hudson and his two main cronies had started calling her "B3" for "Ball-Busting Bitch" after the punching incident.

"Correction: I suck him and then fuck him, Hudson," Blair said flatly, too annoyed to even bother to look back.

Blair sighed as Hudson and his friends snickered. This was their daily routine in the lunch line. The boys would poke and prod her, and she indulged them with dirty talk to prevent them from further bullying her. She knew it turned them on, and she would much rather them be focused on the swelling in their pants than on her specifically—her hair, her clothes, how she smelled, what she ate, whatever.

"What's his favorite position?" one of them asked.

"I bet you let him do anal," the other chimed in.

"How many times do I have to tell you?" Blair raised her voice. "I screw him right in his desk chair and bounce on his big, fat, hard—"

She turned to continue her particularly vulgar tirade, wanting to get to the punch line sooner today, only to see Andrew standing behind Hudson and his two friends. Horrified, Blair immediately turned back around to face the front. The boys were thankfully too busy laughing to notice her terror.

The butterflies were now drowning in anxiety and humiliation.

"Wait, you didn't finish," Hudson plied. "Or should I say, *he* didn't finish..."

More laughter. Then silence.

Blair didn't want to continue, but she knew what would come if she didn't. They would start to turn mean. She inhaled, refusing to turn again, heart thudding.

In a much lower voice, she continued, "I bounce on his big, fat, hard cock until he comes all over my ass."

"Gross," Hudson said, satisfied. "Such a dirty little slut."

Luckily, they were all at the serving portion of the line now, and they couldn't continue talking like that. Blair had never been so relieved to see the lunch ladies. Taking her tray, she practically threw her money at the cashier and told her to keep the change. Head lowered, she hurriedly made her way over to Rachel Dao. She slammed the tray down without realizing it, making her best friend jump.

"Jesus!" Rachel shrieked, holding a hand to her chest. "Blair, you scared me."

"I'm sorry," she mumbled, sitting down and immediately putting her hands on her forehead.

"What's wrong?" Rachel asked, brushing away a piece of dark hair from her tan shoulder. Blair always envied her fine Asian hair.

Blair's shoulders rose and fell as she inhaled and exhaled deeply. "Just Hudson and the A-holes, managing to make me look like a pervert in front of the new guy."

"New guy? What new guy?" Rachel turned to look. "… Oh. Yeah, wow."

"I know."

"Why don't you tell on them? It's wrong that they're making you say sick stuff to them."

"Because I can't. After what happened with Hudson, they never want to hear about me or him in the same sentence ever again. Plus, if I tell, it means he's won."

"Is that really all you care about? Winning?"

"We've got seven months left in this hellhole. I can manage." Blair sat up straight and started poking at her food. Seven more months, and then she'd be free. She would graduate, have a job by then, hopefully, and move out of her parents' house. No more wondering when she would next be belittled, grabbed, or slapped unexpectedly for doing something wrong.

At that moment, some of Rachel's other friends arrived at the table. None of them liked Blair; they only tolerated her presence because of Rachel. It was Blair's cue to eat quickly and get out of there. She shoveled food into her mouth and kept her head low.

Once down to her last few bites, she brought her gaze up to look around carefully. She was done eating when her eyes spotted Andrew sitting at Hudson's table across the room.

Bastard, she thought.

* * *

Blair was more than relieved that another crap day was over with. The halls thrummed with students slamming their lockers closed, chatting, and exiting. She opened her overstuffed locker and forcefully shoved the books she wouldn't need inside. Just as she went to close it, however, her gym shoes came tumbling down with some smaller books and papers. Blair swore, bending down to pick up the spilled items.

Footsteps around her were becoming sparse. As she rearranged the mess inside to shove the contents in again, the hairs on the back of her neck stood up. She turned to see Andrew standing a few feet behind her, waiting. Then she realized that the locker below hers, which had always been empty, must now be his. Arranged alphabetically, that meant that his last name must start with an *S*, too.

The butterflies had disintegrated by this point; this Andrew character had been present for every humiliating moment of her day. Angrily throwing her gym shoes back into the locker, Blair turned away from him.

"You know, you can say 'excuse me' to get into your locker instead of just standing there staring like some fucking weirdo," she barked.

Andrew said nothing.

She turned after slamming her locker door shut. "By the way, Hudson is a predator who likes to sexually harass women. Probably even raped one or two at a party. If you're friends with him, you'd better stay the *fuck* away from me."

And with that, in true bro fashion, Blair shoulder-checked Andrew's arm to get past him. It didn't have the same effect as someone else his size, but it was enough to make a statement.

"Oh, and another thing—you should probably get some new shoes. No one wears those ugly fuckers around here," Blair said to Andrew as an afterthought. She made sure she seemed like she was down the hallway, then turned to look back, happy to see him staring down at his feet.

Who feels stupid now? she thought with a smirk.

But Blair felt a twinge of guilt somewhere deep inside. There was absolutely nothing wrong with Andrew's shoes.

Chapter 3

Like Christmas Colors

When Blair got home, her mother, Angela, was in the living room, ironing a dress top. Her presence startled Blair, as she was used to coming home to an empty house. Her mother was usually working long hours in the city, often staying at her apartment there. Her father was at work.

"You're ... you're here," Blair stuttered.

"Did you bring the mail in?" Angela asked without looking at her.

"No, I forgot."

Angela scoffed. "Quit being so stupid," she hissed.

"I'm sorry."

"Well, go get it."

Blair turned around and went back outside to the mailbox, the winter air biting at her. She brought a few pieces of mail back inside.

"Where do you want them?"

"Put them on the kitchen counter."

"Anything else?"

"No," her mother said tersely. "You're free to go."

Blair didn't need to be told twice as she hastily made her way upstairs. She couldn't wait to move out. Most of her interactions with her parents were negative. She was always walking on eggshells when they were around. Numerous times, she had thought of getting a job to save up money for an apartment, but her nerves always got to her. At present, her only choice was to grit her teeth and bear it.

Once in her room, Blair threw herself onto her bed, too exhausted to take off her school uniform. Her body was now heavy, as she finally felt safe in her surroundings. She lay on her stomach, eyes closed, lying to herself that she would rest for a bit ... just a little bit.

Drifting into sleep, Blair thought of Andrew. Andrew S. She wondered what his last name could be. She felt a pull to him for reasons she didn't understand, as if she knew him from somewhere. Like he was someone she could trust and confide in. She was curious if they would have any morning classes together, given that he had shown up at lunchtime. Highly unlikely—not after seeing his AP Bio textbook. Here he was, taking college prep courses, and she was taking the "I'm barely going to graduate high school" courses.

Blair always felt something stir inside her when a sympathetic teacher pulled her aside and gave her the "you're smarter than this" speech. It was meant to motivate her, but it just made her feel bad for disappointing yet another adult. She preferred when they just sent her down to Mr. Davis's office.

Ms. Holland was perhaps the last teacher who believed in Blair. She would be lying if she said she didn't hang onto that. It was Ms. Holland who had advocated for Blair when Mr. Davis finally said "screw it" last year and wanted to expel her.

If It All Fades Away

* * *

The following morning, Andrew was at his locker before Blair. She noticed he was still wearing the same shoes, which annoyed her. He grabbed his backpack and rose as he finished, walking past Blair like she wasn't there.

Blair was irritated that he didn't even look at her. Was he really that hurt that she'd told him his shoes were ugly fuckers? *Grow a pair, you baby,* she thought.

Her first period was study hall. This was usually when Blair would complete the homework she didn't finish the night before (if she decided to do it at all). Just as she was entering the massive library, her phone buzzed with a text from Rachel. She wouldn't be in school today because she didn't feel well—possibly a fever. Great... Lunch was going to be a blast.

Blair sat in her usual spot at the end of a long wooden table near the windows. She begrudgingly pulled out her English textbook for Ms. Holland's class. It was the only one she still tried to care about. She didn't want Ms. Holland to give up on her, too. She had started to read when she caught motion in her peripheral vision. Looking over, she saw it was Andrew making his way across the library. He sat several tables away from Blair and began to take out huge, thick textbooks.

Blair looked down at her own textbook. She still had another day to complete the assignment. She might have to do the work at home. With her mind made up, she slammed the book shut and put everything back into her backpack. Glancing at the clock, she noted she had been there for five minutes. That meant she had another forty to mess with Andrew.

Approaching slowly, Blair swallowed at the sight of a

vein in Andrew's neck, protruding upwards from beneath his crisp white collar and dark green wool sweater. His black hair was long enough to cover his ears and came to rest along his jawline. Arriving at the table, Blair pulled out an empty chair in front of him. She wished the floor were tile instead of carpet, so she could make more noise to annoy him, but as it was, she would have to settle for abrupt movements. She plopped down and sighed loudly, throwing her key chain lanyard and phone onto the table.

Andrew was busy writing with a pencil, paying her no mind. One glance, and the math problems intimidated Blair. She then leaned over Andrew's book. *Andrew Stormant* was written in a scribble at the top of the paper. She also saw *AP Calculus* on the textbook page.

"Jesus, no one needs to take that many damn AP courses," she said, throwing herself back into her chair.

Andrew continued to write.

Making a big show of peering under the table, Blair held onto the edge and pushed her chair back onto its hind legs.

"I see you're still wearing those fucking ugly brown shoes," she remarked.

Still nothing.

Blair let her chair down with a loud thud.

Perturbed, she had finally had it. She reached over and snatched Andrew's assignment, causing his pencil to drag a line across the paper and then into his book, where his hand remained. She held the paper up before her to take in Andrew's face, pleased to see his eyes slowly come up to look at her. She smiled a shit-eating grin, then looked back at his paper. "Your handwriting looks like a child's."

Lame. But it was the best she could come up with.

Andrew now had his hands interlocked and rested his chin on them, patiently waiting for Blair to finish.

"I don't understand any of this crap," Blair said, placing the paper down in front of her. She was now looking at Andrew. "What exactly are you going to college for, anyway?"

She was genuinely beginning to wonder what it would take to disarm this smug bastard before her. And then, just as she went to open her mouth to launch another pathetic assault —he spoke.

"Your eyes have central heterochromia," he said in a low, deep voice.

Blair felt like someone had just thrown a bucket of ice-cold water into her face.

"Wha—"

"It's when the inner ring of your irises is a different color from the outer ring. I have it, too. But I must admit, yours look more striking than mine—prettier, almost like Christmas colors, with the red and green."

Blair tried to discern the color in Andrew's eyes, but was too self-conscious now and tucked a piece of hair behind her ear. Thrown off her game, she tossed the paper back at him.

"I, uh... I gotta go," she said, standing up. She quickly grabbed her key chain lanyard, phone, and bag, leaving the library. There was still a lot of time left in study hall, but she didn't care.

Once in the hallway, she heard a voice. It was Hudson, always managing to be nowhere and everywhere simultaneously.

"Skipping class, B3?"

"Not now, you fucking stalker!" she snapped. Her fast pace turned into a run. She was running.

Once in the girl's restroom, she threw her backpack onto the tiled floor, causing it to slide under the sinks. She hastily made her way over to the large powder mirror. Ignoring her disheveled brunette hair, she leaned in close, peering deeply into her own eyes.

Andrew Stormant was right: she had two different colors in her eyes. A reddish-brown on the inner iris, and green on the outer edges. She had stared at her eyes a million times before and knew what she looked like, but she was trying to see them now with new eyes—with Andrew's eyes. She hadn't known that such a thing had a name. She heard his voice in her head again, speaking matter-of-factly. *"Central heterochromia... Prettier, almost like Christmas colors..."*

Fuck.

Chapter 4

Her Name Is Blair

Blair could hardly focus on any of her classes that morning. She was still thinking about how Andrew Stormant had completely dodged her bullying tactics, and she was also worried about how lunch would go. Unless Rachel was sick, she never missed school. Worse still, Blair had to deal with Hudson and his two cronies in the lunch line, and if Andrew was there again, she was sure she would die from humiliation.

The last class before lunch was gym. Blair desperately hoped they wouldn't be doing any partnered activities today; her nerves couldn't handle much more. Changing in the girl's locker room, she tugged at her shorts that were too small. She needed to ask her parents to get her some new clothes soon. As usual, the request would undoubtedly be met with annoyance and scorn.

Blair didn't pay much attention to the fact that she was the only girl in gym. She was just thankful they were a class of twelve, and not twenty-five, like middle school used to be. All the other girls in her grade at least had the good sense to participate in a varsity sport.

As she walked sheepishly out of the locker rooms, Blair's stomach dropped when she saw Andrew standing beside Hudson. Surely, he could do any varsity sport, based on his build and stature. What was he doing in gym? She wanted to scowl, but it became apparent that Hudson was talking his ear off. Andrew dutifully listened, giving Blair the hope she needed to believe he wasn't actually becoming friends with Hudson.

"Hey, Blair," Julian Lewis greeted her as he passed.

Julian. A genuinely nice guy. He was tall and handsome, with dark skin, and Blair felt that on more than one occasion, she should have tried to talk to him more. He hadn't been there the day she decked Hudson, but he did make a sly comment when she returned from suspension: that she had done them all a favor.

Andrew glanced in Blair's direction, then turned his head back to Hudson.

Poor guy, Blair thought. *He'll never get away if he doesn't tell him to shut up or interrupt him.*

Mr. Parks entered the gym. "Alright, everyone, we're doing some exercise drills today."

A collective groan could be heard.

"We're going to do ten laps around the gym to get our heart rates up, and during that time, I'm going to be setting up some agility stations in the middle of the court. When you're done with your laps, go ahead and stretch and then get a drink of water."

All the boys scuttled over to the designated starting corner. Blair made sure to get behind all of them, not wanting to interfere with their dick-measuring contest of who was the fastest.

Sneakers squeaked and thudded as they stampeded around the gymnasium. Blair did her best to stay at least within range of the boys, not wanting to get lapped, though it would inevitably happen anyway. Hudson always overexerted himself to try to beat Julian, and it amused Blair that he failed every time.

Turning one of the corners on the second lap, Blair saw that Andrew and Julian were striding together, Hudson flailing behind them. They both looked at ease, while Hudson looked like he was trying not to die. His freckled face was bright red, matching his hair, thus making his whole head look like a giant red dot bopping around in circles. Blair stifled a laugh.

She quickly felt her lungs and legs start to burn. She stopped focusing on the boys and instead concentrated on her stride. Though her lung capacity had improved since the beginning of the school year, she still struggled to keep an even running pace. But she preferred this cardio over the agility drills that would come next.

Thinking of what she would do about Rachel not being at lunch, she didn't realize that Julian, Andrew, and Hudson were now passing her on the fifth lap. Blair tried to move out of the way and got clipped by Hudson. This infuriated him, and he abandoned his desperate attempt to stay with Julian and Andrew.

"Get the hell out of the way, B3!"

He must have stepped on the loop of one of her laces, because, like in a bad high school movie, Blair felt her whole shoe come off, and just like that—BAM—she was sprawled out on the floor. She hit hard. The other boys continued right past her. Mr. Parks was too busy getting cones and ropes out of one of the utility closets to see what had happened.

Blair blinked. Her eyes instinctively closed on impact, and her vision was black momentarily. She began to sit up when she saw Andrew's legs near her.

"Are you okay?" he asked, offering her his hand.

"Fine," she said, standing up with his help and dusting herself off. She looked down at her elbow, which had burned on the floor. She retrieved her shoe and quickly put it back on, tying it hastily, then started running again. Only this time, Andrew stayed alongside her.

"You don't have to run with me out of pity," she informed him.

He didn't respond, only kept alongside her. Then Julian passed them both.

"Are you okay, Blair?" Julian asked.

"Yeah," Blair breathed.

"Don't worry about B3!" Hudson called after Julian, breathless and lagging behind, but now passing them. "She gets plenty of cardio each week with Mr. Davis."

Suddenly, Andrew stopped. Surprised, Blair turned to look back at him.

"Her name is *Blair*!" he shouted, his deep voice echoing in the large gymnasium.

All the boys looked over from a straightaway, stunned. Mr. Parks was stupidly standing in the doorway of an attached hallway, holding cones, confused as to what had just happened.

Hudson looked frightened. "I—I know," he called back awkwardly from a distance.

Andrew wore an angry expression, but then he quietly resumed running. A tense silence overcame the room. The thudding of shoes sounded more intense than before.

Blair kept her head down as Andrew came back up alongside her. She couldn't remember the last time someone stood up to Hudson for her that had gone unchallenged. Rachel's attempts were always viciously shot down, making Blair hurt

If It All Fades Away

for her friend. She insisted that Rachel stay out of any taunts or put-downs aimed at her.

Blair tried to stay away from Andrew for the remainder of the class. She could already sense that Hudson was not particularly happy that Andrew was staying close to her, nor was he pleased to be humiliated in front of everyone.

With legs like jelly from agility ladders and cone sprints, Blair hobbled to the locker room, where she showered quickly.

As she exited the gymnasium, Blair felt the dread of lunchtime that she had managed to forget due to physical and mental exertion. She could just … not eat. But then her stomach rumbled, reminding her that she was famished. Not eating could mean she would faint later. It had happened before. Blair remembered how furious her mother was in her sophomore year, forced to leave work early to come and get her. She could still hear Angela's voice ranting on the car ride home, about how a "skinny little bitch" like her needed to eat more—that no one wanted to sleep with a skeleton, and to "never pull a stunt like that ever again."

Yes, Mother—fainting from not eating because of the severe anxiety of being bullied was definitely an elaborate stunt.

Blair sighed, her legs weak from exercise and nerves, her hands trembling. Today, like every other day, she would just have to suck it up and put on a brave face. *Just get through it*, she told herself. *It'll be okay. And even if it isn't, you'll find a way to be okay later.*

Chapter 5

Who Hurt You?

Blair grabbed a Saran-Wrapped sandwich and scurried out of the cafeteria. She was relieved that Hudson didn't notice her. Equally relieved that the girls didn't seem to spot her looking over to confirm one of her worst lunchtime anxieties—that they would never leave a spot open for her if Rachel wasn't present. While sneaking out, Blair also noticed that Andrew was not sitting at Hudson's table. He wasn't sitting anywhere, actually.

Walking down the hallway, Blair crammed the sandwich into her mouth, not wanting to get in trouble for eating outside the cafeteria.

Opening her den of trash in the senior hall, Blair resolved that it was perhaps time to try cleaning out her locker. Probably worthwhile, after the spectacle she'd made of herself yesterday. She had plenty of time before Ms. Holland's class; might as well be productive with it. Blair began to sort through old papers, walking over to a trash bin and tossing them as needed. She also had a few empty water bottles, Starburst wrappers from when she was given the yellow ones that

Rachel didn't like, and some spare clothes that smelled of locker now.

She heard footsteps coming around the corner, not thinking anything of it. Blair's stomach leaped when she realized it was Andrew. She refused to give him more than a sideways glance, however. She didn't want to seem overly interested, but she didn't want to seem completely disinterested either. She wasn't exactly sure how to behave with him —not after this morning in study hall or gym.

Blair should have been grateful that Andrew stood up to Hudson for her. But truth be told, it filled her with dread, because now Hudson would be hyperaware and focused on the two of them. Maybe Andrew hadn't snapped at Hudson because he was defending her; perhaps he was using her as an excuse to tell Hudson off, a quick and easy way to get rid of him. Whatever Andrew's motives were, be it making her blush in study hall or offering her a hand when she fell, Blair didn't know what to do with any of it. Sure, she wanted to get his attention by messing with him, but somehow, he thwarted her every attempt to disturb him.

Looking down at him as he opened his locker, staring at the top of his head of black hair, Blair hated that at every turn, she was the one looking like an idiot. Andrew managed to subvert all of her efforts to fuck with him. As he pulled thick textbooks out from his locker, Blair felt contempt creep up inside—contempt for his laser focus, his unflappable demeanor, his commitment to schoolwork that would surely grant him favoritism, and his attempt to play nice by complimenting her eye color, offering a hand in gym, and defending her to Hudson. She hated all of it. That was what she had convinced herself of, anyway. She hated that she was so easily disturbed and an outcast, and he got to be the cool kid on day two—the studious good guy.

Their locker doors had been flush together while open. Blair stayed to the side of Andrew, slowly sifting through the papers in her hand. Andrew was crouched down, examining his schedule, probably still getting used to which classes he had on different days. Ever so slightly, Blair reached over him and quietly positioned her locker door right above his head. She smirked and mindlessly stared at her papers, completely unfocused—waiting for Andrew.

He folded his schedule and slipped it into his binder within his bag. Zipping up the backpack, he rose, just as he had done many times before—and a loud, metallic *WHACK* came from the sharp metal corner smashing right into the back of Andrew's head.

Blair howled with laughter. She shouldn't have, but she couldn't help it.

"Oh, I got you good!" she managed. "Gotta even the playing field by knocking out a few of those brain cells." She held her stomach and continued to cackle.

Andrew remained motionless, his right hand on the top of his head. It had to have hurt; Blair had banged her own head into plenty a cabinet door at home. Sometimes, the pain was so sharp and excruciating that she wondered if she would need medical attention.

Still laughing, Blair jumped when Andrew raised his hand, still looking down, and slammed her locker door shut. He stood up quickly and faced her with serious eyes.

Blair was so frightened by the rapid shift in energy and sudden movement that she punched Andrew in the chest on reflex. Then, before she could pull away in horror at what she had done, he snatched her wrist. His grip was firm, his massive hand wrapping easily around her tiny wrist.

Blair looked up to see that Andrew's eyes were glassy. He looked ... wounded? Sad? Concerned? Something. And it was not at all what she was expecting. She didn't know what she thought would happen, but certainly not this.

"Who hurt you?" he asked. His voice was low and quiet —one of concern, like a teacher trying to convince a child to report abuse at home.

She felt the terror flicker through her body, and it surely flashed in her eyes, because she saw that Andrew caught it. She quickly forced herself to switch back into regular Blair mode.

She looked down and snorted. "Wow. Really? 'Who hurt you?' Stick with bio and calc, you big-nosed freak."

Why were her insults so juvenile when it came to him? She tugged her wrist to break his hold, to no avail. His grasp was firm, but not threatening—not like the death grip when her father had grabbed her by her upper arms and shoved her into the fridge once, furious over something that Blair couldn't recall. She only remembered that she had been terrified of the brute strength she felt.

Was this the part where she told him to let go?

Blair kept her gaze on the floor. She didn't want to look into his eyes again ... but she also strangely didn't want him to let her go. She looked up and saw the sadness in his eyes again—and something about it stabbed her.

Blair slapped him across the face with her free hand, for reasons she didn't understand.

He caught that wrist, too.

"You take hits like a pussy," she said weakly.

Andrew now had both of her wrists, a red mark on his face, and a look of deep melancholy in his eyes. It was a suffocating gaze that Blair could hardly stand. She felt like a rodent in a cage, desperately trying to get out while scientist Andrew watched, taking notes and thinking how interesting this little rodent was.

"Let me go," she said finally.

And to her utter surprise, Andrew did. Immediately.

She didn't know what to think of that. She rubbed her wrists and lowered her head, blinking tears away.

And then, Andrew stepped closer ... and wrapped his arms around her.

Her arms, which had been released and remained up to her chest, came to curl into his.

A *hug*? What the hell was this?

Blair stood like a feral child, unsure of what to do with Andrew's contact. He smelled good. *Really* good. It was something musky, but faint—a scent that you could only smell when you were this close to him.

Blair couldn't come up with one single smart-ass remark to say. All she could do was stand, her legs now put through the roller coaster ride of a lifetime in one day. First a fall, then intense exercise, anxiety, and now—a strange and painful euphoria that Blair had never experienced, making her weak again.

She couldn't remember the last time a male had hugged her. If it was her father when she was a child, she had no memory of it.

Walk away, Blair told herself.

But for some reason, her body wouldn't let her.

Blair decided she would just ... accept it. Whatever Andrew's intentions were, she would accept them at this moment. She allowed herself to lean into him slightly, arms still folded into his chest. She closed her eyes when he brought his hand to rest on the back of her head, petting her.

Affection. That must be what this was. As a feral animal, even Blair knew petting like this was good, kind, and safe.

She was safe.

Safe in the arms of Andrew Stormant.

Chapter 6

The Student Advocate

"Did you get enough to eat?" Andrew asked, bringing his hand to a stop on the back of her head.

"Hmm?" Blair hummed into his chest.

She opened her eyes when she felt him move. He had pulled his head back slightly to look downward at her.

"I was in Mr. Singh's classroom, asking him some questions. I saw you walk by and shove that whole sandwich into your mouth. Did you get enough to eat? Are you still hungry?"

"I… I'm fine," Blair said.

She *was* still hungry.

"Well, I have an unopened bag of Oreos, if you want them."

When Andrew released his hold on her, Blair wanted to cry out.

He crouched down and opened a front bag compartment to pull out the cookies. "Dessert…" he said, offering them to her.

"… Thanks," Blair said, slowly taking the bag.

More time must have passed than she thought, because some students were now trickling into the hallway. Then the bell rang, signaling the end of lunch.

"What class do you have next?" Andrew asked, pulling his backpack over one shoulder.

"English with Ms. Holland."

"Oh, she's nice. I have her for AP English."

"Oh, for Christ's sake..." Blair muttered, letting her hands fall to her legs in annoyance.

Andrew smiled, raising both hands. "It's the only other AP class I have, I promise."

Blair twisted her lip, trying to stop a smile from forming on her face, but Andrew's grin was too infectious, and she felt her teeth show. She also realized that her face was becoming warm again, as it had in study hall that morning.

The hall was now full of seniors coming and going to their lockers.

"I'll see you later?" Andrew asked.

"Yeah," Blair said.

And with that, Andrew disappeared around a corner on his way to his next class.

Blair picked up her bag from the floor and opened her locker. Surprised, she had completely forgotten how much trash and papers she had cleaned out. She grabbed the textbooks she needed for the rest of the day, conscious that her mouth could not stop smiling. Making her way to Ms. Holland's class across the building, Blair felt a lightness in her step and a giddiness that lingered in her stomach. She inhaled deeply, cherishing the faintest hint of Andrew's scent particles clinging to her.

"Blair." Ms. Holland nodded to her with a smile when she entered.

Blair bowed her head in return with a genuine smile

today. Ms. Holland appeared pleased to see that, checking her name off for attendance.

Blair daydreamed as the lesson began. She watched with glazed eyes as Ms. Holland's head of purple hair moved about. She used to wonder how they let her get away with that at St. Michael's. Then she got to see why last year at her possible expulsion meeting for biting a teacher.

* * *

Blair sat outside Mr. Davis's office with her head between her knees, waiting for her parents to arrive. She was more terrified of her mother and father than of expulsion. Feeling sick, she jolted when the reception door swung open.

Ms. Holland stormed in, charging for Mr. Davis's office, bursting through the door without a knock.

Immediately, Blair and Mrs. Welsh heard yelling before the door could even click shut.

Ms. Holland loudly told Mr. Davis that they only cared about the big donors at St. Michael's—that as long as they got their money, they didn't give a shit about the other kids. Mrs. Welsh breathed an audible "Oh, dear" at hearing the word "shit." Blair usually would have been amused at that—but not today. Not with the dread of her parents on their way.

Ms. Holland then mentioned a handful of students who had done far worse than Blair. She noted drugs and alcohol on campus, and the horrific vandalism of a hotel after an away football game that was kept quiet thanks to powerful connections. She name-dropped both boys and girls.

Mr. Davis immediately countered with a reference to Blair's freshmen year, when she had punched a junior girl in the stomach, and how the parents wanted to press charges—that she should have been expelled then. Or what about when she was caught cheating on a final exam in her sophomore year? Suspensions and academic probation weren't doing much.

Ms. Holland retorted that they hadn't even tried counseling yet, adding that the school counselor was an imbecile, and that Blair needed real help—maybe even medication.

Blair caught Mrs. Welsh quietly shaking her head in pity as she typed on her computer—as if the problems with Blair were so trivial that she could still manage to focus and type while a full-blown argument was taking place. It hurt Blair to see that. However, what hurt her even more was when her parents arrived. She wanted to throw up at the sight of her father in his greasy work uniform, contrasted against her mother's grey pencil skirt and matching grey jacket slung over her arm.

Ms. Holland made her case to the whole room—Mr. Davis and her parents. Blair sat as still as possible. A resolution was finally agreed upon. Blair would have to serve three days of suspension and would get six private counseling sessions.

When they left that day, her parents said nothing to her as they walked out together. Her father got into his pickup truck and said he was going back to work. Her mother audibly sighed, placing her purse and jacket in the back seat of her car before she closed the door and got in the front seat. Blair joined her with trepidation.

Once inside, and not a moment too soon, Angela slapped her across the back of the head. One of her nails caught and dragged awkwardly through Blair's hair as she pulled away.

"I can't fucking believe you," she breathed, immediately reaching to turn the keys in the ignition as if nothing had happened. "Counseling... Medication..." She muttered to herself, disgusted. "I swear to God, Blair..."

If It All Fades Away

Blair curled her left ear into her shoulder to prepare for another blow, before she realized her mother was just reaching to put the car into reverse.

"If we have to come up here one more time, you're going to regret the day you were born."

Blair got six sessions of counseling, and that was that. She wished she could have gone for longer, as she had liked her therapist—but of course, her parents refused. She never did get on any medication. She wasn't sure what she would have needed or been put on, but she would've at least liked to try something.

* * *

Snapping back to the present, Blair was reminded that Ms. Holland got to wear a head of purple hair at St. Michael's because Ms. Holland was a badass. Blair smiled at the memory of her yelling. She wasn't intimidated by Mr. Davis or anyone, not one tiny bit, and she wasn't afraid to lose her job if it meant she was doing the right thing. She was the very definition of "no shits given."

If Blair could think of one adult she would like to be like when she grew up, it would be Ms. Holland.

Chapter 7

Cherry Red

Blair could hardly get to her locker fast enough at the end of the day. She wasn't sure what to say or do around Andrew; she just wanted to be near him. Stalling for as long as possible, she felt disappointed when he didn't show up. Maybe he was talking to a teacher again, or had already gone home.

Once outside, Blair pulled the hood of her coat up. The November air was bitterly cold. She was thankful she only had a few neighborhoods to walk through to get home.

A text buzzed in her pocket—Rachel, asking her if the day went alright. *Oh, Rachel.* Thinking of Blair even while she was sick at home. Blair told her not to worry about her, that it all went fine, and to rest up.

Blair's Mary Janes crunched on the snow as she walked. Her cheeks were the coldest part of her body at the moment. Head down and almost to the edge of the school premises, she heard a vehicle slow next to her.

"Do you need a ride?" Andrew called through the passenger window. "It's way too cold to be walking out here."

If It All Fades Away

"I don't live far," Blair said, her cheeks cherry red.

"Come on, get in, I'll take you."

Blair hesitated for a moment, then agreed.

Climbing inside the SUV, she shivered. Andrew quickly turned the heater on full blast, and Blair placed her hands on the vents.

"You really walk in this?" Andrew asked, looking at Blair's knees, just as red as her cheeks.

"It's not that bad," she responded, fisting her plaid skirt downward.

"Where do I need to go?" he asked, ignoring the cars going around him to get to the stop sign at the end of the drive.

Blair was still shivering as she directed him, but was warming up quickly.

"I'm sorry I didn't see you at our lockers. I'm still getting used to where everything is."

Blair said nothing. She didn't want to seem like she had been expecting him.

Another wide turn, and they were on her street. It was really close in a vehicle.

"It's that blue house up there." Blair pointed.

Andrew slowed down once they got closer, then pulled into her driveway.

Now comfortable and toasty, Blair reached for her bag at her feet. She slowly gripped the door handle, trying to think of something to say other than just thank you. Just as she was pushing the door open, Andrew spoke.

"Were you able to get your homework done?"

"… What?"

"You didn't come back to study hall this morning. I was just wondering if you were able to finish what you needed to get done."

It felt like an eternity since first period. So much had transpired in one day, Blair could have sworn he was asking about last week. At St. Michael's, there was never-ending reading, writing, studying, and projects to do.

"I didn't ... but I'll get it done tonight."

"I can give you my number ... in case you need help with anything."

"Okay." Blair pulled out her phone, and they entered each other's information.

"Do your parents work late?" Andrew asked.

Blair realized that *he* was stalling now.

"They do. My dad usually works second or third shift, depending on the week or month. And my mom works odd hours. Sometimes she doesn't come home at all. She has an apartment downtown for when she has to work late and be up early, too."

The heater was blasting, and Andrew turned it lower now that they were becoming too hot.

"Well, be safe, then," he said.

"Um, thank you for the ride," Blair said, exiting the vehicle.

As she was walking up the pathway to her front door, she heard Andrew call out.

"Blair."

She turned to look.

"If it's okay with you, and your parents don't mind, I can take you home each day. It's not a problem for me, and it's not that far. It's too cold for you to walk home."

How sweet. He was worried about what her parents thought, even though he knew nothing about them or how little they cared about her. The only time they cared was when she messed up or inconvenienced them, which felt like a lot.

"Okay," she called back to him.

He waved and pulled away. Blair returned the gesture, watching him go, then unlocked the front door and entered.

Chapter 8

Good Morning

Blair could hear her father snoring down the hall when she awoke the next day. He was working thirds and would go straight to bed when he got home. Her mother was at her apartment. Checking her phone, Blair still had about ten minutes before her alarm was supposed to go off.

There was a text message from Andrew:

Good morning, Blair. I asked my parents, and they said it would be okay if I picked you up and dropped you off each day. What time do you usually leave? Is it alright if I come and get you this morning? I don't want you walking outside in the cold. -Andrew

Blair smiled and texted back. She thought it was cute that he'd told her good morning and signed his name. It was nice to hear from him first thing in the morning.

After showering and getting dressed, Blair ate toast with jam while she waited for him. Watching the dark SUV pull into her driveway, she grabbed her bag and hastily exited the front door.

"Good morning," Andrew said as she opened the door.

"Ugh, you're one of *those* types," she said, climbing in.

"What?" he asked, confused.

"You actually say 'good morning' to people, verbally. Just … say 'hi' or something. 'Good morning' is such a huge 'screw you' to me."

"… Okay." He laughed nervously.

"I'm still not fully awake yet. When someone says, 'Good morning,' it just feels like they're trying to start shit."

Andrew chuckled as he started driving down the road. She could tell he was amused and conceptually understood her distaste for morning greetings, but not quite literally. Probably the result of a better upbringing, she told herself.

Blair remained silent for the rest of the ride. Once parked and walking up to the building, Blair slowed when she caught the back of Hudson's head entering. Andrew noticed she was lagging and turned back to look at her, then back to Hudson's head disappearing through the double doors.

She could see his breath in the cold air as he spoke. "How long has he been bothering you?"

"Hudson? Oh, since freshman year. I'm used to his bullshit by now, though."

Andrew was not convinced.

"I punched him in the face earlier this year." Blair laughed as if that was supposed to appease him.

Andrew's eyes widened. "What happened?" he asked. "Come on, let's get inside."

They continued through the double doors, Hudson now out of sight down another hallway.

"He snapped my bra strap during basketball. I got mad and punched him in the jaw." Blair shrugged with a nonchalant expression. Andrew stopped again now that they were inside. "He had been pissing me off for weeks in gym, and I'd finally had it," she added.

"Wha—what happened next? Did he get in trouble?"

Blair snorted. "No, actually, *I* got in trouble. I had to do a three-day suspension. Although I did hear Ms. Holland was pretty pissed, because she didn't know I got suspended until I didn't show up to class. There was an ugly rape here about two years ago." Blair felt her cold nose starting to warm up. "I guess Ms. Holland practically dragged Hudson in by his ear to Mr. Davis's office and made him confess." Blair laughed. "She threatened to make a bigger deal out of it than it was. Pretty sure she scared him into getting his mom to back off of talks of assault and shit. I think she knows he's done some other stuff to girls ... she just can't prove it."

Blair's words did not calm Andrew. If anything, he looked horrified. Blair was starting to feel self-conscious, like perhaps she had said something wrong. Andrew was supposed to laugh it off like she did. Why wasn't he laughing? It made her uneasy.

"That's disgusting," he said finally. "Him, not you. My God, why haven't they done anything about him?"

"Why do you think?" Blair threw back at him. "Because he has *money*. More than me, anyway. It's always about money... You should know that."

"I'm really sorry that no one's done anything for you," Andrew said, with that familiar sadness in his eyes again.

Blair's breath caught in her throat. "That's not true," she said quietly. "Ms. Holland's done a lot for me. And besides, Hudson doesn't bother me all that much," she lied. "He's just an idiot."

"He's a *dangerous* idiot, Blair."

Blair looked down at her black Mary Janes. "Did you ... did you hear what we talked about in the lunch line on your first day?"

"Only the end of it," Andrew said. "I didn't know the

context of the relationship between you two. I didn't think much of it until Hudson talked about you at the table."

Blair was both curious and mortified. "What did he say?" she asked a little too quickly.

"Stupid shit. Nasty stuff that's obviously all in his head. It's not worth repeating."

"No, I want to hear it," Blair insisted.

"I don't want to repeat it," Andrew said firmly.

Blair gave him an angry scowl, feeling petulant and betrayed simultaneously.

The bell rang, signaling the start of first period. They had five minutes to get from class to class. She and Andrew had been so caught up in their conversation that they had forgotten to go to their lockers. They both made haste to get there, putting their coats and belongings away in tense silence.

Blair made sure to close her locker door first, loudly and definitively, so that Andrew knew it was closed before he stood up.

Chapter 9

Church Duty

Blair and Andrew sat together for first-period study hall. Blair decided to read the chapter required for world history.

Blair rested her head on her fist and began to read. She had a hard time focusing. Glancing up at Andrew several times, she was dismayed to see him so intently working on ... whatever it was he was working on. She wasn't sure how to get his attention without being obnoxious. But she also couldn't be mean to him again—not after he had been so nice to her repeatedly. When was a good time to try to flirt with him?

Blair watched his brow furrow as he glanced back and forth between a page and his paper. His intensity was admirable, and ... sexy, Blair decided. She bit her lower lip and choked back a laugh. Thankfully, the librarian was super chill about students talking a little. It also helped that her office and checkout counter were farther away, near the door.

Andrew looked up at her, then returned to his work.

"I'm sorry." She giggled.

"It's okay," Andrew said, not looking at her now. "I like

If It All Fades Away

seeing and hearing you laugh." He continued to write before pausing. "That is ... as long as a locker door isn't smashing into my head." He flashed her a grin.

Blair's smile faded away as she looked down and cleared her throat, grabbing her other arm across her body. "I'm ... I'm sorry about that."

"Don't apologize," Andrew told her without hesitation. "I'm grateful for it."

Blair blinked up at him from beneath long lashes. *Grateful? Really?*

They held each other's gaze for a moment. Then Blair's phone buzzed quietly, distracting them both. It was Rachel, who informed Blair that she would be out of school again today and would be going to the doctor. Blair felt her stomach drop at the news. It was the same hollowness she'd felt yesterday. What was she going to do about lunch?

"Will you sit with me at lunch today?" Blair blurted out, the thought spilling out before she could take it back.

Andrew picked up on her anxiety. "Where do you usually sit?"

"With Rachel Dao. She's my best friend. You haven't met her, but she was sick yesterday and today ... and I don't have a seat at our table unless she's there."

"Why not?"

"Her other friends that sit there, they, uh ... don't really like me. So ... unless Rachel is there and saves me a seat, I have nowhere to go."

She saw a realization dawn on Andrew's face as he put two and two together from yesterday, when she'd stuffed that sandwich into her mouth while walking down the hall.

"I guess I don't really have anywhere to go, either," he said to soothe her. "Yesterday, Mr. Singh told me to bring my lunch to his room to chat, but I hadn't thought about where I would sit today. Definitely not with Hudson."

Blair didn't know what to say to that. She couldn't fathom just ... not thinking about her seating arrangements until the time came. That level of confidence Andrew had, not worrying about where his place was in a totally new environment, galled her.

"We'll find a spot, don't worry," Andrew told her.

And for once, Blair believed she could not worry, if Andrew was at her side.

Thankfully, gym was only on Mondays, Tuesdays, and Fridays. Today—Wednesday—Blair had church duty. Her responsibility was to clean up the cathedral, to pick up any litter and ensure that everything was ready for Thursday Mass for the school. She looked forward to being on church duty more than anything else each week—even more than Ms. Holland's English class. Blair wasn't stupid, though; she knew this was a charity class for her—an attempt to keep her away from Hudson (and out of trouble as much as possible), and to hopefully bring her closer to Jesus.

Blair wasn't sure what she felt about God or Jesus. She had prayed many times, but she still felt ... alone. Still, there was something to be said about the solitude she experienced each week when she cleaned. The genuinely good people involved with the church, like Sister Eugene and Father Patrick Donovan, made any type of Catholicism worthwhile to Blair.

Entering through a back door, Blair announced her arrival to Sister Eugene.

"Good morning, Blair," she said warmly.

"Good morning, Sister Eugene," Blair replied politely.

Sister Eugene. Probably the only person who could get away with a "Good morning" greeting anytime. She managed the reception area for Father Donovan and never gave Blair a hard time about anything. Super sweet and in her eighties, she seemed genuinely happy to be of service to the Lord and the Church.

Blair hung up her coat and asked if anything special needed to be done.

"Just the usual, my dear." Sister Eugene smiled. "Do you want some candy? I stocked up."

"Of course," Blair said, walking over to the crystal dish at the front of her desk. "Oooh, you got my favorite!"

"I always think of you, dear."

Blair plucked out the Werther's Original hard caramel candy and immediately unwrapped it, plopping it into her mouth.

"Mmm. Is it okay if I take another?" she asked, indulging the kind older woman.

"You take as many as you want, dear. Hardly anyone else is ever back here."

Blair grabbed at least three more and put them into her skirt pocket.

Entering from behind the altar, Blair always stopped to take in the grandeur of St. Michael's Cathedral. It was old-school, with rows of pews and tall stained-glass windows. At this time of the morning, if the sun was out, it shined through the windows just right, illuminating a section of the pews and center aisle with a beauty rarely rivaled by everyday occurrences—except maybe legitimate rainbows that could be seen after a summer rain.

Blair took a deep breath and then got to work, checking the pews for any possible litter and rearranging the pamphlets and hymnals in their back slots accordingly. Next, she would change the song board to reflect tomorrow's hymns accurately. She would then check the bathrooms to make sure toilet paper was stocked and trash bins were emptied. Simple work, but work that her overactive and anxiety-ridden mind never seemed to tire of. Blair was just fine in solitude; that was how she usually liked it.

Except today. Today, she wished that somehow Andrew could be doing this work alongside her. Just the thought of him diligently cleaning and ensuring everything was perfect made Blair smile.

Chapter 10

Calm

Blair made her way to her locker to put her coat away. Just as she was about to close it, Andrew arrived.

"You weren't in gym," he told her, as if she were unaware.

"Oh… Yeah… I forgot to tell you. I don't have to go on Wednesdays. Church Duty."

"'Church Duty'?"

"Another one of Ms. Holland's attempts to keep me in this shithole's good graces … and to spare me Hudson's bullshit in gym. She wanted to get me out of there completely, but you know how that went. They'd rather girls be sexually harassed than possibly gain weight."

Andrew made a face. "What is even going on here?"

Blair laughed loud and hard at that. His genuine confusion at the fuckery that was St. Michael's Catholic High School could no longer be contained—and he was only on day three.

Blair composed herself, still amused. "We have Mass every Thursday, as I'm sure you've already burnt into your memory from that little schedule of yours. Anyway, I'm the one that makes sure everything's clean and tidy for that."

Andrew shook his head. It was all beginning to make sense to him.

"Are you ready to eat?" he asked earnestly.

"No," Blair muttered.

"It'll be fine. Let's go."

They silently made their way down to the lunchroom. Blair's mind and stomach did multiple jumps and twirls, trying to figure out how the next forty-five minutes would transpire.

Arriving in the side hallway, Andrew could fully appreciate how badly Blair hated this time of the day.

"It's going to be okay," he told her.

She said nothing as she stayed behind him.

And then, it began. Hudson and his two cronies were coming their way. Blair glanced sideways and then quickly looked away. But she could tell Andrew was facing them, chin held high and proud. She saw from her peripheral that Hudson had stopped talking, slowing down a little, taking in the sight of Andrew and Blair together.

"Bentley, good to see you again," Andrew said, as if they were pals. Blair knew they had both just had gym together, but the formality in Andrew's voice was more of an upper-hand tactic. She instinctively knew it was a manipulation technique, as did Hudson. They all did. However, Andrew's level of maturity and confidence to be that bold to Hudson, with Blair at his side, could not be challenged; it simply worked.

"Hi, Andrew... Blair."

Blair couldn't believe her ears. Wait—did he actually call her by her name? All she could do was nod in acknowledgment, but she did not make eye contact. *Coward*, she told herself.

"So, like I was saying..." Hudson said to one of his two cronies.

And that was that. Hudson left her alone for one fucking day. Blair was stunned, and eternally grateful to Andrew. Even if he left St. Michael's tomorrow, forever, Hudson had a new respect for Blair, which moved her.

Without realizing it, Blair suddenly found herself in front of Andrew, and she noticed for the first time in a long time that she could actually think about her food and drink choices. The cashier even looked confused when Blair calmly and carefully handed over her lunch money without an attitude or grimace.

Now came the tricky part. Blair stood with her tray nervously, waiting for Andrew to pay as well.

"Where do you sit again?" he asked.

Blair looked to a long corner table. "Over there." She gestured with her head.

"Okay," Andrew said, as if it were no big deal. And without hesitation, he headed straight for her table.

"Andrew—what, no! Wait!" Blair called out, but it was too late.

Andrew arrived at she and Rachel's usual table. At least four of the girls looked up as he arrived. And two to three more would come soon.

"Hi, I'm Andrew," he informed them all. "I just got here on Monday. Is it okay if Blair and I sit here with you today?"

Again, the confidence. Blair would typically have laughed, if it weren't for her gut-wrenching anxiety. Be it because he was a male, or because he was new—or because he was a male *and* new, and hot (at least to Blair)—she could practically see all the girls jizzing their panties.

"Yeah, sure, of course," one of them said.

"No problem," another said.

The girls on each side of the table moved chairs out for them.

You've got to be kidding me, Blair thought. *Seriously?*

Seriously.

And just like that, she and Andrew were seated across from each other.

"Blair, have you heard from Rachel?" one of them asked. "She hasn't been in school, and we're all worried about her."

Blair could hardly believe what was happening. This wench was seriously talking to her like they were friends.

"Umm..." Blair cleared her throat. "She's, uh, she's going to the doctor today. She's had a fever since yesterday."

"Oh my gosh, that's terrible," one of the other girls said, holding her hand to her chest as if she actually gave a shit.

"Oh no, I hope it's not too serious," another said.

"I ... I don't know. But I should hear from her by the end of the day," Blair informed them.

"Yeah, totally let her know we're thinking of her," the last of them said.

"I will," Blair lied. Too disgusted to continue the façade, she angled her body away and began to fork at her food. Andrew had been waiting for her to start eating before he began.

"Is she going to be okay?" he asked.

Blair had forgotten momentarily that she had also failed to inform him of Rachel's condition. "I think so?" she said. "She's had bad ear infections and stuff in the past, so maybe it's that again."

"That's rough," he said sympathetically. "I used to get them really bad, too, as a kid."

Blair felt her stomach and body soften at Andrew's

If It All Fades Away

mention of his childhood. And it distracted her from the fact that Rachel's supposed friends were glancing over at her and Andrew frequently, clearly dying for them to leave so they could gossip about the two of them. And something about that made Blair feel smug, confident, and validated inside. In some small way, her being friends with Rachel, and Andrew asking them if he and Blair could sit there, meant that Blair was winning. She wasn't exactly sure what she was winning at, but it was evident that she was no longer just Rachel's weird friend—she was something else entirely. And neither she, they, or Andrew was sure exactly what that was. But it was tangible—and Blair felt it most of all.

Chapter 11

House Invite

Rachel did end up having an ear infection and a bad cold. She would be out of school for the rest of the week on antibiotics. Far too much had happened for Blair to convey via text, and she wasn't about to put her best friend through the misery of a phone call with an infected ear. Blair told her that she and Andrew were sitting with the girls at lunch, and Hudson was now leaving her alone—a miracle. Rachel was both happy and relieved for Blair and excited to meet Andrew.

When Blair entered the house on Wednesday afternoon after Andrew dropped her off, her mother was home, sitting on the sofa near the front windows.

"Who was that?" she asked, with a cup of coffee in hand.

"Oh—" Blair said. "Hi, Mom."

"Who was that?" she repeated.

"Andrew ... Stormant?" Blair timidly said. "He's new."

"Why is he taking you home?"

Blair didn't know how to respond except honestly. "Because he says it's too cold to be walking outside."

Her mother scoffed. "It's really not that far."

If It All Fades Away

Blair expected her to give her shit about a boy bringing her home, but she didn't. She got up and took her coffee cup to the kitchen.

"I'll be here tonight and tomorrow, but I'll be in town again on Friday. There's a conference all day Saturday." Blair said nothing. "Would you like to order something for us in about half an hour?"

Blair breathed a sigh of relief. "Umm, sure, what were you thinking?"

"Something with rice. Chinese or Indian is fine. I'm going up to shower."

Blair settled on Chinese, double-and triple-checking that everything was entered correctly. When the food arrived, her heart sank when she realized the restaurant had forgotten the egg rolls. "No, no, no," she said, frantically searching the bag. Then she gripped her hair. "Fuck!"

When Angela came down, Blair's heart was racing so fast that she thought she might faint.

"Smells good," she said. "Get some plates."

Blair shook as she opened the cupboard to grab plates. She was hoping Angela wouldn't notice the missing food. As she scooped rice and sweet-and-sour chicken onto her plate, Blair watched as Angela searched the bag.

"Where are the egg rolls?"

"There ... there aren't any."

"What do you mean, 'there aren't any'?"

"I ordered them, but they weren't in there."

Angela removed the last box and spread the empty bag out, peering inside.

"You had one task," she breathed.

"I'm sorry," Blair said. "They must have forgotten."

"Or you're just stupid."

Blair held her head down, flinching as Angela slapped her on the side of her head. "Get out of my sight," she snapped.

Blair shrunk away and grabbed her plate to go upstairs.

"Where do you think you're going?"

"I-I was going to eat in my room," Blair said, voice so low that she could barely hear herself.

"You're not eating." Angela snatched the plate away from Blair. "*Now* you can go to your room."

With a rumbling stomach, Blair left the kitchen and retreated to her bedroom. Once there, she curled up on her bed and stared at the wall until night fell. She wished she wasn't such a coward and had the balls to get a job to save up money. Closing her eyes, Blair fantasized about the day she could move out.

Eventually, her stomach stopped hurting, and she fell asleep.

* * *

Thursday Mass came and went. Blair and Andrew sat with the other seniors in one of the back pews. Julian sat next to Andrew, and it was nice for Blair to see them forming a friendship.

As they left school on Friday and Andrew began to get closer to her house, Blair felt her heart thudding in her chest. She was shaking slightly, worried that she would lose her nerve.

"So, did you have a good first week of school?" she asked.

Andrew looked over to her as he slowed on her street. "I did," he said. "It was … interesting, to say the least. And kinda weird in some parts, but it was good." His voice emphasized "good" at the end, and Blair knew he was talking about her.

They were now pulling into her driveway. Blair could sense that Andrew had no expectations. He was just dropping her off as usual.

Reaching for the door handle, Blair's hand shook.

"Do you want to see what my house looks like?" she asked awkwardly.

The sentence came out of her mouth clumsily. *What the hell was that, Blair?* She couldn't believe she couldn't even ask Andrew properly if he wanted to visit.

His expression changed, and she saw him contemplate her offer momentarily.

"Are your parents home?"

"No."

"… I don't know that I should be going into your house if your parents haven't met me yet," he said.

Blair instantly regretted her offer. *Too soon, Blair, much too soon*. But she refused to let rejection get the better of her. Not yet, anyway.

"Andrew, my parents don't give a damn about you," she said, a little too harshly. "And by that, I mean my mom saw you drop me off the other day and basically said nothing. My dad works third shifts for twelve hours every day, and I barely see him anymore… It's not a big deal."

Andrew still seemed reluctant. But at the end of the day, he was still a teenage boy, and Blair was a teenage girl—and she was offering him the chance to come into her house while her parents weren't home. She could tell he was thinking about it, but the good boy in him was agonizing about not following some proper protocol.

"My mom is at her apartment for tonight," Blair pushed. "She has a big conference tomorrow at the Hilton. And my dad just left for work thirty minutes ago. They're not going to be coming home at all. It'll be okay."

Andrew sighed, then turned off the car. "Okay," he said, still a bit nervous.

Blair was giddy all of a sudden and opened the door. Andrew followed her hesitantly up the front pathway, his hands in his coat pockets. It was the first time Blair had seen him out of his element.

Unlocking the door, she suddenly felt aware of every aspect of her home. Andrew stood until she told him to take off his coat and shoes. An old wooden clock with a pendulum ticked methodically on the wall.

"Are you hungry?" she asked.

Andrew looked around and shook his head.

Blair gestured to the living room, dining room, and kitchen layout and remarked that it wasn't as big as other people's houses. Instinctively, she knew that his home had to be bigger and more expensive.

"It's nice," Andrew said.

Blair stood, unsure of how this whole thing was supposed to go.

"Umm ... if you want, I can show you my room?" Her voice was slowly becoming smaller and smaller.

"Sure," Andrew said.

Blair started up the stairs to the second floor, maybe a little too quickly, entirely aware that Andrew could get a look up her skirt if he wanted to.

Chapter 12

Lightning Strike

Blair slowly opened her bedroom door, and Andrew followed her cautiously, as if every step he took in her home was dangerous.

"So, this is where I sleep," she said with an outstretched hand.

Andrew again looked around, seemingly surprised at how plain it looked. Blair didn't have a lot of belongings—no band posters typical of someone her age, no collage of pictures, just a bed pushed up against the wall, a TV facing the bed on the dresser to the side, and a bookcase with some books, magazines, and a DVD collection.

In that moment, Blair realized how entirely ill-thought-out her plan was. Truly, she had no plan. The plan had just been to get Andrew Stormant into her house. And here he was, and here she was, standing in her room, saying nothing and doing nothing.

Just before Blair thought she would turn into a puddle on the floor, Andrew's eyes widened, and he immediately went to her bookcase.

"You have *The Secret of NIMH*?" he asked in disbelief.

Blair smiled. "… Yeah?"

"Oh my God, I haven't seen this movie in years!" he said excitedly. "Can I…?"

Blair gave a nod of approval for him to grab the DVD.

As he was looking at the back cover, she spoke. "Do you want to watch it together?"

Andrew looked up while holding the case. "… I'll have to text my mom to let her know where I am," he said. "But it shouldn't be a problem."

Blair took the DVD from him and sat on the edge of her bed, opening the case and placing the disc in her player. She gestured for Andrew to come and sit next to her.

"Sorry … I don't have any chairs in here," she said.

"This is fine."

As the movie started, Andrew kept repeating how he hadn't seen the film in years and how it had been one of his favorites as a child. It was one of those movies he would sometimes think about, meaning to look it up to watch it again—but then he would forget about it the moment the thought had passed.

After about fifteen minutes of sitting without support, Blair felt pressure in her neck and upper shoulders. As the winter sun went down, the room became darker and darker. Blair realized that this was usually when she would fall asleep after school. She couldn't fall asleep now—not with Andrew sitting next to her. But she also couldn't sit on the edge of her bed in agony for a whole movie.

"I, um… I need to lay down. My back and neck are hurting," she finally said to him.

"Oh—uh, where would you like me to be?"

Blair was too tired and sore to be particularly shy about it.

"You can just ... put your legs over mine and put your back against the wall, if you'd like."

Andrew began to move, and Blair lay down to face the television. She made sure her skirt was tucked under her, and once she was comfortable, Andrew sat as she suggested. He was trying to keep the contact of his legs over her to a minimum.

They watched in total darkness now, the screen illuminating them. They were coming up on Blair's favorite scene. Her eyes were heavy as the kaleidoscope of mandala-like shapes and DNA strains flashed on the screen—when the rats and mice emerged from the other side of the scientific experiments.

Nicodemus's deep and wise voice narrated.

Blair had always loved the scene of Jonathan opening the latched door to rescue the other mice from the lab, how cute he looked, wiping his forehead. Poor Mrs. Brisby's sadness at seeing her dead husband's heroism.

Blair could no longer stay awake afterward; the sound of Mrs. Brisby and Nicodemus's voices were too soothing. Andrew must have seen her eyes close or felt it was the right moment, because Blair felt his warmth shift just as her eyes shut. Andrew was now behind her. He wrapped his arm around the front of her waist and snuggled up to her. Blair welcomed his head behind hers, his breath in her hair. She desperately wanted to stay awake to enjoy it, but she simply could not keep her eyes open any longer. She was lulled into slumber by Andrew's large hand caressing her hair behind her ear repeatedly.

Sometime later, Blair heard her name.

"Blair," Andrew whispered. His breath was hot on her ear.

She stirred. As she came to, she felt Andrew's hand rub

her sweater-covered stomach, giving her flutters of excitement. She rolled over to him.

He was smiling.

"The movie's over," he told her, still in a whisper. Blair could hear the song playing during the credits.

She looked up at him, taking in how happy he was and how beautiful his hazel-brown eyes looked in the light of the television. It was the first time she could really look deeply at him.

Moving his hand from her stomach to her face, Andrew leaned in and kissed her.

A pulse shot through Blair's body, instantly hitting the center of her thighs—like a lightning strike. *This is really happening.* Andrew kissed her softly, warm and wet, his lips larger than hers, but gentle. He was staying relatively at the front of her lips, mouth only slightly open with a bit of tongue—encouraging her to yield to him, but only if she wanted to.

Blair slipped a hand behind his neck, pulling him into her. She pushed her tongue against his, forcing a deeper kiss between them. His breath on her upper lip, the smell of him, his hands—firm, but never aggressive... Blair welcomed all of it. She felt a flash of worry at seeming too easy, but quickly shoved that mental attack back into the depths it came from.

And while there was the "mature" side of Blair that wanted to go a little bit further, there was still a pang of fear lingering behind her arousal. She didn't know what it was or what it meant, just that she wasn't ready for whatever was supposed to come next. Pulling away, Blair caught her breath. Andrew was trying to pace himself, too, it seemed.

He then stroked her hair around her face, looking at her forehead, eyes, and lips, searching.

If It All Fades Away

"Blair," he said softly.

She gazed at him with her full attention. He looked as if he had something profound to say.

"Can we be together?"

Blair's breath felt faint and shallow. She couldn't be sure she was hearing him correctly. And while she was overjoyed to be asked that question by him, another part of her brain—the protective part—instantly jumped in front of her soft-hearted side, like a big sister, demanding an answer to one single question: why would he ever want to be with someone like her?

Blair stared at Andrew, searching for any ill intent—as if at any moment, he could pull a "just kidding" on her. But all he did was smile.

"Why?" Blair croaked.

Andrew's eyes flicked back and forth over hers, waiting for her to ask her whole question.

"Why do you want to be with me?"

Andrew blinked, briefly organizing his thoughts, then spoke almost immediately.

"Because ... I feel like I've known you my whole life already. Because you're funny, and kind—"

Blair's face cracked like a doll's when Andrew said the word "kind." Her eyes shifted downward, unable to look at him. Her throat squeezed shut as she attempted not to cry, but the tears flowed anyway. Andrew seemed unfazed by it. As she cried, he continued brushing the hair away from her forehead.

"Because from the moment I first saw you through that window in the office, I knew I wanted to be closer to you."

Andrew kissed her temple.

"Because you're beautiful," he whispered into her hair.

Blair's whole body shook as she sobbed, choking back

ugly throat noises. Andrew put his arms around her, pulling her into him. She cried into his chest. He was deliciously warm, and so big compared to her tiny body. She wished she could bottle up his smell and keep it forever. His sweater was becoming wet from her tears. He rubbed her back and stroked her hair repeatedly.

Eventually, Blair was able to breathe. Her face was puffy, and her head hurt from crying. Finally, she was still.

"Almost everyone," she said, her voice thick from crying.

Andrew looked down at her, hand on the side of her face, thumb on her cheek. She was still looking downward. Again, he waited for her, listening.

"The answer to your question—'Who hurt you?'—is 'almost everyone.'"

"Oh, Blair," he said, so sorrowful. Squeezing her tight, he rocked her as best he could. "I can't promise anything, because I know life can get messy ... but if I ever did hurt you, I just want you to know that it would never be on purpose. Ever."

The pressure in the top of Blair's skull and sinuses was immeasurable. Eventually, she pulled away from Andrew and lay on her back. They were silent as Andrew lightly traced his fingers over her neck and face.

"I feel so sad for her," Blair said, staring at the ceiling. "Elizabeth Hartman."

"Who?"

"The actress who voiced Mrs. Brisby."

She could tell that Andrew didn't know.

"*The Secret of NIMH* was the last movie she ever did. She left acting after that, and died five years later by suicide."

Andrew seemed crestfallen at hearing this.

"My God, did she have a beautiful voice," Blair said. "I just think ... how alone she must have felt at the end, because

If It All Fades Away

I think that people always feel ... so alone when they get to that point. I know I have... I'm sorry." Blair cried, shuddering, bringing her hands to her face. "I'm so sorry. You asked me one question, and I didn't answer it at all."

"Blair, it's okay," Andrew said, snuggling closer to her.

Blair breathed deeply, her chest filling. Then she exhaled.

"Yes," she said.

Andrew perched himself to be over her once more.

"Yes, we can be together," she said, smiling. She sat up and pushed him down onto her pillow, kissing him deeply.

Chapter 13

New Status

It was official: Blair Simons was dating Andrew Stormant.

That was how Blair thought of it, abstractly and objectively, because she still couldn't believe it. Rachel couldn't believe it either when Blair texted her.

Rachel: *I get sick and am gone for a few days and you end up with a boyfriend?!*

Blair: *You should probably get sick more often, and we can see what else improves in my life, lol*

Rachel: *No kidding! OMG*

Blair thought of Andrew all weekend—how badly she wanted to see him again, to kiss, cuddle, watch movies, and hold hands. She couldn't stop smiling at random moments. Her father was home on the weekends, but he was practically a zombie in front of the TV. Meanwhile, Blair dutifully did her required weekend chores—cleaning the upstairs and

If It All Fades Away

downstairs bathrooms, sweeping, mopping, and any laundry that was undone.

Her mother came home on Sunday morning, and Blair avoided both of her parents as much as possible. The tension between them as they tried to maintain some semblance of a connection one or two days a week was soul-sucking at best. Usually, the discussions in the living room revolved around bills and housework that her father was too exhausted to complete, but simultaneously refused to hire anyone else to do.

* * *

Monday morning, Blair was nervous, as Angela was awake and drinking coffee in the living room. She had the day off. Blair timidly made herself toast in the kitchen. As she ate slowly and deliberately, each minute that ticked by felt excruciatingly slow.

Blair couldn't shake the feeling that her mother would start something with her as she tried to leave the house.

"That Stormant boy picking you up again today?" she finally asked.

"Yes."

"What do his parents do?"

"I haven't asked yet."

"Jesus, Blair, do you ever think of anyone but yourself?"

Blair remained silent. She finished her glass of water and threw away the piece of paper towel she had been eating off of. Andrew would arrive in five minutes.

Blair knew the real issue wasn't that she hadn't asked Andrew what his parents did (although she did feel guilty at the mention of it), but rather, that her mother wanted to see how she herself measured up to *his* mother. She didn't put much stock in measuring her marriage against others anymore, but as far as being a powerful woman in a corporate job, she was always competing. Even if other women were more successful, Angela Simons always found a way to try to cut others down to her level.

The lights of Andrew's SUV crawled across the back wall of the dining room, cueing Blair to get up and head out.

Just as she was about to open the front door, Angela spoke.

"We'll have to schedule an appointment with Dr. Brewer."

Blair paused.

Her mother sipped her coffee and grinned. "You don't look like that and not end up pregnant. I was seventeen once, too, you know."

Blair blushed. "Mom…"

She chuckled. "Have a great day, cauliflower."

That was her nickname from being a colicky baby, "colick" sounding like "cauliflower."

Blair opened the front door and was so happy that her mother seemed to approve of Andrew. She had her charming moments, for sure—which always broke Blair's heart when they disappeared in an instant. She could never predict when she would be "cool" or "crazy"—because there was no in-between to Blair. She was forced to suffer the whiplash of Angela's ever-changing moods.

Once inside Andrew's car, Blair wanted to kiss him, but knew her mother was watching.

"One of your parents home?" Andrew asked.

"My mom," Blair said, buckling her seat belt. "She thinks we're banging already and wants to take me to get on birth control."

Andrew's eyes got wide.

"I didn't tell her we're dating, but she already knows. She's always had a sense for that kind of stuff. Probably pretty obvious, since I've never mentioned any other boys."

"Hudson?"

"Gross. But yeah, no—my parents still don't know about that."

Andrew was driving down the street. "Wait—what?"

"I begged Mr. Davis not to call them. He just told me to do my suspension out of school. So, I did. He probably broke some protocol or something by not telling them, but I think he's just so jaded with me that he doesn't care anymore."

Andrew's brow was furrowed. Blair wasn't giving him anything more than that at the moment.

"Do you have any projects you're working on?" Andrew asked, changing the topic.

"Just a sociology project. We had to research female criminals. I decided to do mine on female gangs in the United States."

Andrew laughed. "Of course you did."

"Whatcha implying over there, Stormant?"

"Oh, nothing. It's just so very … you."

"I can get down with some sister loyalty," Blair said, nodding. "Step to me or my loved ones, and I'll cut a bitch."

Andrew just shook his head and laughed.

* * *

Blair was happy to see Rachel was back. Although she was still taking her antibiotics, she was feeling much better.

At lunch, Rachel was always the first at the table. Then came Blair and then the other girls, usually. As it was, Blair and Andrew now arrived together, the same as they had since last Wednesday.

Rachel was waiting for them both. In true Andrew style, he introduced himself and shook Rachel's hand. Anyone else, and it would have been too much, but anyone who interacted with him could tell that his interest in others came from a genuine place. Rachel was flattered, and Blair was proud.

They sat, talked, and laughed as the other girls slowly arrived at the table. Blair did her best to ignore it, but once the girls had expressed their condolences to Rachel for being sick, they ignored her completely. Instead, they started talking to Blair excitedly. She hated it, but she also didn't know how to be mean to them now that they sat together daily.

One glance over to Rachel, and Blair could sense that she was baffled about what had happened while she was gone. Blair couldn't put it into words, except that the queen bee of the little clique, Claire, now seemed to regard Blair as an equal. That devastated Rachel, because she had worked all four years to level up with these girls, to be something to them. And here, in less than a week, Blair had achieved something that Rachel never would with them. A seat at the table, figuratively, not just literally. And it hurt Blair to see that this bothered Rachel. Immediately, she felt terrible for her friend and managed to turn the conversation back over to Rachel to take control of it.

Andrew, while a sweetheart, could not pick up on any of this. And why would he? He was a new student, a boy, and the whole reason all of them were behaving differently anyway.

Blair hated the moment that a dick was added to the equation—for anything. It meant that suddenly, the women involved started a henpecking order, assigning value as to who was at the top. With Blair now dating Andrew, none of the girls at the table, including Ms. Queen Bee herself, wanted to admit that it was Blair. Blair was the one on top. She didn't think like this on purpose, but they all thought about it subconsciously and had known it all too well since infancy: where their places were, where they stood in the world of men, and particularly, where they stood in the world of women—formed *around* the importance of men.

Chapter 14

1984

Blair hadn't known it was possible to be this happy. She thought of Andrew all the time and wanted to be with him all the time. They coordinated their class routes as best they could, either walking together, or reaching out to touch each other's hands in passing.

Blair looked forward to every morning when Andrew would pick her up and when they had first-period study hall together. She found that being happy compelled her to study harder. Watching Andrew work hard at his studies made her also want to work hard. Blair realized that even though they were dating now, she weirdly wanted to impress him, to match his level of commitment to learning.

To be worthy of being his girlfriend.

Mrs. Dakota was surprised when Blair finally turned in the paper that she had told her to "go get some dick" over. She had marked it off in her grade book as incomplete, but had to go back in and erase the mark. She checked it as completed, though she was forced to take off a few points for it being late.

"I'm sorry for what I said to you last week," Blair said, handing her the paper after class one day.

The look of shock on Mrs. Dakota's face was a Kodak-worthy moment. Blair realized that Mr. Davis hadn't actually followed up with her about whether or not Blair apologized. And why would he? She was a seventeen-year-old senior who had been a troublemaker since day one. They were all just going through the motions at this point.

* * *

On Friday, Blair stayed after school to ask Ms. Holland some questions about that week's assignment. She texted Andrew where she was. He arrived quietly as Blair was sitting in a front desk, casually chatting away. Ms. Holland turned and smiled.

"Blair tells me you guys have been discussing Orwell."

Blair scoffed. "He read all of his books when he was, like, ten."

"That's not true, just *1984* and *Animal Farm*," Andrew corrected. "My mom had them from when she was in high school."

"Whatever." Blair waved her hand. "Still a weirdo reading dystopian shit before you had pubes growing."

"Language, Simons," Ms. Holland said, but only out of obligation.

"Sorry." Blair grinned.

Andrew took a seat at a desk next to Blair.

"I was just telling her how we were talking about the movie," Blair said to Andrew, "and how I got mad at you that you haven't seen it."

"Oh, yeah, Blair's upset that I haven't seen it," Andrew confirmed.

"John Hurt—what a phenomenal actor," Ms. Holland remarked.

"Then we were talking about the *1984* Apple Super Bowl commercial, and how I got really mad that he hadn't seen that either."

Ms. Holland laughed. "Stormant, you're going to be submitted to a lot of visual media while you're with Blair."

"Yeah, she literally busted out her phone and pulled up YouTube to make me watch it."

They all laughed.

"I remember seeing that live when I was young," Ms. Holland added. "It was really something to experience firsthand."

"So jealous," Blair commented.

There was a moment of silence. Ms. Holland was still smiling at her desk, chin on one hand.

"You two are so cute together."

Blair and Andrew both squirmed a little, then smiled.

"Say, since I have you both for English, I'll give you both extra credit if you watch the movie *1984* and compare it to the book, plus explain why you think the movie and the Apple commercial being released during the actual year 1984 was so significant."

Blair groaned loudly and exaggeratedly, throwing herself across the desk. "I should have known we can't talk about anything without it becoming some sort of assignment."

"Make it a date night," Ms. Holland said, chipper. "Stormant, you don't need the points, but knowing you, you'll want them anyway."

Andrew didn't protest. In fact, he got out his small notebook and jotted down the assignment.

"You really need to write that down?" Blair asked him.

If It All Fades Away

"I just want to make sure I'm getting all the details," he said, his tone serious.

"Is that a 'yes,' then?"

Blair and Andrew both said "yes" in unison.

"Great," Ms. Holland said. "Blair, do you own the movie, or do you need a copy?"

"I don't have it, actually. So, a copy would be great."

"I'll be right back." Ms. Holland left the room with a smile plastered on her face, and now Andrew and Blair were alone.

"So … when can we watch it together?" Blair asked, all too eager.

"Umm… I was thinking of us watching it separately."

Blair laughed. "Andrew, it's just extra credit."

"I know," he said. "I'm just worried I won't be able to focus if we watch it together."

"I'm not letting you borrow it," Blair teased. "So, if you want to watch it alone, you're going to have to rent it."

Andrew was looking at her with sweet eyes, but also like he wanted to object.

Ms. Holland returned a moment later. "Had to get it out of the media storage closet across the hall." She handed Blair the case.

"Is there a due date for this?" Andrew asked.

"No," Ms. Holland said casually. "Just make sure I get it before the end of the semester. That way, you can get the points for your report card." She was now seated at her desk again.

"We should get going," Andrew informed Blair.

"Right," Blair said, standing up.

Andrew and Blair waved their goodbyes.

As they walked down the hallway to leave school, Andrew was quiet. He was quiet on his way out to his vehicle as well. Blair didn't ask why, but she felt something was wrong. Once inside his SUV, she spoke.

"Did I say something to upset you?" she asked.

Andrew looked over to her, as if he didn't realize he hadn't been speaking, then back to the steering wheel. "Oh—uh, no... I was just thinking about what I remember from the book. I'll have to read it again—I haven't read it since my freshman year. And I was just thinking of when I can find time to read it, because we're already reading three books at the same time in her class right now."

Blair swallowed. "Andrew."

He turned to look at her again. She had a look of disconcertion on her face. She waited for him to realize what she was getting at, and his face was searching hers, waiting for her to speak.

"Andrew, it's not that serious."

She saw his eyes scan her whole face, then he smiled.

"Yeah," he said, "you're right." He laughed. "I'm probably overthinking it."

"You are," Blair insisted.

Andrew turned the key in the ignition.

They were silent for the rest of the ride to Blair's house.

* * *

When Blair got into the house, she was startled to see her father, Gerald, looking out the window.

"Who was that?"

"Oh, that was Andrew. He's in my grade."

Her father scoffed, rubbing his greying beard.

"Did you eat the last of the potato chips?" he asked out of nowhere.

"What? No."

"Don't lie to me."

"Dad, I'm telling the truth."

Her father covered the short distance from the window to the door rather quickly. He grabbed Blair by her ponytail and yanked back, hard. Involuntary tears sprang up from the force.

"Then you're going to go to the store and get more. Got it?"

Blair sniffled and nodded. She smelled alcohol on his breath.

He shoved her away. "Useless," he mumbled.

"Do ... do you have any money for me to get more?" Blair asked carefully.

Her father pulled out his wallet and handed her a ten-dollar bill. "And be quick about it."

Wiping her eyes, Blair left the house and walked to the liquor store nearby. Her toes and fingers were freezing cold by the time she returned.

"Grab me another beer," Gerald barked as soon as she got in the door.

"Yes, sir."

Tasks completed, Blair retreated to her room as quickly as possible. She rubbed her neck, feeling a kink in it from being yanked back unexpectedly. She would stay in her room for the rest of the evening.

Hurt and angry, she counted the change she had in her piggy bank. A whopping $24.06. She had been saving up her money for a special-edition movie she wanted. If she wasn't such a coward, she would go out and apply for a job. As it was, she was relegated to saving what little money she had and counting down the days until graduation.

She couldn't wait to move out.

Chapter 15

The Cat and the Snake

Blair got on birth control the following week. The pelvic exam wasn't as dreadful as she thought it would be. Her mother was actually a good sport about the whole thing. Blair figured it probably had something to do with her parents having her so young. As her aunt Natalie told it, both sets of her grandparents had been furious and horrified when they found out Angela was pregnant. They met at the kitchen table and discussed what to do, agreeing to wed the young couple. The shame and scandal from the greater Catholic community would be too great to bear.

Walking to her locker on Wednesday after Church Duty, Blair spotted Claire standing at a locker nearby, talking to one of the other girls. Little Ms. Queen Bee herself—maybe not of the whole senior class, but certainly of the middle tier of girls. Blair was not fooled for one second by her motives. She handled her carefully, expecting her to bite at any moment, like the snake that she was.

"Blair!" she called out to her.

"Uh, hi," she said.

"So, um, we're having a thing this Friday. At my place. And we wanted to invite you."

Blair must have stared like a cat spotted, ready to pounce on said snake, because she felt her head move forward unnaturally. She had a specific reaction, as if to say, *"What the fuck did you just say to me?"*

"But ... only you," the other girl, Annabelle, added. "And Stormant, if you want to bring him."

"What about Rachel?" Blair asked immediately.

The two girls looked at each other, surprised, perhaps, that Blair wasn't getting the hint.

"It's, umm, for couples only ... and anyone trying to hook up..."

"Yeah, there'll be other guys there and stuff, so it's not just us girls," Claire noted.

Blair could see exactly what was happening here. Rachel was being put into the square-virgin category—the goody-two-shoes innocent bookworm, who had no business going to a party that would most definitely involve drinking and people humping in back rooms.

"I'll, uh ... have to talk to Andrew," Blair said, taking her coat off and putting it on an inner hook.

"Great!" Claire said.

"You going down to lunch now?" Annabelle asked her.

"Um, I will... I gotta use the bathroom first."

"Oh, good, 'cause we have to go, too."

Dammit.

Blair wasn't getting out of this. And where the hell was Andrew? He was the one usually waiting for her. She sent him a quick text message. The girls practically shoved her down the hall.

Once in the lunch line, Blair tried to avoid Claire and Annabelle as much as possible. She knew Rachel would already be seated and eating, but she tried not to provoke her anxiety about these bimbos if she could help it.

Thankfully, just as she was turning to look back, Andrew arrived behind some other people in line. Thank God. Blair told the girls to go ahead and that she would get her food with Andrew.

"Hi, Andrew!" Claire said obnoxiously.

Andrew nodded respectfully, as he always did.

"Hope it's okay that we stole your girlfriend away," Annabelle said.

"It's not a problem," he said with a smile.

Blair walked up to him and put her arms around his waist playfully. She was truly smitten to see him, and just as he was leaning in to kiss her—she caught it out of the corner of her eye. A flicker, a dash, a moment—in Claire's eyes. She still had a smile on her face, but her eyes betrayed her. Blair knew what it was instinctively, and a moment of cockiness overcame her. Instead of just a peck, she slipped Stormant some tongue, not looking at the two girls.

"Jesus, get a room, you two," Hudson said behind them. Blair hadn't realized he and his cronies had arrived.

"Screw you, Hudson," Blair said, so flippantly dismissive, turning away from him.

Andrew stayed with his back to Hudson, holding Blair's hand. Once she glanced in the direction of Claire and Annabelle again, she could see that Annabelle was fully facing forward, but Claire was not. Blair could tell she was watching them from the corner of her eye. She talked as if she were fully engaged, but she was still tracking their movements. Blair knew the tactic well, because she had to use it her whole life, too, the same as Claire—always on the lookout for potential dangers.

Blair. Blair was the danger now. She had to remind

herself not to get too carried away with this feeling. This security. This cockiness.

But for once, it was nice to be seen, and not just as the weirdo girl who told other girls to "shut up or you'll get done up"—or B3, the overreactive bitch who'd punched Hudson. No, now … now she was an actual person. Someone worth respecting.

* * *

Walking to Thursday Mass with Rachel, Blair could tell she was not her usual self. Once they got into the church, seated in the back row of pews, Blair tapped Rachel's arm and mouthed, *"What's wrong?"*

Rachel mouthed back, *"I'll tell you later."*

Blair had a sinking feeling that it had something to do with the party tomorrow night.

The way the pews had filled in, Andrew wasn't seated with her today; he was a few rows up with Julian.

After the second reading, Blair saw a teardrop hit Rachel's arm. Blair opened her mouth, but Rachel got up and left before she could say anything. Blair waited for a few moments to avoid being obvious, then followed Rachel to the church bathroom.

Opening the door, she could see Rachel crying.

"Rachel, what's wrong?" Blair asked.

Rachel was startled at the sight of Blair. She wiped her eyes, went to a stall to get some toilet paper, and blew her nose.

"Hi," Blair said, not looking at her. "What's going on?"

"I feel so stupid," Rachel said. "I shouldn't feel this way, but I do."

Blair's heart was thudding.

"It's just..." Rachel sniffled. "Ever since I was gone because of my ear infection and cold ... and coming back, and Andrew is sitting with us—which don't get me wrong, it's great—it's just like ... I'm invisible at the lunch table now."

"Rachel, those girls are monsters," Blair said.

"I know, but it's like..." She blew her nose again, then took a deep breath. "It's like they don't even want to talk to me anymore."

"Why do you care so much about what they think?" Blair asked.

Rachel exhaled, somewhat annoyed. "Blair, is it true?"

"Is what true?"

"That Claire invited you to her party tomorrow night?"

"Yes. And I have no intention of going."

Rachel started crying again. Blair put her hand on her back, rubbing slowly. She wasn't sure if that was what Rachel needed. It certainly wasn't how anyone comforted her, until Andrew recently. Blair thought momentarily and then found what she hoped were the right words.

"Rachel, I think they shit on you because they know you care so much."

"I know, that's my problem! I always care too much."

Blair had an idea.

"What about Julian?"

Rachel's head perked up. "What?"

"He sits at a different table, but what if we sat with him instead? Andrew and him are kinda friends now, I think, so it wouldn't be too weird."

"But his table is always full."

Blair could see that Rachel was thinking about it. She had a massive crush on Julian, but was always too shy to do much about it.

"Honestly, they'll probably be shocked if we stop sitting with them. God knows Claire will act like one of her lapdogs escaped... No offense."

"No, it's true," Rachel said. "I'm freaking pathetic."

"You're not pathetic, you're just too nice for them. Like, actually nice and kind, and they're all fake as shit."

Rachel stared off now, her face becoming slightly less strained. Her tears dried.

"I can talk to Andrew about it?" Blair offered.

"Yeah, okay," Rachel agreed.

"Come on," Blair said, wrapping her arm around Rachel's shoulders. "Let's get back out there, so we can wish that Father Donovan's ass wasn't covered up in a robe."

Rachel laughed, and Blair could see that she was feeling much better.

* * *

Rachel and Blair sat with the girls at lunch as if nothing was amiss. Any evidence of Rachel crying was long gone. Watching Claire prattle on about next month's Winter Wonderland Dance and what she planned to wear was nauseating. Blair had only vaguely thought about it, but Claire's mouth yapping reminded her that it was only a few weeks away.

Rachel and Blair had gone last year, and their sophomore year. As non-dancers, they just migrated back and forth between the gymnasium and the hallway. Other hall minglers were out there as well, in little groups, socializing. A few girls humored Rachel during dance breaks, while Blair stood by awkwardly.

Thankfully, this year would be different. Blair would have Andrew to go with. And if this whole lunch table thing worked out, maybe Rachel would have Julian to go with, too.

Blair texted her mother about the dress situation after lunch. She had never gone dress shopping before, but this time she would. In previous years, Rachel's older sister, Rebecca, had let Blair borrow dresses for homecoming and the Winter Wonderland Dance. This year, Blair really wanted one of her own—something that would wow Andrew.

Chapter 16

Blue

Blair had to forgo she and Andrew's Friday night date plans. (One of Andrew's conditions of dating was that they could only see each other after school on Fridays.) Angela said that if they were going to go dress shopping, they should do it now, before all the good ones were picked over. She made time in her schedule to take Blair to the mall.

They had now looked in a few stores without much luck. It seemed that a lot of the dresses were too childish. Blair had a vision of what she would like to wear, but was too afraid to ask her mother, fearing she would say it was too expensive.

Blair could never understand how her mother and father worked so much, yet they always argued about money. They acted annoyed or told her she didn't need it if she asked for something new. She supposed her tuition, her mother's apartment, the house, and car payments must add up. What little money she was now saving for an apartment was not nearly enough to even hope to buy a decent dress.

Blair tried not to sulk when they hadn't found anything yet and only one store was left: Carmen's Prom & Bridal

Shop. It was most certainly where all the lunch table girls got their dresses, and Blair could only imagine that Claire would make sure to get something outrageously expensive.

Her mother stopped at the cross section of the mall, putting her hands on her hips with a sigh. Blair said nothing. She knew the body language, even if she was behind her. Angela was contemplating something, but wasn't sure if she was ready to commit to whatever it was. Could it be…? Then she turned to Blair.

"If we do this, I expect some serious good behavior from you until the end of this year, and when Aunt Natalie visits. Any smart-ass remarks to me in front of her, and I'll bring that dress right back here."

Blair couldn't help a grin forming across her face.

It was about seven o'clock in the evening now, and nobody else was at the bridal shop. It was located on the far end of the mall, tucked in a corner. Entering the store, Blair realized she had never actually gone into it. She felt like she was crossing over some forbidden threshold. The mannequins were beautifully adorned with formal dresses for young ladies, and of course, bridal gowns. Blair admired them individually as they approached the center, where a consultant was standing. She was curvy, with short-cropped hair and expertly applied makeup. Her face lit up as Blair and her mother approached.

"How can I help you this evening?" she asked enthusiastically.

"We're shopping for a winter dance dress," Angela informed her.

"St. Michael's?" she asked.

"That's the one."

"Well, you've come to the right place. We have a wonderful selection of unique, one-of-a-kind dresses, so you never have to worry about another girl wearing the same dress."

That thought had never occurred to Blair before. Then again, she wouldn't be familiar with that kind of thing—that a boutique would ensure that no two dresses were identical.

"If you want to just come over here, dear, and I'll take your measurements real quick. Then I can look and see what we have that's closest to your size."

Blair approached the panel of three mirrors and stood on a raised platform. The consultant pulled out a loose tape measure and looped it around Blair's bust, waist, and hips.

"You're a tiny thing, aren't you?" the woman said, finishing the last measurement around her hips.

Angela was seated on a nearby white chaise longue, watching, her elbow and head resting on the back.

"If you'll follow me, I'll show you some of what we have."

Blair and Angela followed her to the back of the store, not far from the mirrors and dressing rooms. Dresses were hanging there, and the woman stopped just before them.

"You have any idea of what style you'd like to wear, and what color?"

Blair glanced at her mother, who gestured to the woman, like *"She's asking you."*

"Umm…" Blair mumbled. "Something blue?"

"Perfect color for a winter dance. Let's see what we have here."

She moved down the way a bit to where some blue dresses were hanging. Blair moved closer.

"You can come over here, dear."

Blair then walked up to the blue dress section.

She sifted through them. Some had very deep V-cuts, plunging too far down for Blair's comfort. There were spaghetti-strap ones, which reminded Blair of the nineties. And still more with long sleeves.

Then Blair saw it. It was a completely strapless gown with subtle sparkles all over—the kind that wasn't too much, but stood out. She loved that it had a sweetheart neckline. And there was a slight slit up the side—tastefully sexy and beautiful.

Before she could get carried away, she tried to sneak a look at a price tag ... and there wasn't one.

"Umm, Mom, I think I like this one."

Angela came a little closer. "What about that one with the long sleeves and open back?"

Blair turned to look again. She had considered it, but she didn't like how low it went in the back.

"I ... feel like my back would get cold," Blair said.

Angela scoffed. "And your arms and shoulders aren't going to get cold in that one?"

One glance at the consultant, and Blair was thankful that she knew when to intervene.

"We can try a few on. Sometimes what you think looks good on a hanger doesn't always look good once you try it on."

That seemed to satisfy Angela. Blair agreed to try on the long-sleeved one, the sweetheart-neck one she liked, and a third one with a nice turtleneck-like collar exposing the shoulders. The consultant placed all three dresses in a large dressing room.

"You let me know if you need any help. Otherwise, just come on out when you're ready."

"Okay," Blair called, slipping out of her street clothes.

She looked at all three dresses and contemplated which one to try first. She decided to go with the turtleneck one, as neither she nor her mother seemed particularly invested in it.

If It All Fades Away

Slipping it on and shimmying her butt into the fabric, she took one look in the mirror and didn't like it. She didn't hate it, but it certainly wasn't the one.

She came out.

Her mother looked up at her, and Blair knew that she didn't care for it either.

"What do you think of this one?" the consultant asked.

Blair opened her mouth to speak.

"Go ahead and step up on the platform, that way you can get a better look."

Blair stepped up and looked at herself in the three mirrors.

"I just … don't like it," she said. "It's not bad, it's just … kinda boring."

She turned to look at her mother again.

"Agreed," she said flatly.

"Okay," the consultant said, as if that settled that.

Blair stepped down. "I'll, uh, try on the next one, then."

The consultant came in and helped Blair get out of the dress.

Looking at two dresses now, Blair knew in her heart what she wanted. She had known the moment she saw it, but she had to try this one on for her mother. Blair wasn't sure how she was going to tell her no. Stepping into the gown, she put her arms through the see-through sleeves with floral designs. There was no back to zip, but she adjusted as needed. There was a gap in the lower back region, which went far too low for her taste.

She stood and looked in the mirror. It wasn't her. It wasn't her style. It wasn't what she wanted at all. She sighed, then opened the dressing room door.

"Oh, I love it!" her mother said, putting her hands to her mouth.

Blair smiled a little because Angela was smiling. She

sheepishly stepped up onto the platform again. The consultant came over.

"I think it's a little too big in the back," Blair said.

"Anything can be altered, my dear, so that's not a problem."

Angela stood to the side, in front of Blair and the mirrors. "My God, Blair, you look stunning," she said.

Blair lowered her head, feeling her eyes getting a little glossy. She couldn't remember the last time—or ever—that her mother had paid her a compliment like that.

"I ... I still need to try on the other one," Blair said.

"Yeah, yeah," Angela said enthusiastically with a downward wave. "Try the other, honey, but I think this is the one."

Blair saw the consultant's face behind her in the mirror's reflection. The woman had been in the business a long time, that was obvious, and she had seen it all. Blair knew she saw a familiar situation unfolding before her, but it was still upsetting for her to witness.

Returning to the dressing room, Blair easily slipped out of the open-back dress; it fell to the floor in a pile. She didn't bother picking it up. She took a deep breath and then reached for the sweetheart one. Her bra straps were visible as she stepped into it and pulled it up to her chest. However, the dress had a built-in bustier. Blair knew she wouldn't need a bra for this, so she slipped hers off. She got the zipper all the way up in the back. Immediately, once she kicked the dress on the floor aside, she felt a small gasp escape her.

It was the most beautiful dress she had ever seen on herself. The lights caught the subtle glitter spectacularly. Blair loved how good her shoulders and collarbones looked in it. She could see herself with a little updo, a clutch, maybe even some heels. She imagined Andrew in a suit, with a look of admiration as he saw her in it for the first

If It All Fades Away

time. Blair could see it all. Them dancing under the lights together. Her with Rachel and Julian. All of them having a good time. She was smiling. Opening the door, she stepped out.

The consultant involuntarily let out a small noise of approval.

Blair, still smiling, stepped up onto the platform.

"Tell me what you think, dear," the woman said.

Blair couldn't stop smiling. She did a little twirl, and with all the lights focused on her, the glitter sparkles dazzled everywhere. She felt beautiful.

"I think this is the one," she said.

"I have to say, that's the most breathtaking one I've seen you in so far," the woman said.

Blair had almost forgotten about Angela, though. She was so happy coming out of the dressing room in a daze that she hadn't even looked at her mother's face; she just wanted to get up onto the platform right away. Now she turned to look at her. She immediately regretted that decision.

Her mother had her arms and legs crossed, her lips pursed.

"It does nothing for me," she said.

Blair swallowed. "But I really like it…"

"And I don't, so take it off."

The consultant looked terribly sad.

Blair looked down, the sparkles on her dress becoming obscene in her watery eyes. She started crying.

"Oh, don't tell me you're going to cry now? I just said it does nothing for me."

Blair was trying to stop the tears, but they kept falling.

"Come on, let's go," Angela said, standing up and grabbing her purse.

Blair felt a fire building inside of her chest. It was rushing upwards, like a river of flames, until finally it burst forth, up and out of her, violently.

"You don't even fucking *know* me!" Blair yelled through angry tears.

Her mother looked stunned, her eyes wide, clutching her purse strap; she had already been turned to leave.

"Excuse me?"

"I hated that dress!" Blair sobbed. "I hate it so much! And you only like it because it's some stupid shit *you* would wear."

"You know what?" her mother snapped, reaching into her purse. "You want that slutty dress? Fine." Shaking, Angela opened her wallet, pulled out a credit card, and threw it at Blair. It hit her upper arm and fell to the platform. "It's yours." She jammed her wallet back into her purse angrily. "Find your own way home."

And with that, she turned her back on Blair and left the store.

Blair's sobbing deepened. So thoroughly humiliated. So hurt.

The consultant came over to Blair and stepped up onto the platform. "Oh, sweetie," she said, wrapping her arms around her. "I'm so sorry."

Blair could not stop the tears from flowing; all she could do was accept a hug from a kind stranger.

* * *

When Andrew arrived to pick Blair up, he insisted on coming into the store to get her. Blair was sitting on the chaise longue when she saw the consultant stir and knew Andrew must have arrived. Coming into the center area, he looked over to Blair. She suddenly realized that this was the first time they had seen each other without their school uniforms. He looked good.

Blair stood up and started apologizing immediately for inconveniencing him, saying she wouldn't have called him if she had any other options. Andrew wordlessly came over and hugged her. It took all Blair had not to start crying again. He stroked the back of her head just the way she liked.

When Andrew turned to the consultant, he was still petting Blair's hair while they both looked at her.

"Like I said, dear, I can hold the dress for you, if you'd like."

"I … I don't know what I want to do."

Blair didn't want to buy the dress now. Not with her mother's credit card. She would be beholden to her for a year or more over that damn dress. They hadn't even purchased it, and already it had caused a huge disaster.

"What's going on?" Andrew asked both of them.

"I don't want the dress anymore. I'm not using my mom's credit card. I'll never hear the end of it. I'll just … borrow another one of Rachel's sister's dresses."

"I'll buy it for you," Andrew said immediately.

Blair pulled away from him. "What? No! You can't do that!"

"It's your senior year. It's the last winter dance you'll ever have. I want you to be happy."

"I … I don't want you to see it before the dance," Blair protested.

"All dresses come with a storage bag with the contents hidden," the consultant chimed in. Blair noticed she'd had a small affectionate smile on her face since the moment Andrew arrived.

"See?" Andrew said.

Blair didn't want Andrew to spend his money on her. But

she also knew this was her only chance to get the dress without her mother's help.

"... Okay," she said hesitantly.

"Is there anything else you need?" Andrew asked.

Blair hadn't even thought about it. "Well... I'll need some heels, I think. But I can always check the thrift store."

"No, that's ridiculous."

The consultant waited, and when Blair didn't object, she spoke.

"Would you like to look at the shoes we have?"

Blair nodded.

Andrew sat down on the chaise longue, and Blair and the woman went to the front of the store, where a selection of formal footwear was on display. Blair had no clue what would look best. With the consultant's help, she grabbed two pairs of silver heels. The woman wanted Blair to try them on with the dress, so back into the dressing room she went. She tried on the first pair, and the heel was too high, and the straps dug into the tops of her feet—definitely a no. The second pair was a pretty silver satin, open-toed, with an adorable raised bow detail in the front.

Blair hadn't thought it was possible, but she was smiling again.

"Alright if I take a look?" the consultant asked.

Blair opened the door. Andrew was on the other side of the large mirrors, so he wouldn't be able to see.

"Oh, those are adorable!"

Blair looked down. "They're adorable *and* comfortable."

"Hold on one second," the consultant said. And Blair waited for a full minute.

The woman came back with two clutches. She held one out in front of Blair, standing in the doorway, then the other.

"Definitely this one," she said, handing the first one to Blair.

Blair took the silver clutch with an elegant jewel adornment and looked at herself in the mirror.

"What do you think?" the consultant asked.

"It's beautiful... But this is too much. I can't have him buying me all this stuff," Blair said, shaking her head.

"I tell you what..." The woman lowered her voice a little like it was a secret. "I had planned on it anyway, but I'll give you fifty percent off the dress. And the clutch will be on the house."

"Oh, no—you don't have to do that! Gosh, I was so upset, I forgot to ask how much this cost."

"I want to do this for you, honey. And the original price for the dress is four hundred," the woman informed her.

"Oh my God," Blair said. "No!"

"I can hear you, you know," Andrew called from over the mirrors. "We're getting that dress. And anything else you need."

Blair laughed a little.

"He's a keeper," the woman whispered to Blair.

Blair was sincerely touched. "Okay," she agreed.

The woman unzipped Blair's back.

"I need to come out there to bag this dress up. Can you be trusted to close your eyes?" the woman called over the mirror to Andrew.

"Yes."

"Alright, I'm coming out now!"

They all laughed.

Blair watched as the woman whisked the gown away to a back room in the corner.

Once dressed, Blair carried the heels and clutch back to where Andrew was.

"Umm, she said she's going to give me a fifty percent discount on the dress—so you won't have to pay as much," Blair said. "And the clutch will be free," she quickly added.

"It's not an issue," Andrew assured her.

After a few minutes, the woman returned with the dress in an opaque fabric storage bag. She then took the clutch and heels, boxed them up, and put them into a nice, sturdy white bag with the shop's name on both sides.

Blair stood at Andrew's side with her hands in front of her. Her heart thudded as the woman calculated the total on the computer.

"Total is going to be $318.06," she told Andrew.

Blair had forgotten about the shoes. "Oh my God," she said, touching her forehead.

Andrew said nothing. She watched him swipe a card and then intently sign his name.

Coming around the desk, the consultant handed Blair the gown bag.

"You can handle these, I presume?" she said to Andrew, handing him the other bag. He laughed a little.

"Um, thank you so much," Blair said. "I'm sorry I didn't ask your name sooner…"

"Oh my goodness, I did forget to introduce myself, didn't I? And I don't usually wear a name tag. I'm so sorry about that. I'm Sally, the store manager. It's on the card in the bag."

"I'm, uh, Blair." She always hated telling others her name. "I really appreciate everything."

"It's not a problem, dear," Sally said. "You two are going to have the best time."

Blair wasn't one for giving hugs, but she was incredibly grateful to this woman.

"Can I give you a hug?" she asked shyly.

If It All Fades Away

"Oh my God, yes," Sally said, as if waiting for Blair to ask.

Blair awkwardly held the dress bag out, and the two embraced. Sally squeezed her tight, saying so much with her hold.

"If you need anything at all, my number is on that card. If I'm not here, just ask for me."

"Okay," Blair said over her shoulder.

As they pulled apart, Sally looked to Andrew, then back to Blair. "Now, you two remember me when you return here in a few years," she said with a wink.

Before it hit Blair what Sally was implying, Andrew spoke.

"We will," he said with a warm smile.

"Take care, now," Sally said with a smile.

Blair mumbled a goodbye as they left the store. Her head spun at what Andrew had just said—that one day, just maybe, Blair would be here shopping for a wedding dress.

Chapter 17

Money Money

Once in Andrew's car, her dress hanging in the back, Blair realized how exhausted she was from the whole experience.

"I'm so tired," she said, putting her elbow on the windowsill, resting her head on her palm, eyes closed.

"What happened?" Andrew asked.

Blair sighed. "She didn't like the dress I wanted and said she hated it, then when I started crying, she said, 'Let's go'—and I blew up on her. I told her how much I hated the dress she liked. So, she threw her credit card at me and walked out. Told me to get my own ride home."

"All of that over a dress?"

"Yup. That's Angela Simons for you."

Andrew was quiet for a moment.

"Blair, that's abuse."

"What?"

"What she did to you was abuse."

"She's just nuts," Blair said, completely dismissing what Andrew said.

"Nuts or not, that's no excuse to humiliate your daughter

If It All Fades Away

in public, throw a tantrum, and then abandon her with no way to get home."

Blair's face bunched up, and then she started crying again. God, why couldn't she stop crying? Andrew's simple summation of what happened illustrated how completely messed up the whole situation was.

"I was so happy!" Blair cried. "And then she had to shit all over it, like she always does."

Andrew brought his hand up to brush her hair, trying to comfort her.

Blair was ugly-crying now. "I hate her!" She couldn't see, the tears streaming down her face. Again. "It's like, *nothing* I ever do is good enough."

She started wiping her eyes and nose. She looked out the window, taking shuddering breaths. Glancing at the time, Blair realized she had no idea how long she had been in Carmen's. It was close to nine already, and the mall was closing soon.

She inhaled and exhaled deeply.

"God, I don't want to go home. She'll be waiting for me and ready to let me have it."

Blair didn't want to ask, but she had hoped Andrew would offer.

"Well … maybe you can come to my place for a bit? And then if you decide you want to go home later, I can take you. Otherwise, you're welcome to stay the night. We have a guest room, and my mom already knew I was coming to get you."

Blair turned and blinked at him, wiping her nose again. "… Okay."

Andrew kissed the side of Blair's head. "It's going to be alright."

He started the car and then brought his cell phone to his ear.

"Hey, Mom, I'm coming back now. Blair's with me."

She could hear a woman's voice on the other end.

"Yeah, she's okay. But she might stay the night. We're not sure yet."

Blair was floored. She'd had no idea how good of a relationship Andrew had with his mother, but she did now. One short phone call told her everything she needed to know.

He hung up.

"Are you hungry? My mom has some zucchini pasta left over from dinner."

Blair hadn't checked in with her body in a while, but the small snack she had eaten before they left for the mall was long gone. They were supposed to get fast food or something on the way home. That obviously didn't happen.

"Umm, I am pretty hungry," Blair admitted.

* * *

Arriving at Andrew's gated community, Blair suddenly realized, *Oh—they have MONEY money.* The houses were huge, just ridiculous.

Eventually, they pulled up to Andrew's house. Blair could see a high window over the entrance, with light from a chandelier peeking out amidst the other lights. Walking up to the door, she realized she was nervous. This wasn't how she wanted to meet Andrew's parents.

When Andrew opened the front foor, a smell of clean and something floral hit Blair's nose immediately.

"I'm home," Andrew called.

One step inside, and Blair couldn't contain herself. She looked up at the chandelier hanging above them from the high ceiling.

"Holy shit," she breathed.

If It All Fades Away

There was a massive living room off to their left, with an actual fireplace going. Some music was faintly playing somewhere, but the house was so large that Blair couldn't tell from where, exactly. To their right, a formal dining room, untouched, but certainly used for special guests. The table, an expensive wood, could easily seat twelve or more. A lengthwise chandelier hung above the table, dimly lit. She could see light from the kitchen coming through another entry point. In front of her, a staircase led to the second floor, and a hallway ran down the center of the house.

Andrew led the way while Blair gingerly padded behind him.

As they entered the kitchen, there was an informal dining area that perhaps Andrew and his parents ate in each night. Tall glass windows overlooked what must have been the backyard. There was stainless steel everywhere. The kitchen was fit for a chef. Hell, they probably *had* a personal chef.

An older woman with grey hair wrapped up in a simple but elegant hairdo was seated at the counter, playing with her phone. As soon as they arrived in the room, she lit up.

"There she is!" she said excitedly.

Blair was stunned. She almost looked behind her to see if there was someone else she was talking about.

The woman came over to Blair with open arms, pulling her into a hug. She smelled good—an expensive perfume.

"Blair," Andrew said with an amused face, "this is my mom, Lily."

"Oh my goodness! He's told me so much about you. We've meant to have you over for a proper dinner, but it's been so busy around here, and we're still getting settled in."

Andrew had mentioned that they had moved recently because his mother had accepted a new position as dean of the College of Health Professions at the local university. Blair couldn't help but smile. Andrew's mother practically threw up kindness all over her, and it was hard not to get coated in it. She could not remember the last time her own mother or father had hugged her. And here Lily was, throwing her arms around Blair within seconds of meeting her.

"Hi," Blair said shyly, overwhelmed.

"So, Andrew tells me he was picking you up from dress shopping?"

Lily said it as if Andrew picking up his abandoned girlfriend at the mall was just an everyday occurrence. She didn't seem deliberately dismissive, but she knew precisely how to evade an obvious problem at hand.

"Umm, yeah, I was shopping for the Winter Wonderland Dance."

"Andrew is so excited to take you. Is the dress in the car?" Lily turned and asked him. He nodded. "Well, go get it, Andrew. We don't need it hanging out there getting all cold and wrinkled!"

Andrew had no expression of protest as he turned and left. Blair thought it was cute that his mother called him "Andrew" while lightly scolding him.

"Come, come." Lily signaled for Blair to sit at the raised counter. Blair sat on a cushioned stool carefully.

"Are you hungry? I have some leftover zucchini pasta. Are you allergic to anything?"

Blair could barely keep up with Lily's energy. "Umm, no, I'm not allergic to anything. And that sounds really nice, thank you." She could feel herself hunching forward, not wanting to intrude.

Blair could hear the front door opening again.

"Where do you want me to hang it?" Andrew called.

"The first guest room is fine," Lily called back, opening the massive fridge.

"First" guest room, Blair thought. *Jesus Christ.*

Lily began to reheat the leftovers, and they smelled amazing. A short time later, she placed utensils in front of Blair with a place mat. She then gave her a napkin—a cloth one, with an actual napkin ring on it. It was all too much.

"What do you like to drink, dear?"

"Water's fine," Blair said.

"Nonsense," Lily said. She then listed off a wide variety of drinks they had available.

"Um, Sprite is good."

Blair wanted Coke, but didn't want to be awake all night. The thought of having to go home to bed suddenly entered her mind, and she quickly shooed it away.

"Eat, eat," Lily urged her, setting the beverage before Blair.

Blair placed the cloth napkin in her lap and then slowly began to eat the noodles. She hummed instantly.

"This is delicious, thank you."

Andrew came back down into the kitchen. He got himself a glass of water and leaned up against a counter on the other side of where Blair was sitting. Lily then came over and pulled out a stool at the end of the counter.

"Andrew tells me your mother is a paralegal, and your father works at a metal manufacturer?"

Blair swallowed a mouthful of noodles, blotted her mouth, then spoke. "Yes, that's right."

"How wonderful. Andrew says you're very smart, but haven't decided what you want to do after graduation?"

Blair shot a look over to Andrew. She wasn't smart.

"Yeah… I'm not sure yet."

"Well, you've got time to figure it out. I keep telling Andrew he should consider surgery, just like his father, but he said he wants to have a life outside of being on call. That's where Henry's at now—the hospital."

Blair squirmed a little. She wondered if Lily was saying it in passing, or if there was actual pressure on Andrew to follow in his father's footsteps.

"He's already been accepted to several universities, but we'll see. He doesn't know what he wants to do yet either. And that's okay."

Blair knew all this already, but she could tell it still made Andrew uncomfortable. Any time the topic of his future came up, he got a little dicey about it—the same way he had dodged her question when she first asked him in study hall. He had hit her with that shit about her eyes, making her forget about it altogether. When she'd inquired again later, he said he had some ideas, but still didn't know. He was weirdly quiet about it. In the same way, he had gotten weirdly quiet about the *1984* assignment.

After more chitchat, Lily eventually excused herself.

"Well, I'm going to sit by the fireplace for a bit. And Andrew, if Blair decides to stay, you show her the guest room. I'll be going to bed in an hour."

Blair glanced at the clock. It was ten.

When she finished eating, Andrew took her bowl to wash it.

"I'm really tired, and if it's okay with you, I'd like to stay the night," Blair said hesitantly.

She had checked her phone several times. There was nothing from her mom—the silent treatment. *Classic Angela*, Blair thought bitterly. Fine by her; she'd had enough of her shit for one day.

"It's okay," Andrew said. "I'm glad you feel comfortable enough to want to rest here. I'll show you the guest room. We have pajamas and stuff, too."

If It All Fades Away

Just then, her phone pinged. It was Claire, saying the party was starting if she and Andrew still wanted to come out. Blair had forgotten all about her stupid gathering. She almost snorted. Claire was the last person she wanted to see, besides her mother. Especially given the day she'd just had. She just wanted to not think about any of the people in her life who made shit more difficult.

Just for one night, maybe she could do that.

Chapter 18

Need

Once upstairs, Andrew opened one of the guest room doors, revealing a space larger than any Blair had ever slept in. There were two nightstands with lamps turned on a low setting. She could see a large closet open with her dress bag hanging inside, the other bag with the shoes and clutch on the floor.

"There're towels and everything you need for a bath or shower. We keep spare pajamas for men and women in the dresser here."

Andrew opened a few drawers to show Blair. Someone had folded them neatly inside—probably a maid.

"Thank you," Blair said.

"I'll just be down the hall reading if you need anything," Andrew said.

"Okay."

Andrew went to close the door. Blair stood, overwhelmed yet again. At this point, the entire experience of this house was almost obnoxious.

Blair moved to the attached bathroom, chuckling in disbelief when she turned the light on. The tiles beneath her feet were heated. It looked like a spa—a full-size, deep-soak tub and a separate glassed-in shower with an overhead rainfall nozzle. There were double sinks, fresh flowers placed in one corner, and a chair to sit in if needed. Towels were rolled up in view, perfectly placed in the recessed cupboards, which were lit inside.

After the long day Blair had had, she decided she would take a bath.

Nearby were some bath salts and the like, sitting on a small table. Blair didn't need anything of the kind. She just needed warmth. The tub didn't take long to fill up. After undressing, she stepped into the hot water, slowly lowering herself.

"Oh, for Christ's sake," Blair said, realizing there was a remote on the side table to control the lighting, floor temperature, and apparently, music from a wall speaker. She didn't want to touch it; she knew she would drop it and ruin it somehow, even if it was waterproof. Instead, she leaned back into the tub curve and closed her eyes. The incident with her mother was now a million miles away. She refused to let Angela take up any more head space. Her muscles relaxed, and she was able to enjoy the moment.

After a while, Blair stepped out of the tub and made her way over to the shower. She washed and shampooed her hair, feeling like one of those women in those ridiculous commercials with the rainfall water streaming down. Stepping out, she felt amazing. She dried off, lightly towel-dried her hair, and returned to the bedroom. Opening the drawers, she found summer and winter pajama bottoms and tops. She realized that she couldn't put her old underwear back on and was now in the weird position of putting on pajamas with no panties. Oh, well. It wouldn't be the first time.

Blair didn't like to get too hot in her sleep, so she opted

for a summer set—short sleeves and shorts. They were a pale pink with little roses all over. Blair didn't care for collared pajama tops, but would have to deal. She finished towel-drying her hair and put all her belongings on a chair in the corner.

Blair's phone's battery was at fifty percent—enough to get her through until she went home tomorrow. Turning her phone on silent, she pulled back the plush comforter and sheets underneath. The corners had been tucked in, which she always hated. She gave a hard tug and released one corner. She could now poke one of her feet out if she wanted and not feel trapped.

Two clicks on the cord switch turned off both lamps.

Blair lay there, unsure of what to do. Everything felt so foreign and strange. There was an outside light somewhere casting shadows of naked tree branches on the ceiling. She watched them sway gently in the winter air.

There was a low hum of a heater switching on from another wall. It wasn't loud and rattly, like hers starting up at home. In fact, this house barely had any sounds. Blair stared at the bathroom entrance for a while, then rolled over and stared out the window on the other side of the bed.

She didn't like sleeping alone in a bed this big. She was used to her tiny single bed. Eventually, Blair reached over and checked her phone. It was a few minutes past midnight. Sitting straight up, she looked at the crack under the door to see if there was any evidence of Andrew still awake down the hall. The light was very faint.

Blair went to the door, hesitated, and slowly turned the handle. She was used to being quiet while she crept around at home, not wanting to upset her mother or father if she made too much noise, especially while they slept.

After one look into the hallway, Blair realized that the

If It All Fades Away

dim light was actually a series of nightlights. She looked down at Andrew's door and saw that it was cracked ever so slightly, but dark inside. He was probably sleeping. She listened in the hallway for a long time; this house that barely spoke was unnerving. She had no sense of what noises it made or where. She was nervous about going down and seeing Andrew.

He had mentioned on the way up that his parents had a massive master bedroom on the house's first floor in the far back. Andrew's room was closer to the front. Still, what if Lily could hear her downstairs from where she was? Blair carefully opened the door and lightly stepped onto the middle of the hallway carpeting. She then closed the door as gently as possible without making any noise. She wanted his mother to think she was still in there if she did come upstairs.

Step by step, Blair made her way down to Andrew's room. Once at his door, she held her breath and pushed it open slowly.

Andrew must not have been sleeping, either, because he stirred immediately. She saw him sit up slightly. Once in his room, Blair closed the door quietly.

Andrew had clearly been waiting for her. He scooted away from the edge of the bed, lifting the covers, wordlessly inviting her in. Blair crawled into the bed, and he dropped the covers over them. Immediately, she kissed him, his hands unable to wrap around her fast enough. Blair realized that Andrew must have showered, too, because he smelled really good, and his hair was still damp.

They made out for a long time, Andrew's hands wrapped around her.

Finally, Blair spoke.

"I couldn't sleep," she whispered.

"Me, neither," Andrew said, brushing a hair away from her face.

There was a pause; Blair had a few things to say.

"Thank you for coming and getting me earlier."

"Of course."

"Your mom is really nice."

"She's been really excited to meet you."

"It's not how I wanted to meet her."

"She doesn't care about stuff like that. I mean, not that she doesn't care about what happened, but she won't think negatively about the circumstances of meeting you. She's just happy to meet you."

Blair paused, then rolled onto her back, Andrew's arm underneath her neck, between her and the pillow. She exhaled. "I'm not looking forward to going home tomorrow."

Andrew said nothing, or didn't know what to say. He just kept petting Blair here and there.

"Try not to think about it," he said after a moment. "You're here with me now."

Silence. Blair blinked, then spoke.

"Am I good, Andrew?"

"Do you mean are you a good person? I think so."

Blair cleared her throat. "I'm not good. And my parents remind me all the time. I always feel like I'm doing something wrong. Maybe it's because I've done a lot of wrong things."

Andrew kept stroking her hair. "Like what?"

"I used to always make fun of this one kid in eighth grade —for how poor he was. His uniform was always ratty. It felt good to have someone else be beneath me for once."

Blair paused before continuing, going through a laundry list of examples.

"My freshman year, I punched a junior girl in the stomach

If It All Fades Away

—hard—just because she was doing that stupid shit where you try to step around a person, and then they match your steps, back and forth. It was literally the first time she did it to me."

Andrew kept listening.

"God, I didn't even know her. But she was a lot taller than me. Looking back, I think she was joking, but I couldn't tell or take it. She dropped to the floor and started crying. A bunch of girls came to her side and immediately started yelling at me. I remember feeling so scared when one of the girls told another one to get a teacher. She started running down the hallway, and I just knew I was screwed."

Blair had light tears trailing down the sides of her face.

"I cheated on my sophomore final exam for geometry and got caught. And I've stolen stuff from people—things I couldn't afford, but wanted, like earbuds and expensive makeup, perfume. I've name-called people 'slut,' 'whore,' 'stupid,' and 'ugly'… I've made fun of struggling peers for dumb stuff like reading too slowly in class, even though I'm no better."

Andrew wiped the tears away on his side, and Blair wiped the other. She watched the tree branches dance on the ceiling.

"I'm not a good person, Andrew."

Andrew moved in and kissed her temple.

"You're a good person to me. And you're still young. You've been through a lot. It's not like you're an adult and still doing some of those things."

Blair closed her eyes, the tears streaming down the same path they had traveled.

"And even if you were an adult—there's help out there. I think you're good," he said, as if his judgment was final. "You've just been hurt a lot, that's all."

Blair turned her head to him, eyes still closed, kissing

him. Andrew understood she needed him, needed his praise, needed his touch.

"You're so good," he said, coming up over her. He trailed soft kisses along her jaw, making his way down her neck. His breath tickled her flesh. "Tell me what you need."

"I just need you," Blair said, kissing him, pulling him closer.

"You're so good," he repeated softly in her ear, his hand sliding into her shorts. Blair gasped as Andrew's fingers found her center.

"Is this okay?" he asked.

Blair nodded.

She was breathless as he inserted one finger, then two, pumping slowly. Their tongues tangled together as Andrew's hand moved within the confines of her shorts.

Blair felt a pressure building. "Andrew..." she breathed.

"I'm right here," he whispered.

With their foreheads pressed together, Blair looked into Andrew's amber eyes. As he curled his fingers and moved faster, Blair cried out when her climax hit her like an ocean wave. Her eyes fluttered shut as the white-hot sensation rolled through her. Falling away into a boneless heap, she took shuddering breaths.

"That was amazing," Andrew said.

"Stop." Blair laughed and covered her face with both hands. She winced as Andrew removed his fingers.

"Are you okay?"

"I'm fine."

Catching her breath, Blair reached for Andrew, palming him through his boxers. He made a low hissing noise when her hand slipped beneath his waistband. He assisted in pushing his boxers down to give her better access. She wrapped her fingers around him and began stroking him. "How should I—"

"You're doing great," he breathed.

Blair didn't know what she was doing, but she was trying her best. Andrew, however, seemed to be enjoying himself, eyes closing and head falling back onto the pillow. Finding a comfortable and steady rhythm, Blair kept her pressure consistent as low moans escaped Andrew's mouth. Stroking him to completion, Blair startled as he spilled onto her hand and his stomach.

"I'm sorry," Andrew breathed.

"For what?" Blair asked.

"For coming so quickly." He laughed.

Blair laughed with him, her hand sticky. Andrew left for the bathroom and returned with a wet washcloth for her.

Shortly after, Blair curled up into Andrew's arm. She wouldn't remember falling asleep.

Chapter 19

Freedom

When Blair awoke the next morning, Andrew wasn't next to her. Outside of his bedroom window, light snow was falling. She had no idea what time it was or how long she had slept; Andrew didn't have a clock on his nightstand. He probably only used his phone. His bedroom door was closed.

Blair went to Andrew's adjoining bathroom. It was essentially modeled the same as the guest bathroom. After she used the toilet, she looked at herself in the mirror while washing her hands. Her brunette hair was a bit messed up from sleeping on it damp, but nothing unmanageable.

Opening Andrew's door, she could hear talking, and the smell of bacon hit her nose. She went to the guest room where she was supposed to be sleeping. Checking her phone, she still had no messages from her mother. Angela's silent treatments were always the worst, because if you had really pissed her off, you didn't know how long she would keep the grudge going.

Rachel had sent a message, probably out of anxiety,

If It All Fades Away

asking if she went to Claire's or not. Blair briefly told her what had happened.

She wasn't sure if she was supposed to get dressed in yesterday's clothes, or if coming down in the guest pajamas was okay. She texted Andrew.

You're fine to come down as you are. Breakfast is ready.

Blair went down the back set of stairs she and Andrew had taken from the kitchen last night. Once in the back hallway, she made her way to the sound of voices and the smell of food.

"Oh, you're awake!" Lily said enthusiastically. She, Andrew, and Andrew's father were all sitting at the table in various sleepwear. Any other family, and Blair would have laughed at them, looking like something straight out of an advertisement. But this was Andrew's family, and she found them rather adorable.

The counter she'd sat at last night offered fresh-cut fruit, a glass pitcher of orange juice, a large French press of coffee, and bacon on paper towels in a basket.

"Blair, honey, do you like eggs?"

"Umm, yes?"

"How do you like them?"

"Anything is fine."

"Andrew, you've been working on this with her, right? To ask for what she wants? My goodness, she's way too modest."

Once Blair was seated across from Andrew, his father introduced himself. "Hi, I'm Henry," he said, extending a hand. "Sorry we didn't meet last night. I got called into surgery at the last minute. Did you sleep alright?"

"Yes, I slept very well, thank you," Blair replied, praying she wasn't blushing.

Lily soon served Blair scrambled eggs with bacon, fruit, and toast. "Coffee or orange juice? Water?"

"Um, orange juice, please."

"Andrew says you like movies, Blair?" Henry asked her as she slowly ate her eggs.

"Yes," she said. "I don't think it's more than the average person, but Andrew hasn't seen as many as I have."

"He's always had his head in books since he was very little."

"Blair has a good book collection, too," Andrew added, as if to defend her a little.

"I mostly read at the library," she added.

"Oh, which library?" Henry asked. "We're still not really familiar with the area."

Lily returned to the table with a fresh cup of coffee to sit with them all.

"The Hutchinson–Genesis Library," Blair replied. "It's very close to where I live, and to St. Michael's."

Henry grunted in approval.

Blair finished eating as Henry, Lily, and Andrew talked about this and that. She felt like an observer looking in. So, this must be what normal families looked like? Andrew and his family were good people, even if they were stupidly rich.

Just then, her phone buzzed. It was her father. That was never a good sign; he rarely texted her.

Will you come home sometime today to do your chores, or will you keep running the streets?

Blair sighed. She was glad she had already eaten, because her stomach tightened at the message.

Andrew looked over. "Everything alright?"

She sighed again. "I should probably get ready, so I can go home."

Henry and Lily stopped speaking and looked over to her,

too. Blair couldn't keep a good poker face with them. She had been living in another life, another world with them, and the illusion had been shattered by a single text message.

Blair got up. "Thank you so much for breakfast, Mrs. Stormant."

"Oh, honey, call me Lily, please."

Blair forced a smile and left the kitchen. Sullen, she made her way up the stairs in the front section of the house. Once in the guest room, she began to tidy up the bedding and moved her belongings from the chair to the bed.

There was a soft knock at the door. It was Andrew.

"You okay?"

"No," Blair said.

Andrew looked a bit sullen himself. "I can take you home whenever you want."

"I've got to go now. My dad texted me, and he never texts me. My mom must still be super pissed."

Her mother and father were both home, and it all hung over Blair's head like a dark cloud. Andrew approached her and wrapped her in a big hug, kissing her head. He smelled so good. Blair never wanted to leave him, never wanted to leave his home. She could have stayed here with him, with his parents, forever.

* * *

When they pulled into Blair's driveway, it was still lightly snowing. A few inches had accumulated on the ground. Blair's hand trembled as she grabbed the door handle.

Andrew reached over and stroked her hair. "It's going to be okay," he reassured her. "If anything happens, or you need me to come back and get you, let me know."

"I will," Blair said.

She gave Andrew one last look, and she could see his hurt for her in them, but also reassurance. And that alone was enough to convince Blair she could handle anything that lay in wait beyond that front door.

Once inside, Blair saw Gerald seated in the recliner, watching television as usual. Angela was also seated, reading a book. The contempt practically emanated from her.

Her father spoke once she closed the door and Andrew had pulled away.

"That's not going to happen again," he told her.

"What?" Blair asked, trying to conceal her anger at yesterday's events.

"You running the streets and acting improper," he replied.

She looked to her mother, who licked her finger and turned the page in her book. The little head movement she made told Blair that she was enjoying every second of her father's slut-shaming.

"Nothing happened."

"I don't care. It's disgraceful. And you're not going to embarrass us like that again."

"Andrew comes from a good family."

Angela stilled.

"You're saying *we're* not a good family?" Gerald demanded.

"No. I'm just saying ... he's not like that."

"If he's not like that, then why haven't we met him yet?"

"When was he supposed to meet you both at the same time again, exactly?" Blair asked incredulously.

Her father was up and across the living room in an instant. He backhanded Blair so hard that she stumbled backwards, his wedding ring catching her cheek bone. "Watch your mouth!"

Finally, her mother looked up, placing the book in her lap.

If It All Fades Away

"I see you didn't bring that harlot dress home. Did you even buy anything?" she asked, completely unfazed by Gerald hitting Blair.

"I-I did." Blair winced, hand to her cheek.

"So, where is it?"

"At Andrew's house."

"You're going to use *my* credit card and not even bring home what *I* bought?" Angela's nostrils flared.

"You didn't buy it," Blair said in a small voice. "Andrew did." Cautiously, she reached into her small purse and pulled out Angela's credit card. She set it near the key dish at the door. "May I be excused?" she asked quietly, head lowered.

Gerald returned to his recliner, while Angela sat unmoving with a look of shock plastered on her face. When neither said anything, Blair went upstairs to her bedroom and closed the door.

She'd made it—just barely. It could have been a lot worse, but something felt different about getting into it with them this time. Something new. Something miraculous.

A taste of freedom.

Chapter 20

Sharp-Smart

Monday morning, Blair was more than happy to see Andrew again. Thankfully, her parents had left her alone over the weekend. She did her chores and came out of her room only to eat peanut butter and jelly sandwiches or cereal. Even when her father gruffly called up Saturday evening to report that they'd ordered pizza, Blair said she wasn't hungry. She later came down to eat only after her parents went to bed. It wasn't easy, but she did it.

"What happened to your cheek?" Andrew asked immediately.

"Oh," Blair said, touching the ring mark on her face. "It's nothing."

Andrew reached out to touch it.

"It's okay," she said, pulling away.

He didn't seem convinced, but said nothing else.

Making her way to her locker with Andrew, Blair glanced over to see Rachel.

Crap.

If It All Fades Away

Blair had forgotten to mention the lunch table arrangement to Andrew. It was the last thing on her mind.

Rachel gave Blair a look and came up to her. She could tell that she had been agonizing about it all weekend, and about Claire's party. Blair felt awful after seeing Rachel crying last week, then telling her she would talk to Andrew and not following through. She also knew they couldn't take one more day with Claire and the girls.

Rachel timidly approached. "Did Andrew talk to him?"

"Not yet, but he's going to," Blair lied.

"Oh my God, Blair..." Rachel brought her hands to her forehead.

"It'll be fine, I promise."

The first bell rang.

"I'll see you at lunch," Blair told her. "We won't be sitting with those wenches anymore."

"Okay," Rachel said, unconvinced.

Blair could see Rachel's trust in her as a friend was slipping, and she couldn't handle that. She decided to take matters into her own hands. Julian was a nice guy—he always said hi to her, had commended her on punching Hudson, and then asked her if she was okay when she fell while running. Even though she wasn't good at schoolwork, Blair was fairly proficient at reading people. Furthermore, Blair also understood that people, even if uninterested, perked up at the news that someone else was interested in them. It was human nature.

Blair caught Julian as he was on his way out of the boy's locker room.

"Hey, Julian!" she called.

Julian turned to face her. "Oh, hey, Blair. How's it going?"

Blair came a little closer. "Can I talk to you for a second?"

Julian's pupils widened slightly. They moved to a side corner.

"Yeah, sure, what's going on?"

Blair had no time for beating around the bush. She had to push things a bit if she had any hopes of them getting out from under Claire's claws, and for the possibility of a double date for the dance. She made herself as cute and mischievous as possible. She felt like she was in seventh grade all over again.

"Umm… So, this is a little awkward for me," she began. "But, uh, Rachel likes you. And she wants to know if you'll go with her to the Winter Wonderland Dance … if you don't have someone to go with."

Julian's eyes were still wide, but he said nothing. Blair prayed that this wasn't a big mistake and she had just humiliated her friend.

Julian inhaled. "I, uh—actually don't have a date yet," he said, a bit stunned.

Blair could tell he wasn't repulsed at the idea of Rachel, so she decided to push a little more.

"Even if you don't feel the same, you've always been a cool dude to me, so promise you won't say anything to embarrass her."

"No—of course not," Julian said, a little eagerly.

Yes, Blair thought. He was in, he just hadn't said it yet.

"But yeah, she's liked you since sophomore year."

That part was true.

Julian's head came forward a bit. "Really?"

"Yes. She's just too scared to ask you herself. Also, Andrew and I had hoped you guys could go to dinner with us —like a double date. Before the dance."

If It All Fades Away

"Wow," Julian said, reflecting.

"Just … give it some thought."

"Yes," he said.

"Yes, you'll go with her?"

"Yes," he said.

"Okay!" Blair grinned, a little too pleased with herself. "I'll, uh… I'll let her know you said yes."

"Cool," Julian said, trying to act nonchalant.

As Blair turned to leave, she remembered the more immediate ask.

"Oh, Julian, one more thing," she said. She could tell that he was committed now. "Listen, Claire Miller and her little crew have been mean to Rachel lately. They treat her like a lapdog. And Andrew and I sit with her at lunch to support her. Would it be cool if, like … me, him, and Rachel sat with you today?"

Blair knew his lunch table was always full, but she was surprised to hear what he said next.

"Yeah, sure, it's no problem at all. We all sit wherever we want, so it's super chill. If you want to sit with us, the guys will be okay with moving elsewhere."

Blair sighed with exaggerated relief, so Julian would know how much he was saving their asses. "Oh my God, THANK YOU! Those girls are so mean to Rachel, and she was hurt when they didn't invite her to a party this weekend. So, I said, 'screw them,' and promised we would move to another table. Thank you so much for saving me, her, *us* from those wenches."

Julian laughed. "It's no problem at all," he said again.

"Great," Blair said. "So, we'll see you in a few?"

"Absolutely," Julian said. "I'll let the guys know what's happening before you arrive. So it won't be awkward or anything."

Blair clasped her hands together, half tempted to hug him. "Thank you so much!"

Julian laughed a little nervously. "Of course, Blair."

As they parted ways, Blair wondered why she hadn't made more of an effort to be friends with Julian Lewis over the last four years. Maybe things would have been different from the start if she had.

* * *

Blair texted Rachel to wait for her before entering the lunch line. Once she and Andrew approached, she spotted Rachel biting her fingernails.

"We're all set," Blair informed her.

"We are?" Rachel asked, her voice unnaturally high. "'Cause I just saw Julian go by, and he told me he was looking forward to going to the dance together. Blair, I about fainted! What the hell is going on?"

"Well…" Blair said, a little too cheeky.

"Oh my God, Blair—you didn't tell him I *like* him, did you?!"

"No," Blair lied. "But I think he likes *you*, because he said yes to going to the dance with you."

Rachel playfully punched Blair in the arm.

"Ow," Blair said, holding herself.

"What's going on, exactly?" Andrew asked.

"We're sitting at Julian's table from now on. And Julian and Rachel are going to the dance with us."

Andrew blinked twice. "Okay, then."

Blair and Rachel laughed.

"You just follow along, okay, babe?" Blair said, patting his arm.

"Of course." Andrew smiled.

If It All Fades Away

Approaching the cashier, Blair saw that Julian was true to his word. Some of his friends had gone to other tables, and he was eating and chatting with a few sitting nearby. Blair glanced over to Claire, who was squawking as usual.

This should be interesting, she thought.

Once through the line, Blair made a beeline straight for Julian's round table. She glanced back to see Rachel tucking her head down like a shameful turtle, while Andrew was as chill as always.

"Hi, guys!" Julian said enthusiastically.

Rachel put her tray down and pulled out a chair, tucking a piece of hair behind her ear as she sat. "Hi," she mumbled.

Andrew and Blair sat as well. Blair turned to look over at Claire's table across the cafeteria. She saw all of the girls looking their way.

If looks could kill, Blair would have been dead by now.

Claire was angry. And while Blair usually wouldn't have been afraid of her, something sinister lay in wait behind her gaze. Blair knew she and Claire were not of the same breed. Claire would pay her back for this; Blair just wasn't sure how or when. And while Claire might be the type to enjoy such drama, Blair honestly just wanted to get through the rest of high school with a minimal amount of crap.

At study hall the next day, Blair sighed and groaned. She was struggling to focus. Again. She felt itchy and hot. All she could think about was kissing Andrew. As she looked at him from across the table, she also wondered what his ears looked like beneath all that hair. They were protruding slightly through his luscious waves.

Andrew, however, was intently focused, completing

calculus problems. Blair groaned again and threw her head back, staring at the old lights above her.

"Doing okay?" Andrew asked.

"No," Blair said tersely.

Silence.

"Blair."

She brought her head back to face him, a little dizzy from staring upwards for so long at the overhead light. She could see the afterimage of it in his face.

"Don't take this the wrong way..." He paused.

Blair tensed at the words. Oh no. What was he going to say?

"But have you been tested for a learning disability?"

Blair could only blink. "What?"

"It's just ... you're very smart. Brilliant, actually. I know you don't think that, but it's true. You can remember many facts and details about movies and get hyper-focused on stuff. But with schoolwork and things you aren't interested in, it's a lot harder for you."

Blair scoffed. "No, I've never been tested. And I'm sure Angela would rather *die* before she had to admit that her kid is *actually* stupid, in addition to being a troublemaker."

"Please stop saying that," Andrew said.

Blair froze. She could tell that he was starting to hurt from her constantly putting herself down.

"You're not stupid."

Blair blinked back tears. She felt like Andrew was scolding her a little.

"It's too goddamn early in the morning for this," she said, looking down.

"Blair, I'm not mad at you. Please don't cry."

She was crying. Tears in her lap now.

Andrew came to her side, his knees on the carpeted floor

as he looked up at her. His hands were on her lap, touching her arm.

"Blair, you're not stupid."

He really needed to stop saying that. It was ruining her.

"Let's go outside for a minute," he said.

Blair stood up, her head still hung low. Andrew held her hand as they left the library.

There was an exit at the front of the building. Andrew took Blair into the space between the two sets of double doors. It was cold, but nothing they couldn't handle in their uniform sweaters.

Blair kept crying soft tears, unable to look at him. Andrew hugged her, petting her head as he had done many times.

"I don't know where you got this from," he said, "but I really wish I could take it away for you."

Blair clung to him. "My parents," she said into his chest. "My mom and dad have both called me stupid before."

She could feel Andrew inhale deeply. He was clearly frustrated, but it was as if he was containing himself. He was too good of a person—too kind of a soul—to pass judgment on people he had never met.

"You're not stupid," he repeated quietly. "You're so smart. Sometimes, I wish I could be as sharp as you are."

Blair knew he wasn't pitying her. He was speaking the truth. Andrew Stormant only ever spoke the truth. She didn't know what specific moments he was referring to when he said she was "sharp," but it was simultaneously beautiful and awful to hear.

"I lied to you yesterday," Blair said abruptly.

"What?"

"I lied when I said this mark was nothing." She touched her cheek.

"I figured, but didn't want to push it. What happened?"

"When I got home on Sunday, my parents confronted me about staying over at your place. My dad backhanded me when I back-talked him."

"What a coward," Andrew said bitterly. "Have you thought about reporting him?"

"I'm not going to report him just because he backhanded me." Blair sniffled.

Andrew pulled away to look at her. "Your parents are abusive, Blair. It's not okay."

Blair didn't know what to say to that. She was so used to how her parents were that "abuse" seemed too strong of a word.

"I'm okay," she said. "Really."

Andrew grimaced. "If anything else happens, you'll tell me, won't you?"

Blair nodded.

He pulled her close again. *"You're not stupid,"* he whispered once more.

Chapter 21
Family Visitor

"Christ, Angela, has she gotten any new clothes since I was here last?"

Those were the first words out of Blair's aunt Natalie's mouth when she walked through the door Wednesday evening. She had driven five hours from Chicago to spend Thanksgiving weekend with them. Blair had a half day of school, and the rest of the afternoon had been spent anxiously awaiting Natalie's arrival. Her mother got home just before she arrived.

Blair's bra straps were showing from her off-the-shoulder sweater.

"Those aren't that old," Angela remarked.

"That bra is from last year. I would know, because I bought it for her. Christ, look at her spilling out the front, Angela." Natalie gestured. "I can see it through her sweater. Or have you not noticed her tits because you're too worried about your own?"

Blair had to turn away to suppress a laugh. Her aunt's visits were one of the best times she had with her family, and it was always a sad occasion when she left. She texted Blair about once every two weeks. Blair thought that perhaps she should try to text her more on her part. Sometimes, she wouldn't respond to her aunt's text messages, too tired or depressed to reply. Natalie never gave her shit for it, though. She just kept messaging her funny memes or asking how she was, even if she didn't always get a response.

Blair had learned her lesson, though, to not get too overzealous with Natalie about roasting her mother. Two years prior, Blair and Natalie had shared a few laughs at her expense, and Blair added a few comments of her own. Angela laughed right along with them, as if everything was fine. However, as soon as Natalie left, all the smiles and laughs had faded. Her mother immediately took her phone for a week and grounded her to her room.

Blair desperately wanted to tell her aunt more about how she felt about everything going on. But she was afraid of what would happen if a blowup occurred. Her mother was the type to completely write people off for challenging her. Blair also knew there were a few years here and there when she did not speak to Natalie. Predictably, it was Natalie who had come back around to make amends—or as her mother put it, "came crawling back around." It was never Angela making amends, of course.

When Blair was thirteen, Natalie confessed to her that she had only made amends because of her. Things had been relatively calm in the four years since then. Blair knew something deeper lay between them as sisters, though—something unspoken. Something that had absolutely nothing to do with jabs about Angela's tits or the like. Maybe someday, Blair would find out what it was. But she was also too afraid to ask. Deep down inside, she knew it wasn't something she was ready to hear or understand.

Surprisingly, Angela (in true chameleon fashion) acted

cool at the insults to her mothering and her obsession with her appearance.

"Guess this is the perfect opportunity for you two to go Black Friday shopping again, then, isn't it?"

"It is," Natalie said.

Blair went to take her aunt's suitcase upstairs to the guest room.

"No, honey, I got it."

"Let her take it up."

"I can carry my own shit, Angie."

Angie—what Natalie called her when she was growing impatient with her bullshit. Blair always loved to hear it.

Her father started to rouse at the sound of Blair and her aunt coming up the stairs. Blair grabbed a few of her other belongings anyway, more than happy to give her a hand to save her two trips.

"This house doesn't change a bit, does it?" Natalie remarked once Blair opened the door.

For how dated their home was, it was still a reasonably decent-sized house—four bedrooms, one in the basement, two-and-a-half baths, and a respectable amount of property. It had been built before St. Michael's school and church, inherited from Blair's paternal grandparents.

Natalie made coffee, sat, and chatted with Angela and Blair in the living room. At one point, Blair's father came down, groggy-eyed, gave his greetings, and then retreated upstairs. He would watch the television in their bedroom, realizing he couldn't lord over the living room domain as he usually did—not with Natalie here.

Blair cherished seeing her mother laugh and smile with her aunt, though it did upset her to see how entirely ... *normal* she could be, not acting like a child for a change. Blair felt like an equal in the room for once—or at least, she wasn't sitting in fear. She really wished her aunt Natalie didn't live as far away as she did.

* * *

Once Blair was sent upstairs to bed, she sat on the floor with her ear to the furnace vent to listen to her mother and aunt talk. Her room was over the living room, and she could hear almost everything.

"So, tell me about this boy she's seeing?" Natalie asked.

"He's … handsome… Seems nice. He picks her up and drops her off every day."

"What does Gerald think of him?"

Silence.

"He hasn't met him yet. Well, neither have I."

"What?"

Angela sighed. "It's been busy. Though she did stay at his house this past weekend."

Natalie said nothing.

"She made a big scene while we were out dress shopping for her dance coming up."

"How?" Natalie asked.

"She said she hated the dress I liked. Started screaming at me and crying."

"And I can't imagine that you had anything to do with her acting that way, hmm?"

"She's always been so dramatic."

Blair so badly wanted to scream through the furnace that her mother was a liar.

More silence.

"So, then what happened?"

"Well, I guess her little boyfriend came and got her. She didn't tell me where she was or where she was going."

If It All Fades Away

"Why was *he* picking her up from dress shopping?"

"… I left her there."

Blair could picture Natalie's eyes getting wide.

"Christ, Angie, what is *wrong* with you? And why haven't you and Gerald invited him over for dinner?"

She could practically see her mother rolling her eyes.

"Some of this is on her, too," Angela said.

"She's seventeen years old! Be the damn adult here. My God, Mom and Dad would be horrified if they knew this is how you're treating her!"

"You going to see her this weekend?"

"Don't change the subject. And yes, I am. Saturday."

"I'm going to bed," Angela said, ending the conversation. Her voice had changed. Blair could tell she was moving to the kitchen.

"Unless you have any objections, I think Blair should be able to invite the boy over for dinner tomorrow," Natalie said.

"Fine."

"You really going to make me look like the savior here, or will you tell her yourself?"

Angela groaned. "I'll let her know."

"Good."

Blair could hear the sink running and spoons clattering from their coffee cups into the basin.

"Good night," Angela said.

"Night. I'll be up shortly," Natalie replied.

Blair heard the TV click on downstairs.

She heard her mother making her way up the steps. Blair scrambled to get into bed. Her mother's footsteps approached down the hall.

Her door opened without a knock.

"Blair—"

"Yes," she said, her back to the door.

"Invite that Stormant boy over for Thanksgiving dinner tomorrow. Tell him he doesn't have to stay long. I'm assuming he has dinner with his family, too."

"... Okay," Blair replied.

Her mother closed the door.

Blair knew her aunt could have laid into her mother more than she already did. She had probably restrained herself quite a bit.

Once her mother was settled in the other room, Blair pulled out her phone and texted Andrew. He replied that his house would be full of extended family all day, so it wouldn't be an issue for him to dip out for a while.

Blair was both nervous and excited. She wanted her parents to like Andrew and was excited that Aunt Natalie would meet him.

* * *

The following day, Blair showered, curled her hair for the first time in a long time, and put on her best clothes. Her mother and aunt were up early, preparing the turkey and getting the kitchen ready to prepare the side dishes. Her father was downstairs, watching TV, no doubt passing the time until the big football game came on.

Blair came down and set the table. She cleaned every dirty dish her mother and aunt made and tried to stay out of the way.

As the day went on, Blair kept nervously glancing at her phone. When the doorbell rang, her heart and stomach dropped. She rushed a little too quickly to get to the door.

Andrew stood holding a dish and gently knocked his shoes at the door to remove excess snow. Blair shyly said hello.

If It All Fades Away

Stepping inside, Andrew bowed his head as he entered.

"Hello," he said to everyone.

Blair glanced at her father, who had not gotten up to greet him. He said nothing.

Her mother came over. "Hi, Andrew, it's so nice to meet you, finally," she said. For once, it sounded sincere. But then again, Angela was excellent at putting on a show for people.

"Thank you for having me. Please accept my apologies for not introducing myself sooner. I appreciate you allowing me to pick Blair up and drop her off from school."

Blair saw her father stir. Her mother seemed taken aback by his maturity.

"It's, uh, no problem at all. Do you want me to take your coat?"

"Um, my mother sent this along. She says happy Thanksgiving, and she would like to have dinner with you sometime." Andrew extended the dish. "It's homemade apple pie."

Blair could tell that her mother loved the attention doted on her, and that Lily wanted to impress and befriend her. Angela was as charmed as anyone could be by him.

"Well, that's very sweet of her. Please tell her I would love that."

"I will," Andrew said, removing his own coat.

Blair took it from him as her mother took the pie to the kitchen.

Natalie came over. "I'm Blair's aunt Natalie, if you couldn't tell," she said, shaking his hand. "Lord knows she doesn't get her brown hair from her mother."

Andrew smiled. Blair was surprised she didn't see Angela's head of blonde hair whip around to throw a glare.

"Nice to meet you," he said.

Blair hung his coat in the closet nearby. Andrew removed his shoes.

Now came the real test: her father. He was still in his chair, playing the dickhead dad role all too well.

Andrew came onto the carpet and regarded the television her father was watching.

"Oh, they just made a touchdown? I didn't listen to the game on the way over."

And then, just like that, her father was talking football with Andrew. It was wonderful. Blair didn't give a damn about football, but she could tell her father was softening to him, immediately endeared by him liking "manly" shit.

Then a commercial came on, and Andrew walked over to her father and extended his hand. He introduced himself, and her father leaned forward to shake his hand. It was a huge sign of respect on his part. Blair thought she might die of pride. Andrew was old-school. His parents had raised him right. He knew how to introduce himself, even in a difficult situation.

Blair actually enjoyed the dinner. Andrew spoke comfortably with Natalie and her parents, entirely at ease. They even shared a few laughs. Looking around the table and seeing smiles on everyone's faces, Blair felt for once in her life that she was doing something right: dating Andrew.

Chapter 22

This Right Here

After Andrew left, Natalie and Angela kept talking about what a nice, handsome young man he was. Her father had resumed his place in the living room, but Blair could tell he was in a good mood. Blair helped her mother and aunt put food and dishes away.

Sneaking away upstairs afterward to decompress from the stress and excitement of the day, Blair scanned her DVD collection for something to relax with. She found an old favorite and put it on.

Lying in her bed, she received a text from Andrew.

I got home about twenty minutes ago. I'm happy I finally met your parents and aunt; she was funny. I was a little nervous. Sorry I forgot to tell you how beautiful you looked today.

Blair smiled at Andrew's admission that he was nervous and thought she looked beautiful, acknowledging the extra effort she'd put in. She had mildly scolded him recently not to overuse "beautiful" when complimenting her. Andrew was confused at first, but agreed. Blair didn't think she was beautiful; her mother had seen to that a long time ago. But she was trying not to sound like a mess to Andrew at every turn, so she only said to say it when he meant it. "I mean it every time," he said. Blair still couldn't believe it.

But still, she had tried today, tried for him—and he told her she looked beautiful, and Blair thought it might be true.

I'm glad you got to meet them, too, even if they are assholes. They all really liked you.

Blair curled up and watched her movie, so incredibly relieved that everything had gone well.

* * *

Natalie took Blair out to go Black Friday shopping the next day, while her parents stayed home. On the way out the door, Natalie gave Angela shit about Blair still not having her driver's license. After some sisterly bickering, Angela said it was fine to let Blair drive.

Blair hadn't driven in a while and hadn't had enough practice in the Michigan snow. Natalie told her to relax as she drove, giving her pointers and reminders.

As they made their way out of suburbia, Natalie spoke.

"So … tell me what really happened with your mom and this whole dress thing. I got the Angela version the other night; now I need to hear yours."

Blair groaned. She did not hold back, immediately launching into her side of the story. As she recounted everything that had happened, she could see Natalie with her arm on the windowsill, temple on her fist, shaking her head in silent anger. Her lips were a tight line.

Blair told her how Andrew had ended up purchasing the dress, and what it was like staying at his house and meeting his parents, and what they did for work.

"What's he going to college for?"

If It All Fades Away

Blair laughed, because she knew how much that question made Andrew squirm. "I think he's kinda been thinking about being a doctor? Like his dad, but he doesn't want to be a surgeon."

"You can tell he actually cares about people. Medicine would be perfect for him."

"He said he could also see himself teaching biology or something at the university."

"Teaching would also be good for him." Natalie nodded. "What about you, though? I asked your mother last night, and she said you still don't know."

"I really *don't* know."

They were now pulling into the mall parking lot. Blair was surprised at how quickly the ride had passed while talking. The parking lot was full of cars, and they circled a bit.

"You can always apply to some place in Chicago."

"It's so expensive there, though."

"Blair…"

Blair turned to see her aunt with a look on her face, head tilted.

"I wouldn't want to burden you," Blair said.

"You wouldn't be a burden. It's so wonderful there in the summertime. You'd love it. I've been trying to get your mother back out there—with you—for years."

"When was the last time she went?"

"I think you were nine? I don't know why she didn't bring you then. I really can't remember."

Blair tried to remember being nine. Then it clicked. "Oh, actually, I think I remember now. I stayed at Rachel's for a few days."

"Oh, that's right. How is she, anyway?"

They were exiting Natalie's little car now. Blair filled her in on the latest happenings with Rachel and Julian. The sun was shining, the snow a bit slushy under their feet. On the way into the building, Blair let her mind drift away to a life in Chicago. But what about Andrew? She knew planning her life around him was stupid, but the thought stood at the forefront of her mind.

* * *

Inside Macy's, Natalie asked Blair what she needed for clothes.

"Um, pretty much everything?" Blair replied, embarrassed.

Natalie sighed, so obviously over her sister's crap. "Do they give you money for yourself at all?"

"A little. But not enough for clothes. They get mad if I ask for anything."

Natalie started to make a beeline for some active wear. Blair could tell she was trying not to run her younger sister into the ground completely; her lips kept coming into a thin line with a twitch in her jaw.

Blair tried on sports bras, shorts, leggings, sweaters, jeans, and other clothing, until she was thoroughly sick of trying on clothes.

"I don't think my hair can take any more sweaters going over it." Blair came out with frizzy hair, some strands standing up from all the static electricity.

Natalie laughed. "No, you look pretty well done."

When they were checking out, Natalie looked at her watch.

"Say, it's almost lunchtime. There's that nice restaurant on the corner. Do you want to see if Andrew would like to join us?"

Blair smiled. Of course she did.

If It All Fades Away

* * *

Andrew arrived about thirty minutes later while they were seated with water in a dark booth. Blair was thankful he was available to come out to lunch. She felt *new* in the Macy's top she'd changed into.

"Andrew, long time no see," Natalie quipped.

"Hello again," he said with his usual nod, sitting next to Blair.

Blair felt like a little girl, smiling and smiling. She couldn't understand why at first, until it hit her: she and Andrew had not gone out on a proper dinner date yet. Andrew wanted to take her someplace on a Saturday, but Blair was always too afraid to ask her parents. So, they were relegated to sneaking around on Friday evenings, which always made Andrew a little tense, no matter how often she reassured him. Maybe now, after they'd met him, they would be more inclined to let him take her out.

"So, Blair said you're thinking of being a doctor or something, huh?"

Andrew chuckled. "Something like that."

"What's the hesitation? Both your parents are in the medical field. You seem like a great fit for it. I told Blair you have incredible empathy and people skills."

Blair thought Natalie hadn't quite put it that way, but it was true. Strangely, Andrew seemed at ease with her very forward questioning, when he usually seemed reluctant to give answers.

The waiter came to ask if they were ready to order. Natalie asked for a few more minutes.

"Um … well," Andrew mumbled, as if embarrassed. "I thought I knew where I wanted to go, but now I'm not so sure." He looked at Blair unconsciously, then quickly averted his eyes, as if he knew he should have had a better answer prepared.

Silence.

"Oh, honey, you have fallen hard, haven't you?" Natalie said.

Blair's cheeks flared red, her heart racing. A sideways glance at Andrew revealed a similar pink flush in his cheeks. He typically could hold a gaze, but now he smiled shyly, looking into his lap.

Blair was stunned. Andrew? He was unsure about his future because of her?

"My goodness." Natalie sat back in admiration. "You know, I don't know how else to put this to you guys. And you're so young that most adults won't point this out—because they're too stupid, bitter, or don't believe in such things—but you two were made for each other."

"What?" Blair almost barked in disbelief.

Andrew looked up with only his eyes now, his hands resting in his lap.

"Yeah. This right here…" Natalie gestured to the two of them. "This is some soul shit right here. No question."

Just then, the waiter returned, and all three of them quickly grabbed their menus, ordering whatever they could find the fastest. After they ordered, Natalie continued.

"Normally, I would say you shouldn't hinge your life plans on a boyfriend or girlfriend, but in this instance, I think you guys could make it work," she said, retying her hair into a loose ponytail. "I told Blair earlier that she should apply to some places in Chicago. Then she could live with me while attending school there."

Andrew sat up straighter, his interest piqued.

"And as I'm sure you know, Andrew, Pritzker School of Medicine is very highly regarded."

Blair and Andrew shared a look.

"I … I hadn't considered Chicago, honestly. I was considering the University of Pennsylvania, because I've already been accepted there. And it's where my dad went. I mean, not that that's how I got in—"

"Well, just something to think about," Natalie said, smiling as she sipped from her straw, self-satisfied.

* * *

After lunch, Blair, Andrew, and Natalie meandered around the mall, occasionally dropping into a few stores. Towards the end of one section, Natalie stopped, then glanced at Andrew and Blair with a sly grin.

"Andrew, you're eighteen, aren't you?" she asked.

"Uh … yes?"

"Blair, dear, I'm afraid you'll have to stay here."

Blair glanced up to see it was an adult store for sex toys and lingerie, eighteen and up only.

"Oh my God," she said, a bit mortified.

"Oh, please, like you two haven't fooled around already?"

Blair blushed. Andrew was slightly amused, chuckling softly, his cheeks red.

"Um, well, erm…" Blair stammered.

"Yeah, that's what I thought. Come on, Andrew."

As Andrew and Natalie entered the store, Blair resigned herself to sitting in one of the nearby cushy chairs. Although she felt hot all over, she was in a really good mood. She was going to miss it when Natalie left.

Fifteen minutes later, they came out. Blair buried her face in her hands, sheepishly smiling and laughing at the sight of them. They both had black bags in hand.

"Well, I tried not to be a total pervert, so I let your

boyfriend shop in peace, but I did have to recommend some vibrators on your behalf."

Blair could only laugh in disbelief now.

"Shit—we should have gotten one for your mother, shouldn't we?" Natalie asked, as if she was thinking about it. "Would do her some good... She's wound up so goddamn tight—"

"OH MY GOD!" Blair shouted, both amused and horrified, hands on her head. She did not want to think about her mother using a vibrator. Several people in nearby chairs were looking at them. All three of them were laughing now. Blair noticed that Andrew seemed to be amused and happy.

"Sorry, everyone needs that one depraved aunt in their lives." Natalie raised her hand as if to stop Blair. "BUT— Andrew does have some really nice goodies in there now, so you'll be thanking me later."

Andrew smiled quietly, still a little red from blushing and laughing, but looking adorable.

Natalie glanced at her watch. "I hate to split you two lovebirds up," she said to the both of them, "but I told your mother we would be back by four."

A pang of disappointment hit Blair immediately. The fun had to end sometime. She hugged Andrew, while Natalie also bid him farewell with a hug.

* * *

Aunt Natalie left early Sunday morning. Blair tried her hardest not to be depressed, but it was an inevitable emotion as the high of her visit came crashing down. She completed her homework for almost every class, except for one assignment she would complete during study hall the next day.

Blair barely spoke to her mother Monday morning.

If It All Fades Away

Angela sat with her coffee as usual. Blair noticed she had been staying home the last few Mondays, and her father was also staying out after work. Typically, he would have been home and sleeping by now.

"Where's Dad?"

"Somewhere," Angela said, detached.

"He's usually home sleeping by now."

"I know."

"Are you off Mondays now?"

"Yep."

This was a closed conversation. Blair could imagine her dad escaping for a cup of coffee somewhere. She couldn't blame him, yet he seemed to tolerate Angela just fine on the weekends. Blair also wondered why her mother wasn't staying at her apartment instead if she was this grumpy. She had to accept that she would never understand her parents' dynamic, what they were up to, or what they were doing at any given time.

Just then, Andrew pulled into the driveway. Thank goodness.

* * *

Once in the school parking lot, Blair pounced on Andrew.

"Wha— Blair, we have to go inside!"

She was kissing him sloppily, stroking him through his pants. "It'll be quick."

"Someone might see," he said nervously.

"Your back windows are tinted."

Blair took advantage of his weak objections, clambering her tiny frame into the back seat. Andrew got out of the car and then entered the back.

"We have, like, ten minutes. You're ridiculous. We're going to be late."

"To what? Study hall? You think Mrs. Styre's old ass is going to notice?"

It was true; the woman often hid in her office, sometimes dozing off.

They were parked in a corner at an angle, so anyone who pulled up next to them could not see what was happening. Andrew swore as Blair reached into his pants and slowly lowered her mouth to him.

"Oh, God," he breathed.

She didn't know what she was doing, but she kept a steady rhythm up and down, using her hand to aid her efforts. Andrew groaned when she brought him to completion, emptying into her mouth.

"I have something for you," Andrew said breathlessly after a moment, tucking himself back into his pants. He reached into his backpack on the floor.

"No!" Blair gasped with a hand on her mouth.

"I mean, she did say she recommended some vibrators…" he said, pulling the toy out of a little cloth baggie.

"Why the hell do you have it now?" Blair asked in disbelief.

"To give it to you to take home. What the hell am I going to do with it during the week? Plus, we're usually at your place anyways."

Andrew handed Blair the small bullet-shaped vibrator.

"I already charged it. It has a couple of different settings," he said, proud of himself.

Blair blushed as she pushed the end button, going through the various modes.

"We're really going to be late now," he said, leaning forward and kissing her. "Come on, try it."

It wasn't long before Blair did as Andrew said.

Chapter 23

Never Had a Girlfriend

With some time left after lunch, Blair went to Ms. Holland's classroom. She told her what Natalie had said about her and Andrew going to school in Chicago together.

"Has Andrew applied anywhere out there?" she asked.

"I don't think so—not yet, anyway."

"Hmm. If you guys were to try to do something, he would need to submit his application to med school very soon. If I had to guess, one of the latest deadlines for the fall would probably be mid-December, which is only two weeks away."

Blair felt panicked. Natalie had made it all sound so easy and casual, but the reality of the effort required was starting to sink in.

"Have you thought about what you would apply for, now that your aunt is offering a place to stay?"

Blair felt shy about it, but she knew Ms. Holland wouldn't shit on her dreams, no matter how pathetic.

"Um…" She squirmed a bit. "So … I was considering possibly doing a screenwriting program … at Columbia

If It All Fades Away

College." Blair's voice dropped slightly at the end, still unsure of herself.

"Oh, I think that would be wonderful, Blair," Ms. Holland said.

"Really?"

"Yes, of course. You've always been into movies, and you're very creative. The papers you've written have always been insightful. I think you would do very well."

Blair beamed a little. "I'll probably apply, then," she said.

"Yes! Please do. If you need help or a letter of recommendation, or anything, please don't hesitate to ask."

Blair realized that the ending lunch bell was about to ring. She exited one of the front desks and approached her designated seat closer to the back.

"Oh, and uh, I wasn't going to ask, but the end of the semester is approaching. Were you still planning on doing the extra credit?" Ms. Holland asked.

Blair perked up. "Yeah, Andrew and I just haven't had a chance to watch the movie together yet."

Ms. Holland made a face somewhere between confusion and regret. "Oh... Well ... uh, he already turned his assignment in to me."

Blair felt pain in her stomach, like she had been punched.

"Wha—" She stopped herself. "When did he turn it in?"

Ms. Holland frowned. "The week after I gave you guys the assignment."

Blair felt stupid and couldn't bear to stay in that state any longer. She sighed. "He did say something about wanting to watch it alone." She rolled her eyes. "I'm going to have to give him crap later."

Ms. Holland gave a small smile, and then the bell rang.

Blair sat in contemplation as other students started to shuffle into the room. She *would* have to give him crap later.

Because for the life of her, she couldn't understand why he would watch the movie, not tell her, and then turn the assignment in without discussing it.

As class began, Blair couldn't hear anything as she went from being confused to downright pissed.

* * *

On the ride home, Blair had a scowl on her face the entire time. She had hoped that Andrew would notice, but he seemed somewhat oblivious. As they pulled into her driveway, she remained motionless, head on her fist. She wasn't opening the door.

Andrew looked over.

"Blair, what's wrong?"

"So, uh ... were you just planning on watching *1984* together like you never saw it ... or were you just hoping you wouldn't have to tell me you already turned in the assignment?"

Blair turned to him. Andrew looked down into his lap.

"I ... I was kinda hoping for both. I'm sorry."

"Really? So ... you were just going to watch it with me, say, 'Oh, yeah, great, I'll do the assignment now,' and then pretend you didn't turn it in not even a week after Ms. Holland gave it to us?"

Andrew said nothing, his head hung low, like a dog that had just torn up a shoe and gotten caught.

"I've been a bit stressed out with all of her assignments, to be honest. Her class has a lot more writing than I anticipated. It was the same before transferring, but Ms. Holland is harder than my previous English teacher. So, I just wanted to get it out of the way as soon as possible. It's ... it's hard to keep up with all this schoolwork. I'm sorry—"

"You know," Blair said, "I think the second day we met, I told you that no one needed to take that many damn AP classes, and I can't help but feel a little bit smug right now."

"I have to do well, though."

"You need AP Calculus to become a medical doctor? You're going to be doing equations and shit when you're seeing patients?"

"Well, no, but—"

Blair sighed. "Jesus, Stormant. I'm surprised you let me suck you off this morning if you're that worried about every single subject."

"I hated being late, to be honest."

"No one forced you to get in the back seat."

"No ... but you know I can't say no to you."

Blair could only blink. "So ... you'd rather lie to me than say no to me?"

Andrew looked at her with big puppy-dog eyes. "Blair, I'm sorry, this is all really new to me. I've ... I've never had a girlfriend before. I'm not used to being with someone and trying to focus on schoolwork simultaneously."

Just then, Angela opened the front door as if to say, *"You coming in today or what?"* Blair had almost forgotten that she had the day off.

"I gotta go," she said. She got out of the vehicle and slammed the door.

Blair couldn't get up to her bedroom fast enough. She felt childish and stupid for being so upset at Andrew for watching the movie without her. But it felt like a betrayal. It *was* a betrayal. Ms. Holland had given them the assignment with the sole purpose of them watching and discussing it together. And Andrew had just ... completely disregarded that part of the assignment. Cut her out. Did it on his own. Too impatient and anxious to get it done. He had treated it as an assignment to get out of the way rather than an experience to share and enjoy.

* * *

After her nap, Blair checked her phone. She had a few couple messages from Andrew.

Blair, I'm really sorry. I shouldn't have lied to you.
Please forgive me. -Andrew

Later:

I understand if you're mad at me and don't want to talk. I just hope you know how terrible I feel right now. I hate feeling like this. Just let me know what I can do to fix it.

Jesus, Blair thought. *Talk about anxiety.*

She wasn't sure what to say to him. She wasn't accustomed to someone apologizing to her. Her parents never apologized—not to her, and not to each other. They just resumed normal activities as if nothing had happened.

Blair's stomach growled. She was famished.

Once downstairs and in the kitchen, she popped a frozen dinner into the microwave. She sent Andrew a text message:

We can talk tomorrow. I'm too tired and upset to talk right now.

After dinner, Blair begrudgingly decided to watch *1984* by herself.

Chapter 24

Insulted Motivation

Once inside the SUV the next morning, one glance at Andrew, and Blair could tell he hadn't slept well.

"Blair—" Andrew began.

"Just get to school. I've had a shit night and morning, and I don't think I'm ready to discuss anything yet," she said flatly.

Blair could feel Andrew looking at her side profile, but she didn't look at him. He did as she asked and pulled out of the driveway.

Once at school, Andrew parked in the same spot as the day before. Blair knew she couldn't let their fight fester all day.

"Am I just entertainment to you?" she asked, still looking forward as Andrew opened the door.

He stopped and turned to her. "What? No, you're not just entertainment to me. What kind of question is that? I ... I really like you, Blair."

"I mean, you literally said we were going to be late yesterday, and we still messed around—then once you get confronted in a lie later, suddenly it's all *my* fault that you're unable to focus on your schoolwork. And that you didn't like being late."

"Yes, I wanted to mess around, but I also didn't like being late. It was ... conflicting."

"Mmm," Blair said, her mouth forming a bitter line. "Maybe for the rest of the week, I can stay away from you and see if it makes you feel better?"

Andrew sighed, putting his hand on his forehead. "I didn't think it would be this big of a deal."

Blair turned to regard him. "Andrew, you realize she gave us that assignment so *we* could work on it *together*. Or at least discuss and spend time together. It's like ... I'm amusing to you as long as I don't interfere with your schoolwork. But this one little assignment, just some innocent extra credit, and you totally shit on me."

Andrew had sad eyes, which annoyed Blair, but she was at least glad he was showing remorse.

"It's like ... you'll let me blow you as long as we can do it on Fridays, and you're down to do it in the back seat of your car, which you obviously enjoyed—so long as it doesn't interfere with school. But if it does, I'm the easy slut tempting you."

"What?! Blair, my God, no! Please, don't say stuff like that. That's not true at all. I'm ... I'm really sorry. Please, tell me what I can do to make it better?"

"Why are you so focused on just fixing this immediately? Christ, just listen to what I'm saying! Stop worrying about how *you* feel and think about how *I* feel."

Andrew inhaled and then exhaled. Blair could tell he wasn't used to conflict. She didn't like getting into his ass this badly, either. But his lack of awareness of how this movie thing might have hurt her feelings really upset her.

Blair looked at her phone. "We've got five minutes. I'm going inside," she said, opening the door. "Wouldn't want to make you late again."

Blair quickly walked to her locker and put her coat away, escaping as soon as possible. Andrew was slightly behind her.

In study hall, Blair sat further down the table she and Andrew shared. She didn't find it necessary to sit at another table, but she definitely wanted to convey to him how upset she was. And that she too meant business as far as schoolwork went.

Andrew wore the same melancholy puppy-dog face when he arrived a few minutes later. Blair glared at him, pulled out her textbooks, and studied furiously.

So, Andrew wanted to blame her for being a distraction he couldn't say no to. A default response she had heard many boys complain about through the years—including Hudson. If she and a group of boys were horsing around, she was always the first one yelled at—the one who was clearly responsible for getting the boys all riled up. Blair, of course, always shouldered the blame alone. None of the boys took responsibility for their behavior, and no one else held them responsible for it, either.

And damn it all to hell if Andrew Stormant was going to be able to use that excuse with her, too. Not now. Not ever. It felt like uncharted territory for Blair, but she welcomed the extra motivation boost from her boyfriend's unintentional insult.

Chapter 25

The Apology

Arriving after Julian and Rachel, Blair brought her world history book to lunch. She sat and opened it while eating a sandwich.

"You got a big test coming up, Blair?" Julian asked.

This was the first time she'd brought homework to the lunch table.

"Yeah, the day after tomorrow."

Andrew arrived and slowly sat next to Blair. She didn't look at him. With one glance at Rachel and Julian, she noticed that they could sense something was amiss.

"So, uh … how are you guys feeling about them changing where the dance will take place?" Rachel asked nervously.

"Fine," Blair said.

Andrew cleared his throat. "Um, I'm not familiar with previous years, of course, so…"

"Oh, that's right." Rachel smacked her forehead. "Well, Blair and I didn't have dates to prom last year, so … we don't know what the venue looks like."

Rachel said it as if she were hopeful that Blair would say more than two words.

"Sorry, guys," Blair said. "I gotta study. I'm really nervous about this test."

That seemed to appease them, and they left her alone. But the tension was still palpable, because Blair and Andrew weren't talking.

That afternoon, Blair also sat in silence on the way home. She exited the vehicle, mumbling her thanks to Andrew, then shut the door.

* * *

The next day, Wednesday, Blair welcomed Church Duty. She grabbed a broom and swept her way up and down the pews. They had a janitorial service clean the church, but it was amazing how quickly the floors got dirty. Blair often cursed that she did a better job than whoever was getting paid. Little things annoyed her, like how whoever else cleaned put the toilet paper rolls with the paper going under instead of over. It was like a weird silent battle of the over/under debate playing out in the church bathrooms.

There was no sunshine today. Blair had to turn the lights up a notch to see better. She started at the altar, worked her way down, and continued through the pews, one by one. Halfway through them, she heard footsteps coming from behind the altar entrance.

It was Father Donovan.

"Blair," he said. "Good to see you."

"Father," she said, with a head bow. She resumed sweeping.

"If it's not too much trouble, I'd like to inquire about something with you for a moment."

Oh, God, Blair thought. *What now?*

"Um, sure," she said.

"It'll only take a minute." He smiled.

Blair leaned her broom and dustpan against an outside pew and approached from the center aisle. Father Donovan came around the altar and down the elevated platform to meet her.

"As you know, Christmas Mass is in a few weeks. Your family usually attends, don't they?"

"Yes," Blair said. She hoped this wasn't an ambush about their lack of regular Sunday attendance.

"I've seen you working hard here this past semester. And, well, I think you should be more visible in the church."

Blair had no idea what the hell he was talking about.

"Have you thought about lecturing?"

Blair's eyes got wide. "You mean ... like reading?"

"Yes," he said, still smiling. Anyone else who smiled that much would have been creepy, but Father Donovan was easy on the eyes and not creepy at all. "So, what do you say? Maybe Christmas Mass this year?"

"That's, um, kind of a huge deal," Blair said. "I'm worried I'll get too nervous."

"Well, how about you practice in front of me and Sister Eugene for the next few Wednesdays? The church will survive a lack of cleaning or two. Or, if you want, maybe you can do a Sunday Mass reading as practice."

Blair wanted to tell him her parents didn't attend church, but she lived so close and had no excuse. Her anxiety was kicking in. She remembered that Andrew was now attending Sunday Mass at St. Michael's with his parents, and maybe this would be another opportunity for her to see him, pissed off though she might be at him.

"I'll, uh, have to talk to my parents," Blair said.

"Great. Let me know as soon as possible. I think the Lord has other plans for you here at the church than just cleaning."

"Thank you, Father, I will."

Resuming her cleaning, Blair thought about being a lecturer and reading at Christmas Mass. What the hell had she even agreed to? She loved solitude, not standing in front of a bunch of people, reading.

Putting her wireless earbuds in, Blair finished her remaining tasks in the church: sweeping, shaking out the rugs, cleaning windows, and wiping down ledges. It always amazed her how neglected certain ledges and landings were, completely covered in years of dust.

Making her way out of the church and traveling the short distance back to St. Michael's school, Blair was jamming out on her headphones. She was in a better mood from the activity and solitude of cleaning. She thought about watching a movie later that she'd found in the library's movie dump bin. Going to her locker, she put her coat away. Just then, a new song she enjoyed came on, and she was really into it, oblivious to her surroundings.

When Blair felt a pair of arms wrap around her, she shrieked and jumped. One of her earbuds fell out, and she immediately recognized the arms as Andrew's. She ripped her other earbud out and tried to turn.

"Blair," he said. He was holding her firmly, so she couldn't move.

"What do you want?" she asked with a groan. Blair had enjoyed completely forgetting about their little tiff for the last hour or so.

He put his chin on her left shoulder. "Just listen, okay?"

Blair immediately felt herself relax. How was he able to do that?

"I screwed up—I know that—and I'm sorry."

Blair inhaled.

"I've done some thinking, and ... I didn't realize that movie-watching was one of your love languages."

Love languages? Blair thought.

"So ... I wanted to say I'm really sorry in another way. I, uh... I called your mom."

Blair jumped. "What?!"

"Just listen," he said, still holding her. "I called your mom, and she said it was okay for me to take you to dinner and a movie on Saturday."

Blair closed her eyes. Her chest was full of butterflies, and she tried not to cry. Instead, she felt an involuntary grin form across her face.

"Will you let me take you? To say sorry?" He had angled his long neck around and turned her slightly so he could look at her. Her eyes were still stubbornly shut, but surely the involuntary closed-lipped smile she was fighting back showed.

"I'll take that as a yes?"

"... No," Blair teased.

"Yeah, right," Andrew said, snuggling his lips and face into her exposed skin. Blair squealed in delight and shock and swatted him away.

They pulled apart, and Blair looked up at Andrew, fully smiling now.

His eyes were happy, but serious, too. He brought his hand up to her face and kissed her. Blair's knees gave out; he had to hold her up for the second it took to steady herself. It had been two days, but it felt like two months since they had last kissed or touched.

"How the hell did you get my mom's number?" Blair asked.

Andrew smiled, knowing the charm he had. "Well, you know, when you tell the secretary that you want to surprise your girlfriend with dinner and a movie, and she gushes about how sweet it is, it's kinda hard for her to say no."

"You bastard!" Blair slapped him lightly. "She probably found it immediately, didn't she?"

"She did, actually." Andrew laughed. "Said something about how it was nice to be looking up your mom's number for a reason not related to you being 'naughty.'"

"Oh my God, she didn't actually say 'naughty,' did she?"

"She totally did."

"Gross."

Andrew pulled Blair in again with a silly hug, kissing her playfully.

Chapter 26

The Date

Blair found one of the only dresses she had. It was from her freshman year, but still fit her, all black and falling to her knees. It was not her favorite, but she wanted to look her best for her first real date with Andrew. She also found a pair of heels to wear—practice for the Winter Wonderland Dance.

At the top of the stairs, Blair began to take steadying steps. Her face broke into a smile as she saw Andrew's head of black hair at the bottom, talking to her mother and father. When he saw Blair out of the corner of his eyes, he turned up and smiled at her.

She let him do all the talking as she mumbled goodbye to her parents.

On their way to dinner, Blair kept smiling. She and Andrew were back to their usual selves, and nothing made her happier.

* * *

If It All Fades Away

As they entered the dimly lit restaurant, Blair was surprised when Andrew told the greeter they had a reservation. They were whisked away to a semi-private table in the corner, overlooking some other tables—a nice view of the restaurant. A tea light candle flickered romantically in the center.

The waiter mentioned bottles of wine, but then joked that they were too young to drink. Andrew noted how upset his mother would be. He was always so at ease with literally everyone, and Blair wished she could hate it, but she couldn't. She admired it so deeply about him.

After the waiter returned with their drinks, Blair wondered where the menus were. She mentioned it to Andrew. He gave her a closed-lipped smile.

"It's a course meal; it's already been decided."

"Oh," Blair said. Fancy. She most definitely was not used to this.

The first dish was a small appetizer with a swirl of sauce, with components Blair didn't recognize. Was that fish, or a mushroom? Either way, it tasted delicious. This went on for a while, small dishes prepared and plated by a real chef steadily arriving at their table.

Before the dinner portion arrived, Andrew reached for Blair across the table. She raised an eyebrow at him. He shook his upturned palm, and she reached out to take it. Then he offered the other hand, which she also took.

"I wasn't sure when would be a good time to tell you this, but I suppose this moment feels right."

Blair swallowed. She had no idea what he was going to say. But he looked beautiful in the light, well dressed. He had been smiling at her all evening.

He held her hands gently and smoothed his thumb over one of her knuckles. "I didn't have much time to think about it, but I know in my heart that I'm making the right choice."

Blair swallowed.

"Blair—"

"Yes?"

"I want you to know that I've applied to the University of Chicago Pritzker School of Medicine."

Blair's heart skipped a beat. "What?" She couldn't believe what she was hearing.

"Ms. Holland told me you plan to apply to Columbia College for screenwriting. Said you seemed pretty serious about it. She told me I should apply to Pritzker right away, because the deadline is approaching. So, I did."

Blair felt tears forming at the edges of her eyes.

"I don't think I should have any trouble getting in, but even if I wasn't accepted, I'd figure something out."

She looked down at her lap. "Andrew…"

"Blair, look at me."

She regarded him, broken open.

"I want to be with you. I don't think you're just entertainment, or a distraction."

Blair looked down and laughed through her tears.

He bent his head a little to try to look at her more deeply. "Or just a good time."

Blair also laughed at this, as did Andrew.

"But I do know, it's hard not to think about you being the center of every decision I make. Blair…"

She looked up at him now with soft tears trailing down her cheeks.

"I want to make Chicago happen. Do you?"

Blair was smiling and crying at the same time. "Yes," she breathed.

He leaned forward, and it was awkward to kiss across the table, but they did. Blair's heart was so incredibly full.

She wiped away her tears and was glad the food hadn't

arrived a moment sooner. The plates were set in front of them —small exquisite-looking steaks. Blair could hardly taste it through the joy she felt.

* * *

Andrew had asked Blair the other day if she wanted to see a new movie after dinner, or a previously released movie, possibly from years ago, at the historic movie theater. When he mentioned the options, Blair opted for the older movie, and Andrew said he was curious to see the recently renovated theater.

They bought popcorn, candy, and pop at the concession stand. Blair could not stop smiling. Entering the theater, she gasped. It was old, from the 1920s, complete with an elaborate ceiling, wall sconces, a red curtain, and plush red velvet-upholstered seats. There weren't many people yet—they were a bit early—but Blair could not stop staring at the whole structure in wonder. She could feel Andrew looking at her and smiling. She had last visited a movie theater with Rachel when they were eleven. For what movie, she couldn't recall. But this was something else entirely—something so unforgettably special. The dinner, Andrew's news of applying to Pritzker, the theater—all of it.

When the lights went down, Blair was chomping on her popcorn. She found a way to rest her feet between the seats before her. Her spine tingled when a theatrical trailer came on. She felt a fluttering sense of excitement that Andrew would see *Seven* for the first time with her. She had never seen it on the big screen—it had come out before she was born—and she was giddy at the prospect of seeing it in a theater.

Blair got absolute *chills* when the opening credits and

Nine Inch Nails' "Closer" played on the big screen in surround sound. She could only hope that Andrew was feeling what she was feeling.

Blair glanced at Andrew during certain parts of the movie, trying to gauge his expression as the light and movement shifted in his eyes. She smiled when he laughed at Brad Pitt being a smart ass as usual throughout the film:

"So many freaks out there, doin' their little evil deeds they don't wanna do. 'The voices made me do it.' 'My dog made me do it.' 'Jodie Foster made me do it.'"

Blair liked seeing him smile and laugh at the deadpan delivery of the lines, which still cracked her up, no matter how many times she had seen the movie.

She looked at him during the infamous "box" scene and relished when the box's contents were revealed. She giggled silently, thinking about the meme with Brad Pitt and Grumpy Cat. Brad Pitt's character, Detective Mills, demanded, "What's in the box?!", followed by a clip of his sad, confused, yet somehow stupid expression coupled with Grumpy Cat just below it, with the caption, *Shit. Scoop it.*

Afterward, Blair enjoyed the credits the whole way through, noting to Andrew, in case he didn't notice, that they came from the top down, not the bottom up, as traditional credits did. David Bowie's "The Heart's Filthy Lesson" played.

An indescribable sense of satisfaction swelled throughout Blair's body. She did her best not to lament at the moment, but she wished she could always experience this with Andrew. Perhaps because there was a part of her that hoped his confession of wanting to join her in Chicago meant that maybe—just maybe—things could always be this way once she graduated high school and moved out, away from her parents.

If It All Fades Away

A life with Natalie and Andrew. It seemed too good to be true—but for once, Blair didn't feel that way. She was determined to make it happen now, whatever it took.

Chapter 27

Winter Wonderland

Blair and Rachel sat with their hands under a UV light, sealing the shellac on their nails. Rachel was chatting about something, but Blair could only half listen. Turning her head in the large mirror on the back wall, she smiled at the sight. She liked how her hair looked. It had some unique twisting elements on the top, all gathered into the back in an elegant chignon. She wasn't sure how many bobby pins the hairstylist had put in her hair, but it felt like *a lot*.

Blair had convinced her parents to let her stay at Rachel's after the dance. But that was a lie; she was going to stay with Andrew, while Rachel stayed at Julian's. They had their alibis all worked out. Leaving, Blair paid with the cash that Andrew had given her. It was almost amusing that her mother hadn't even asked about her hair or whether she needed dinner money or not. Fine by Blair.

Back at Rachel's house, she and Blair spent a long time on their makeup, chatting, both excited for the evening. It was the most effort Blair had ever invested in her appearance. She

If It All Fades Away

had been watching makeup artist Lisa Eldridge's tutorial videos, happy to use a Chanel quad stolen from a classmate. She decided to stick with a neutral brown smoky eye. She was pleased with the end result.

Blair packed eye makeup remover for the end of the evening, tossed all her makeup into a bag, and ensured she had everything in order.

Now came the final part: the dress. Blair carefully removed it from its bag. Andrew had given it to her, and she then gave it to Rachel to hang onto—for reasons she still couldn't explain. She could have kept it at her house, but she didn't. Ignoring that weird feeling, Blair stepped into it and zipped herself up. She put her heels on, adjusted her small breasts in the front, and smoothed the fabric out over her thighs.

Bless her heart, Lily was letting Blair borrow some old costume jewelry to wear. It was nothing obnoxious, just a little pop. Blair put on the earrings, the necklace, and then the bracelet.

Looking in the full-length mirror, she grabbed the last item, the clutch, and stood, taking it all in.

Rachel came in from finishing her makeup in the bathroom a moment later.

"Wow."

Blair turned to her and felt a strange little smile on her face. "What?" She was stupidly happy.

"Damn, Blair. You look amazing."

Blair mumbled a thank you. Shortly thereafter, she helped Rachel into her gown.

* * *

Rachel drove Blair over to Andrew's house, where Julian would meet them. Blair's feet were cold getting out of the car. Thankfully, the walk to the front door wasn't too long. Her heels were comfortable, but she hoped she wouldn't get sore later. She had no idea how long the wear was on these.

Opening the door before they could even get to it, Lily shrieked. Blair could feel the sheepish grin on her own face, and Rachel was also smiling.

"Oh my God, Blair!" Lily said. "Andrew's still upstairs, but I think he will faint when he sees you."

"I hope not," Blair said with a wry smile.

"You must be Rachel," Lily said and immediately embraced her.

She whisked their coats away, shooing them into the formal dining room.

Blair was nervous, no question. Just then, Julian arrived, and Rachel went to answer the door. Lily was making conversation with them, and Blair anxiously sat at the table, waiting for Andrew to come down. She stood up when she heard what sounded like him at the top of the steps.

He didn't see her at first from his angle on the stairs. When he arrived, he was focused on talking to Julian, Rachel, and his mother in the foyer. He had a corsage in hand, while Blair timidly held the boutonniere in its small plastic box. Rachel's mother had picked them up for the girls.

Blair wished to never forget his expression when Andrew finally saw her.

He froze as if all time had stopped. His mouth parted slightly, and his eyes widened as if they were seeing her for the first time—like she was so awe-inspiring, he was rendered speechless.

Julian, Rachel, and Lily paused momentarily to regard them, but Andrew paid them no mind. He strode across the floor to see her in the formal dining room, her dress sparkling like diamonds in the light of the chandelier.

Blair wasn't sure if what she saw were tears in his eyes or not, but they appeared a bit glossy. Blair, too, felt her eyes shift, seeing him in a suit, just exactly as she had imagined.

"Blair," he said, breathless. Putting his small box with the corsage on the table, he approached and kissed her gently, then pulled away to look at her head to toe.

"You're beautiful every single day, but I'm ... at a loss for words."

"You can just say she looks hot, Stormant," Rachel called, teasing him.

Blair noticed Rachel was becoming more forward and funny, even in the short time she and Julian had been together.

Andrew carefully removed the corsage from its box and slid it onto Blair's wrist. Blair did likewise with Andrew's boutonniere, pinning it to his lapel.

"I need to get pictures!" Lily chimed. "Blair, Andrew, come over here and stand on the steps."

Julian and Rachel took their places below Blair and Andrew. The four of them squeezed together as Lily giggled and snapped a dozen pictures.

Andrew drove with Blair, while Rachel went with Julian. They all ate at an elegant restaurant. It was not as fancy as the one Andrew had taken her to two weeks prior, but it was still lovely.

Blair couldn't focus on the food; she could only think of her nerves about going to this new venue. She also wasn't sure how much she would actually dance. She had never done it before. Maybe she could manage slow dancing? Would Andrew expect her to do any other dancing? She had no idea; they hadn't talked about it.

* * *

The top floor of the hotel ballroom overlooked the river. It was gorgeous. There was a DJ already playing music, and people were lingering a bit. However, as more students arrived, some started trickling out onto the dance floor like ants to a dropped popsicle. Blair was surprised the chaperones weren't paying that close of attention, or if they were, they didn't care, because many of those dancing were very clearly drunk.

There were tables and chairs set up, like at a wedding reception, and students were claiming them left and right. Julian managed to find one round table in the corner, near an exit. Purple and blue streamers hung from the ceiling like wisteria blossoms. Snacks and beverages were being served in the corner bar window area. Blair and Rachel made their way over to grab some pops. Blair hadn't realized how thirsty she was as she downed her Sprite in one go.

Eventually, the place was packed. The DJ played a mix of music—pop, rap, hip-hop. The speakers thumped with heavy bass that rattled in the chest. When the first decent slow song came on, Andrew stood up and offered Blair his hand.

"What?" she said, shocked.

"Let's dance."

"I..."

Andrew could sense her hesitation. "It's not hard. I'll guide you. It's really simple."

Blair's heart thudded as Andrew led the way. He grabbed her arms and placed them at his shoulders, then let his hands fall to her waist. They started swaying from side to side, and Blair thought this wasn't so bad.

As she started to relax, she could finally take in the totality of the moment. The lights, Andrew, her—finally in

If It All Fades Away

this goddamn dress that had caused so much heartache, which was so worth it to her now. Andrew was smiling at her. He was significantly taller than her, so her arms were extended about as far as they could go, but she wouldn't have had it any other way.

"What are you thinking about?" Andrew asked.

Blair's attention snapped back to him. She was looking at him, but not entirely focused.

"Just—that I'm here… I mean, we're finally here."

"We are," he said.

Just as soon as it began, the song changed to something more fast-paced, and Blair scurried away as quickly as possible. Andrew tried to convince her to stay, but she slipped away faster than he could grab her wrist.

Back at the table, she was breathing heavily. Andrew lumbered over, a massive smile on his face. "I thought I was going to get you to stay out there."

Blair snorted. "No way in hell."

Rachel and Julian were approaching. Rachel was just as shy as Blair.

"No luck, either, Julian?" Andrew asked.

"No. I tried. You girls are just nervous. But you know what—I know how to have a good time. Practically mandatory for my family," Julian said with a wink.

Blair and Rachel exchanged a glance.

Julian gestured with his head to the nearby door, and they all followed. Julian found a dark corner down the hallway and pulled out a flask. Rachel looked at Blair, who looked at Andrew, who had a smirk on his face.

"My mother would kill me, but if this will get you out on that dance floor, then I say let's do it."

Blair laughed. "Stormant…"

"I can surprise occasionally," he said with a grin.

And with that, they all took swigs of the stiff drink, which tasted dreadful. Rachel quickly ran off to get something to chase it with. They did a few more shots, and the flask was gone just as soon as it appeared.

Blair had never drunk alcohol before. But something about Andrew doing it, knowing how goody-goody he was, made her feel safe. He wouldn't lead her astray, but cared for nothing more than for them to have a good time; she hadn't expected that. Not at all. And it was ... kinda hot.

Blair's belly was warm from the alcohol, and very shortly after, her whole body started to feel loose. She felt good. Suddenly, her nerves relaxed, and she was able to fully take in the other people in the room. She noticed Claire and the other girls across the way at their own table. She was with some prick from another school. Annabelle, likewise.

She saw Mr. Parks standing and talking to Mr. Banes. Gross. He was the math teacher who had caught her cheating. She knew she was wrong for it, but she still hated him—okay, maybe not *hated*, but she bristled in shame every time she saw him. The alcohol did, however, help take that sting away somewhat.

And then, a dance number came on, and before she could protest, Andrew gently led her to the floor with a hold on her arm.

"Feel my body," he said, coming up behind her.

If the alcohol didn't bring a flush to her cheeks, him grabbing her waist from behind surely did. They were moving now, strangely but erotically. Other couples were gathering around them, also grinding a bit. It wasn't obscene—well, not to them—but it was enough to give the chaperones pause. They always discouraged this type of dancing, but knew better than to try to stop it. If they had implemented "Leave

If It All Fades Away

some room for Jesus" by force, no one would ever come to these functions.

Blair let her ass rest on Andrew's lap, and he lowered himself to accommodate her height. Probably not an easy feat, but he had her. And that was all that mattered. She felt sensual and wanted. She felt unafraid. She wasn't sure she would have agreed to this had she not done three shots of whatever Julian had, but she was glad she was here with Andrew. She turned her head to him, and they kissed each other deeply.

When the song ended, another dance number came on, and they danced to that one, too, until Blair needed some water. Back at their table, Julian and Rachel were already there. They had danced to the previous song, but didn't stay out on the dance floor. It made Blair happy to see how cute they were together. Rachel, like Blair, had managed to loosen up with a bit of help. Blair could suddenly understand why her father drank as much as he did.

A slow song came on, and Andrew was offering his hand again.

"Okay, but I'm seriously resting after this one," Blair said.

Andrew Stormant loved to dance. Who knew?

Blair would have normally laughed at the song, but Andrew could make anything seem better than it was. How could something she'd never paid any attention to suddenly sound so profound and different to her? She sure as hell was not one to listen to Mariah Carey in her free time, but damn, that woman could sing. Suddenly, the song she and Andrew were dancing to seemed perfect. Blair knew that from that moment on, she would never hear Mariah Carey's "We Belong Together" in the same way again.

She was drowning in his eyes, the smell of him, this

moment. Blair could fall asleep standing against Andrew; he was so big, warm, and comfortable. She closed her eyes and rested her head on his chest. She then felt him resting his cheek on her head, protecting and holding her.

She could stay like this with him forever. There was nowhere else she wanted to be. Blair never wanted to forget it.

Chapter 28

Night

Blair and Andrew left the dance a little earlier than it was supposed to end. She was quite tired. She hadn't taken a nap in the afternoon, like she usually would. On the way out, she hugged Rachel and Julian while he and Andrew shook hands and pulled each other into half-bro hugs.

On the way back to Andrew's house, Blair dozed off slightly. She awoke when they pulled into his driveway. His parents were gone that evening to some foundation Christmas party in Detroit, where they would be staying the night.

Once inside, it was odd not to have Lily rush over and hug her. Blair had her heels in hand. She had switched to flip-flops towards the end of the evening, but her feet had held up fairly well.

"Are you hungry?" Andrew asked as they entered the kitchen.

"I'm just thirsty," Blair said, rubbing the sole of her right foot.

"Water, or something else?"

"Water's fine."

Andrew filled a cup with ice water and handed it to Blair. After drinking it in one long gulp, she set the glass down. Her eyes were heavy. She so badly just wanted to snuggle up in Andrew's bed.

Once upstairs with Andrew, she went into his bathroom to look in the mirror. "Jesus, my eyes are red," she said. She had been up entirely too long. She dug around in her makeup bag, pulling out cotton pads and eye makeup remover. Then she washed her face and began the process of taking the bobby pins out.

"Christ, how many freakin' pins did he put in here?"

She heard Andrew laugh, and the sound of hangers moving in his closet. Finally, after an eternity, Blair pulled out all of the pins. Entering his bedroom, she walked over to the end of his bed and threw herself face first onto it, letting out a loud groan. Andrew laughed when he came back out of his closet.

"Good time, huh?"

"Mm-hmm," Blair said into his duvet.

"I'm just hanging this up, and then I'll be ready for bed."

"Can you unzip me when you get done?" Blair asked. She was so tired and just wanted to close her eyes. "I'll also need a T-shirt or something to sleep in, because I was a dumbass and just brought clothes to wear home tomorrow."

"It's not a problem," he said.

A moment later, she felt Andrew's weight come onto the bed beside her. He rested his warm hand on her upper back, holding the fabric in place. His other hand came up slowly to unzip the back of her dress.

Blair didn't move.

And then, suddenly, she was all too aware that Andrew was weirdly quiet and strangely tender. He didn't make any jokes

If It All Fades Away

like he usually would. Instead, he was taking his time. Blair turned to see him out of the corner of her eye. Her breathing hitched, because it was apparent where this was going—and she realized there would never be a more perfect time than this.

Blair hadn't planned this—not at all. But in that moment between her asking him to unzip her and him getting done in the closet, something had shifted.

Andrew leaned forward and kissed her cheek, and her eyes fluttered shut. Blair inhaled deeply and pushed herself off of the bed to stand. As she did, the dress slowly fell to the floor.

She was standing before Andrew now, completely bare-chested, her disheveled curly hair down, in only her black panties. He was nervous, she could tell, because he was just watching her. They were watching each other. And Blair was all too aware that this was the most skin she'd ever shown to him. The last time she was here, she'd had pajamas on as they messed around. And the other time, they were half-dressed in their school uniforms.

Blair swallowed, stepping out of the dress, her eyes still on Andrew. He swallowed as well, his Adam's apple bobbing. He was wearing a black T-shirt and boxer briefs, dressed for sleep, which she took as a clue that he hadn't planned for this any more than she had.

Blair wordlessly thumbed her panties down, and those, too, fell to the floor.

Andrew reached behind his head and pulled his shirt up and over. Blair's breath caught. This was the first time she had seen his bare chest and shoulders. Then he took his boxer briefs off.

Andrew approached Blair and kissed her, leading her back down to the bed she was standing so close to. He brushed her hair away and gently put his lips on hers. Blair let her hands explore his chest and back.

Pulling away, Andrew gestured for her to move up the bed, and she did. He turned the lights off and climbed under the covers with her. The light from outside was hitting various parts of the room, just enough for them to see each other. The shadowed tree branches on the ceiling looked the same as last time. Blair had forgotten how big and warm Andrew's bed was. He smelled amazing. God, did he smell amazing.

Blair couldn't get over the fact that they were both naked together, in his bed, and not in some semi-state of dress. Her hand fumbled to Andrew again, stroking him, and he wouldn't stop kissing her. She didn't want him to. His hand slid to her center, rubbing her in a downward motion. She wondered if he had planned any of this at all.

"Did you think about this before tonight?" Blair asked.

"Uh—well, not specifically this night. But yeah, I've thought about it." He let out a small laugh as he prepared her with one finger, then another. His lips were on her again.

"Shit," he suddenly breathed, looking at his nightstand.

"What?"

"I ... I was literally going to buy condoms the other day."

"I thought you said you weren't specifically planning for this?"

"Well, no. But ... I mean, I figured we were getting someplace soon."

"You asshole," Blair teased. Then she added thoughtfully, "I... I'm on birth control now... It should be okay."

Andrew paused. He wanted to protest, but Blair stopped him with her lips.

"Don't kill the moment, Stormant," she said, pulling him closer.

If It All Fades Away

"Okay." He smiled.

Blair reached down and took Andrew into her hand. "You're nervous," she said, not realizing until then that he'd been stalling.

"Be quiet," Andrew admonished softly.

He didn't take his eyes off of her. Blair inhaled sharply as she watched his hand come down to fit himself on her outside. He pushed slightly, and Blair commanded her body to relax.

"You okay?"

Blair nodded, trying not to wince as she felt him fit just inside of her. "You're okay, you're okay." He pushed a bit more, pausing to watch her expression, constantly monitoring her. Andrew softened and leaned forward to kiss her forehead, then nipped at her neck and ear. That distracted and excited Blair enough to let him fit the rest of the way through.

Now joined together, they were looking at each other. Blair's eyes danced back and forth between Andrew's, his doing likewise. She pushed her head forward a bit and kissed him. They kissed until Blair moved her hips slightly, letting Andrew know he could continue.

Andrew started slow, with gentle thrusts, and Blair's breath hitched as she felt the weight of his body on top of her. They were still feeling each other, still adjusting to this new experience. She clung to him, wrapping herself tightly around him, and Andrew relaxed into her. Blair felt full in every way possible, and somewhere in her brain, she remembered how Natalie had said she and Andrew were made for each other.

He looked directly into her eyes, his wet, full, soft lips touching hers. He was hungry. Blair felt she would never know how he could simultaneously be so many things. Truth be told, she's always felt very two-dimensional compared to

Andrew. He was *smart*, not just book smart—maybe not what she would consider street smart, but he had a grip on reality that she hadn't thought possible for someone with so much wealth. His parents were wonderful, and it was a painful yet beautiful reminder to Blair of what someone could be like when they'd been loved their whole life.

Blair gripped Andrew's shoulders as whimpers escaped her. He was hitting a spot deep inside, something she hadn't known existed. It was sending waves of pleasure all throughout her body. She whined, the pressure building, barely tolerable. Blair's back arched, her neck to the ceiling, and Andrew was kissing her throat. Just as she felt at the edge of a cliff, Andrew started to speed up. She knew she might not climax with him, but just being on the edge was enough. Feeling him—knowing he was losing himself in her—that was enough.

When Andrew fell still, he released a noise somewhere between agony and sweet relief. Blair regarded his face, his eyes closed as he shuddered. They were still for a moment. Her eyes were barely able to grasp the trees on the ceiling now, their hearts thrumming and pounding together, skin sticky with sweat.

Andrew said nothing, still breathing heavily. Instinctively, Blair brought her hand to the back of his head, running her fingers down through his hair. She kept caressing him until she felt a weird vibration in his body. Then there was a sound.

Blair turned to look at him on her left shoulder. He was crying.

"Andrew—what—"

His whole body was shaking.

"Andrew, what's wrong?!" Blair asked, panicked.

She saw tears on his face, running down his nose, his

If It All Fades Away

mouth partially opened. Blair's eyes became glassy at the sight.

"I hate them," he said quietly.

Blair went to open her mouth again.

"I hate your parents," he admitted. "I've never hated anyone in my life. And maybe I don't even know if what I'm feeling is hate—but it must be close…"

Blair's throat caught, tears escaping her now.

"They … they have their own demons, I'm sure, and I've tried my best to understand. But for the life of me, I don't think I ever will."

He lifted himself to look at her, his face completely wrecked in a way Blair had never seen before.

"I will never understand … why they don't love you the way I do."

Blair's vision blurred. She didn't want to make this moment about her or start really crying, because she knew she needed to be strong for him.

"Andrew…" Her voice cracked.

Andrew grabbed her face with both hands. "Blair, I love you."

"I love you, too," she replied. It came so naturally.

"I want this goddamn year to get over with so badly. I want to get you away from your parents. I just want us to be together and happy in Chicago."

Blair closed her eyes, inhaling and exhaling sharply. She tried to move her head to the side to escape him. She couldn't bring herself to open her eyes.

"Don't try to cry looking away," he told her. "I've seen how badly you try to fight it sometimes."

Blair didn't recognize the noise that came out of her, and she wanted to curse Stormant for holding her head in place, for forcing her to be—right here—

He leaned down and kissed her on the side of her mouth. "Blair, look at me."

She opened her eyes.

His tone evened out. "I want to spend the rest of my life with you. I love you. I want to marry you someday. I want kids—I want all of it."

Blair wrapped her arms around him, hugging him, and she felt his head come to the side of her again. They cried together ... and Blair grasped for the right words, something that could even acknowledge or touch the magnitude of what he'd told her.

She swallowed, calling her voice to return.

"Andrew... If ... if all that I am, all that I've lived—all the pain, all the sadness, all of my memories... If it all fades away ... I want you to know that you're the only thing I want to remember."

Andrew looked at her, and they held each other, crying and smiling, lost together.

"We're going to get through this," Andrew said.

"I believe you," Blair replied softly.

I believe you.

Chapter 29

Christmas Eve

Blair felt like she was going to throw up. Her hands were shaky and sweaty.

As the clamoring of people filled St. Michael's, she wondered why she'd agreed to read in front of everyone for Christmas Eve Mass. Why? *Why?*

Andrew was sitting beside her, saving a spot for his parents, and Blair was doing likewise. When Henry and Lily arrived, they were all smiles. Blair did her best to be responsive and hug them, but didn't hear anything they said. She asked Andrew to keep a lookout for her parents; her nerves were too much of a disaster to try to keep looking back for them.

"They're coming," Andrew said.

"Oh, God…"

"Relax, relax."

Blair's forehead was hot, her stomach in knots. She hadn't eaten anything in a while and wouldn't be able to until after Mass. Her adrenaline was the only thing sustaining her right now.

"Andrewww," Angela drawled, giving him a big hug. Gerald was behind her. Andrew shook his hand with a nod.

"These must be your parents?"

Blair stood aside as Angela didn't acknowledge her, shaking Lily's hand and waving to Henry.

"So nice to meet you, finally," Angela said with her best smile.

"It's so nice to meet you, too," Lily said.

Finally, Angela acknowledged Blair. "Hi, honey."

"Hi," she mumbled.

Soon, there was standing room only in the church. Conversations among the parishioners continued until the music started playing to signal the start of the procession. Blair heard nothing but humming in her ears until she was to go up for the second reading.

Once at the lectern, she felt her throat start to swell shut. Hundreds of people were in attendance. Blair was sure she would get stage fright, but then she looked at Andrew, and he mouthed to her, *"You got this."*

Suddenly, everyone else faded away, and Blair imagined it was only Father Donovan, Andrew, and Sister Eugene, as it was when she practiced.

Blair went slowly, making sure not to let her voice drop at the end of each sentence, enunciating each word carefully. Her right hand was shaking, and her palms were sweaty. She realized she had read the reading so many times that she almost had it memorized. With her stomach in knots, she read the final sentence. Then she slowly descended the platform with weak knees. Relief washed over her as she sat next to Andrew. He gave her a small smile and squeezed her forearm as if to say, *"Good job."*

Blair's adrenaline was subsiding, and she was *starving*. After the gospel and Communion, she comically hoped that

If It All Fades Away

the wine she drank and wafer she ate would sustain her for another twenty-five to thirty minutes. As Christmas songs of praise and glory were sung for the closing procession, she began to feel more antsy. And then, it was time for Angela to speak with Lily and Henry.

"Angela, sincerely, so good to meet you," Lily said.

"Andrew is such a nice young man. We loved having him over for Thanksgiving," Angela chimed. "And your apple pie... Oh, my goodness! Wonderful."

"Thank you," Lily said. Then added, "Blair, honey, you did amazing up there."

"Didn't she?" Angela interjected.

Lily blinked momentarily, then switched to another topic. "She looked absolutely *stunning* in her Winter Wonderland dress. Oh my God, I thought Andrew would faint seeing her."

Blair could practically see her mother's eye twitch.

"I couldn't believe it when I saw it," Angela said. "I almost cried. *Breathtaking*. Oh my, we had such a good time picking it out!"

Blair almost balked as Andrew had; she caught the contempt in his eyes.

"So, Blair is planning to live with your sister while she attends college in Chicago, is that right?" Lily asked, changing the subject yet again, still focused on Blair.

Blair's stomach dropped. *Oh my God, no...*

Angela's face almost wavered for a moment. Her eyes shifted, but her smile stayed. She reached up and placed a hand on Blair's neck.

"Yes! Oh my goodness, Chicago is such a beautiful city." She squeezed the back of Blair's neck. "I haven't been in ages and have meant to get back there to visit, but you know, my job working for John J. Turner keeps me *sooo* busy."

"Oh my goodness, it must! That big case he just won—I mean, that you guys just won."

"Thank you." Angela smiled, not relaxing her grip. "It was dreadful. I thought it would never end."

"Well, congratulations, you certainly have much to be proud of."

Blair could feel the anger in her mother's grip. Something made her feel so helpless as she watched Andrew agonize at her being strong-armed by her mother. Blair had never seen Andrew so angry in the time that they'd been together. The only other time she'd sensed this energy from him was when he had yelled at Hudson in gym class. Andrew had a cool head, but Blair could tell he wanted to snap, to say something. But this wasn't the time or place; it would only worsen matters.

"Thank you," Angela said again, closing her eyes slightly and nodding.

Lily quickly added, "I mean about Blair, too. She's such a wonderful young lady. We couldn't have asked for a kinder girl to date Andrew."

Still holding Blair's neck, Angela looked at her, then pulled her closer into a fake embrace. "Thank you. We're very proud of her."

Lily, Henry, and Andrew were all standing there in awkward silence.

Then Angela spoke. "Oh my goodness, speak of the devil, there's John!"

"Well, we'll let you guys go. Merry Christmas!" Lily said with a wave.

"Merry Christmas to you, too," Angela said. She let go of Blair to shake Lily's hand.

Blair glanced over to see her father sitting on the pew with his eyes closed.

If It All Fades Away

Lily and Blair hugged. Blair shook Henry's hand and then gave Andrew a long hug.

"Merry Christmas, babe," he said.

"Merry Christmas."

They embraced for a long moment. Andrew and his parents were going away on vacation for the next week and a half. She and Andrew wouldn't see each other until they were in school again in January. Blair hated that the last time she would see him for a while was at Christmas Mass. She had hoped to spend time with him before he left, but it wasn't possible.

Before she knew it, Blair was being whisked away from Andrew. She watched with sad eyes, as did he, as she was once again being led away by her mother's hand across the church. That was the last Blair saw of Andrew before she was shoved in front of the prosecutor her mother worked for.

"Blair," he said. "My goodness, have you grown up!"

"Hasn't she?" Angela interjected.

Blair felt slimy just looking at the man. His plain but not necessarily ugly wife was standing nearby.

"So good to see you two here on Christmas Eve," her mother said.

"We couldn't miss this year—not with Blair reading," John said.

Blair was floored. "What?"

Her mother squeezed the back of her neck.

"Oh, um, I mean—thank you," Blair said with a head bow.

"Charlene," Angela cooed, and for a moment, she let go of Blair to talk to John's wife.

People were still emptying from the church. Then, realizing her mother was preoccupied with the conversation, Blair slowly raised her head.

John was staring at her.

Not just looking at her; he was *staring* ... with desperate hunger.

Blair's heart thudded as she frantically glanced at her mother, who was so enmeshed in conversation with his wife that she didn't notice anything else.

"Wow," he said, out of her mother's earshot. "My goodness, Blair, I remember you sitting in the courtroom when you were seven, but who knew this would be what you would grow into ten years later?"

Blair swallowed and averted her eyes.

"Your mother has told me so much about you. But I didn't realize how similar you two looked. It's a little jarring to see you with brown hair, though. I'm so used to Angela's blonde."

Blair nodded.

"So, you got any big college plans?" he asked.

"I, uh—I plan to go to Columbia College ... in Chicago," she said, stealing another look at him. He was about Andrew's height, with a little pepper of grey in his hair, a well-shaven face, and a short goatee. He was broad and handsome, although not exactly Blair's type. But she could see his attractiveness, how he could be someone else's type.

"Chi-town, huh?" he said. "I have a college buddy who lives out there. We used to go bar-hopping all the time there. Good times."

John glanced over to his wife and Angela, aware that they were finishing their conversation. He then leaned forward and whispered in Blair's ear.

"Say, if you need any legal help in the future ... let me know. I know you've had some problems in the past. I'm always available if you need me, with or without your feisty mother knowing about it."

Blair's eyes surely conveyed her shock as he pulled away with a smirk, and then smoothly handed her his business card —right under her mother and his wife's noses.

"I'll, uh… I'll keep that in mind, sir. Thank you," Blair said.

"You're welcome," he said firmly. His eyes remained fixed on Blair until Angela returned.

"Well, we really must be going." She smiled at John.

"Angie," he said with a smile, almost cocky.

Blair froze at *"Angie."* No one—literally no one, except Natalie—was allowed to call her that. Blair felt her mother bristle, which must have reverberated right back from her, because Angela tried to deflect it as quickly as possible.

"Merry Christmas, John," she said. "So good to see you and Charlene here."

"Merry Christmas, ladies. Take care," he said with a slight nod, turning away to his wife.

Angela was practically choking Blair by the nape of her neck as she rushed them back over to their pew.

"Gerald!" she snapped.

His eyes opened. "Yeah," he said, practically drooling awake.

"It's time to go. Now. Get up."

Blair turned and saw that John was still creepily smiling at her. And in a flash, it occurred to her that either previously or currently, her mother had been—or still was—fucking prosecutor John J. Turner … who also happened to have his eye on his paralegal's seventeen-year-old daughter, whom he had just reassured he would be there for should she *need* anything … legal or otherwise.

Blair had thought she wanted to throw up before Mass, but she'd had no idea just how close she would come by the end of it.

Myra King

Merry Christmas, Blair.

Chapter 30

Welcome Back

Walking out to their vehicle, Blair stayed a few steps behind her parents. Her mother's heels clicked on the pavement, which had been salted about four times over. Her father walked decidedly slowly.

She heard her mother when she leaned over to her father. "Can't even keep it together for one damn hour?"

He laughed in response, then stumbled a little. He was drunk.

Blair wondered how she had missed all these glaringly obvious clues about her parents' double lives—her father coming home at odd hours or not at all, his slight bumbling of steps when he would stagger down the hall to bed, and her mother's apartment in the city. But what she couldn't wrap her head around was why these two stayed together. Why did Angela even bother to come home at all?

Blair's heart thudded as she got into the back seat. She was expecting Angela to inquire about Chicago, and was deeply unnerved when she didn't. It was terrifying. Blair watched her mother's face in the rearview mirror, quickly looking away when their gazes met.

Once home, Blair hoped to get inside and upstairs as quickly as possible, and she succeeded. Her mother seemed ... preoccupied. Maybe she was thinking about John J. Turner. His stupid middle initial was the only thing adding any flare to his boring name.

Gerald stumbled up the stairs, and Blair heard him groan as the bed collapsed under his weight. She listened, waiting for Angela to come to her room or call her down. But she didn't. Blair breathed a sigh of relief when she heard the TV turn on.

* * *

Christmas morning came and went. They didn't bother putting up a tree anymore. Blair got a fifty-dollar Meijer gift card from her parents. She knew her mother had probably grabbed it in the checkout lane. She remembered Christmases being a bit better when she was younger, and then, as she got older, they became less and less joyful. Still, she was grateful for the gift card.

Blair was relieved to spend Christmas Day in her room, alone and unbothered. In the evening, she heard her mother say she had to go into town to handle a work problem. *Sure, Angela. On Christmas Day.* She wondered if her father knew about her infidelity, or even cared.

Andrew texted Blair the following morning, saying they were boarding their flight in Detroit and that he loved her. Blair texted back the same and that she was going to miss him. She was surprised when he asked her to send him some pictures with a winky face. Blair wasn't sure if she was comfortable doing that; she always worried someone would

If It All Fades Away

end up hacking the photos. She couldn't bear the thought of others seeing pictures not meant for them.

She texted back, *I'll think about it :)*

* * *

Staring out her window on a shit winter day, her father and mother both back to work, Blair masturbated with her vibrator, painfully aware that she was clenching around nothing. With the end of the semester taking up their time and then Christmas break around the corner, Blair and Andrew hadn't had sex since the night of the dance.

It was going to be a very long week and a half.

Andrew video-chatted with Blair when they arrived in the Bahamas. She was happy to see him happy, but he kept lamenting about how he wished she could have come along. However, everything had already been booked in advance. Blair knew her parents wouldn't have let her go, even if she could have.

She cleaned around the house during the day, doing as she was told. She even did seasonal chores, like washing the windows. She swept and mopped the basement floor, dusted away cobwebs, and organized old boxes in a corner.

Sitting down to rest, Blair got distracted and started going through one of the boxes marked with her name. There were some papers and vaccination records from when she was a child, and a few crayon drawings she had no recollection of doing. She found an envelope with pictures at the bottom of the pile. Curious, Blair opened it and saw some pics of her as a baby, some with her mom and dad in them. Angela didn't have a line in the middle of her brow yet; she looked younger and ... happier. Her father had her on his shoulders outside in the backyard. Blair was smiling in the picture, as was he.

Blair felt her eyes become moist.

Before she could sit with her thoughts for too long, she found other pictures with her maternal grandparents, Florence and Wilfred. Blair noticed the dates and that she was in a photo with them of some variety every month for a year. Pictures with her parents, however, were absent during that period. She really didn't remember her grandparents. Blair thought about what Natalie had said to her mom during her visit: *"My God, Mom and Dad would be horrified if they knew this is how you're treating her."*

She recalled her mother asking Natalie if she planned to visit Florence. Angela always told Blair that it wasn't necessary to go with her, claiming she had dementia and was violent, that she wouldn't have remembered Blair anyway.

Natalie had wordlessly left on Saturday to visit her. And she spoke nothing of it upon her return. Wilfred had died of a heart attack when Blair was ten. She vaguely remembered the funeral.

Flipping through more papers, Blair came across an official court document, the corner ripped. She was bewildered when she saw that it had her grandparents listed as plaintiffs versus her parents as defendants. There was a bunch of legal jargon introducing the purpose of the document: her grandparents seeking custody due to child neglect. And then—it ended. Blair frantically searched the box, trying to find more, but there was nothing.

She found her birth certificate, Social Security card, and a few other papers, but not much else. Blair searched in different boxes and found nothing.

"Blair?"

Shit. Hearing her mother's voice upstairs, she put the lids back on the boxes, frantically stacking them back up and shoving them into the corner. She rushed to the laundry area, started the washer, and threw clothes in.

"Down here!" she called back.

Her mother came to the top of the stairs. She said nothing, seemingly pleased to hear Blair doing laundry.

"Did you need something?" Blair asked, her voice a little too high.

"No. Just wondering where you were."

Later, Blair lay in bed, her head swimming, trying her hardest to remember her maternal grandparents. They looked like they loved her. She was so young in the photos, but even as a baby, Blair was smiling. Rolling over, she looked at her nightstand and saw the business card John had given her propped up against the TV. Something about it felt different now, and she wasn't sure why.

* * *

Blair was only too anxious for Christmas break to end. She was sure she had cleaned every corner of the house out of boredom and obligation. She had rearranged her entire bookshelf alphabetically: books, magazines, and movies. As she looked through her film choices, nothing sounded compelling.

Blair was also sure she'd never masturbated so much in her life. She finally caved and sent pictures of herself to Andrew. He did likewise, and it made her crave him even more. The physical ache of his touch, of his smell, of *him*—almost palpable.

Rachel invited Blair to Julian's for New Year's Eve, but Blair said she was sick. She couldn't bear the thought of the ball dropping and Julian and Rachel kissing, while she stood there pathetically alone. And if there was any alcohol involved (which Blair knew there would be), she was sure to become a pathetic, crying mess about her boyfriend being gone for a week.

With a few days remaining of Christmas break, Blair walked outside each day, the weather fairly tolerable. She kept turning over her findings in the basement. There was something sinister that lay in wait for the answers she sought, and she was terrified to receive them. She wasn't ready for them, and she knew it.

* * *

The night of Andrew's return to Michigan, Blair paced all afternoon. She knew he was probably exhausted from traveling, but she needed him. And she was only too pleased that neither of her parents were home, both at work or off doing whatever—or *whoever*—the hell it was they were doing.

Blair took a long shower, shaving her legs and bikini line. She then used some amazing-smelling lotion and curled her hair. She debated whether to do her makeup, but eventually decided against it.

Finally, at around eight o'clock, Blair saw Andrew pull into her driveway. She ran to the door. When she opened it, he looked tired, but happy to see her.

Blair's arms were around him before he could speak. She had thought she knew hunger, but she didn't until she had been apart from Andrew. His energy from traveling may have been depleted, but Blair had too much energy and was more than happy to take the lead.

Once she led him upstairs, it wasn't long before their clothes were on her bedroom floor.

"I've missed you," Blair said quietly.

"I've missed you, too," Andrew replied with a kiss.

Chapter 31

The Urge

When school started back up a few days later, Blair practically jumped out of bed to get ready, which was truly a first for her. She was dismayed that midterm exams were right around the corner, which meant that every class for the next week would be review, not to mention lots of studying.

At lunch, Blair chatted excitedly with Andrew, Julian, and Rachel. She was glad to be back to a normal routine and to see her friends again.

What took Blair by surprise was how some of the teachers who normally groaned at her, like Mrs. Dakota and Mr. Parks, told her "good job" on her reading at Christmas Mass. Blair humbly thanked them, feeling warmth inside at receiving praise for once. Mrs. Dakota also said she'd noticed Blair's renewed commitment to her homework and said, "Keep it up."

* * *

Blair noticed Claire sitting one row up near their back pew during Thursday Mass. During the entire thing, Claire kept turning back slightly to look at Andrew out of the corner of her eye. From where Blair was sitting next to Rachel, Claire wouldn't have been able to spot her stealing glances.

Falling back as the students started to shuffle out, Blair watched as Claire approached Andrew, who was walking with Julian.

"Andrew!" Claire said with a playful whisper.

Blair struggled to get a little closer without being seen.

"You're still coming to the study group tomorrow after school, right?"

Andrew looked down at her, then back up, scanning the crowd before facing her again.

"Uh, I'll see."

"Cool, cool."

As Claire took off, Blair's stomach dropped. Study group? For what? Blair wracked her brain for whether Andrew had any classes with Claire and came up empty-handed. She wanted to ask him, *"What the hell was that?"*, but simply came up alongside him, hands shaking, throat closed.

"There you are," he said with a smile. "I thought I lost you for a second."

Blair looked up and forced a smile.

Internally, she was screaming.

* * *

When Andrew dropped Blair off that afternoon, she finally worked up the courage to ask about what she'd overheard in a roundabout way.

If It All Fades Away

"So, um, you're still planning on coming over after school tomorrow, right?"

Andrew looked at her. "Well, actually, I'm glad you asked, because I was planning on doing a calculus study group with a few people for the midterm exam."

Blair swallowed. "Oh." She fisted her skirt downward. "You going to someone's house or something?"

"Yeah, Danielle Adamski's."

Blair kept her hands in a fist, afraid they would expose how badly she was shaking.

"Who else is going to be there?" she asked, trying to keep her tone calm.

"Uh ... her, Brendon Rhoades, and Claire Miller."

Blair's whole body thrummed with panic, her gaze fixed on her lap. "I, uh... I don't suppose I could ask you not to go, could I?"

Blair felt Andrew turn to look at her more fully. "What? Why?"

Blair closed her eyes. "Because ... I don't like Claire, and I'm pretty sure she has a thing for you."

Andrew scoffed in disbelief. "I don't know how that's possible. We don't even sit near each other in calc, and I barely talk to her. I didn't when we sat with her at lunch, either."

Blair rested her elbow on the door, head in hand, eyes closed. She took a shuddering breath. "Andrew, please tell me you're not serious right now?"

There was a long pause. "Blair, I'm literally so confused. I honestly have no idea what you're talking about."

Blair took steadying breaths, trying to calm her nerves. Then she opened her eyes to look at him. "I'm telling you, she likes you, whether you believe it or not. And I just…"

Blair sighed. "I just don't want you going to someone's house with her."

Andrew's eyes fell. He momentarily picked at a piece of fuzz on his sweater, then looked at Blair again.

"Blair, I don't like her. Like, literally not at all. She's not my type, and we don't even know each other." Andrew's arm rested on the steering wheel as he regarded her. Something about that seemed odd to her—an unusual mannerism. Or maybe she was just freaking out.

"I really do need to go to this study group, though. I want to review some stuff, and we all decided to meet up already."

Blair gritted her teeth. "I don't want you going!" she yelled before she could stop herself.

Andrew's eyes were wide. He swallowed. "Blair… I … I have to say, I don't like how you're behaving right now."

Blair turned to balk at him, mouth open, eyes wide. "You … you what?"

"It's … a little scary. Because I just told you I don't like Claire, that I have to go to this thing, and you're acting a bit … *controlling*."

Blair felt panic course through her veins. Something was terribly wrong. "Oh—*oh*—you think I'm scary now?"

"No, that's not what I meant. I just said your behavior is a little scary."

"So, your girlfriend—who knows this *cunt* better than you ever will, after four years—suddenly has no idea what the hell she's talking about when it comes to her?"

"I don't like her!" Andrew yelled out of desperation, his hands out.

"I don't *care*!" Blair screamed directly at him, spit flying. *"She's the fucking problem, even if you're not!"*

Andrew was shaking now. He put his hands over his face, exhaling deeply. Blair could hardly believe what was happening. *This can't be happening right now, this isn't happening, this isn't real.*

"Blair," he said, not looking at her. "I love you. I don't know how many different ways I have to show it to you, but I do." He regarded her once more. "But I think you're being irrational and jealous for no reason right now."

Blair's face twisted, and she closed her mouth. She couldn't think straight. She stared at Andrew, not fully processing what he'd just said. It hit her like a brick. But she was aware, very suddenly, of an indescribable and violent *urge* to *hit* Andrew. The thought alone was terrifying to the more logical part of Blair's brain, and whatever ounce of that she had left, she used to move her visibly trembling hand to reach for the door handle.

"Blair—" Andrew said.

There was no love in his voice.

Blair exited the car without a single glance back and slammed the door.

Chapter 32

Knock, Knock, Is Anybody Home?

Blair was a complete and total *wreck* for the rest of the evening. She couldn't think about anything except Andrew and Claire. Worse still, the way Andrew had basically called her a jealous psycho of a girlfriend completely invalidated her feelings.

Blair's fear and panic eventually gave way to a slithering sadness that snaked its way up to her throat, strangling her, until finally she yielded to it and sobbed uncontrollably.

For hours.

She was losing Andrew, had probably already lost him, and she didn't know what to do about it. Blair tried to stop panic-crying several times, to no avail. She managed a few times, giving herself the opportunity to breathe—and then was gripped with the pain once more. She cried until her face, chest, and eyes hurt, snot and tears all over her blanket.

Eventually, Blair fell asleep, utterly exhausted from the emotional hell and turmoil she had just experienced.

* * *

If It All Fades Away

Upon her waking to darkness a few hours later, Blair's stomach physically hurt from hunger, but she paid it no mind. It mattered little now, because *something* had shifted while she slept. Something had *awakened*. Where there was sadness before, it was now completely gone, replaced by an eerie yet soothing sense of calm.

The calm before the storm.

* * *

The next morning, Blair set out on foot for school at the same time she used to. She had checked her phone a few times, but there was nothing from Andrew, which was fine with her.

Arriving at school, she glanced at the clock and noticed that this was the time when Andrew would normally be picking her up. She put her coat away, grabbed her books, and closed her locker door.

As she made her way down to study hall, her phone vibrated.

Are you ready? I'm here.

He had been waiting for seven minutes. Typically, Blair was out the door within thirty seconds of his arrival.

Five minutes later...

Are you at school? I just spoke with your dad, and he said you're not in your room.

Blair ignored the message.

Once in the library, she sat at the old spot where she used to sit. She hadn't realized how much she'd missed the view out the window. How little time had passed since she had last sat there alone. It was comforting, actually, the familiarity.

Blair did her best to focus on her reading, but she couldn't help but keep glancing at her phone and out of the corner of her eye. Andrew eventually arrived, and her heart started thudding, but she kept her head down to her book. She noticed him pausing at their usual spot. She could practically feel the shock emanating from him.

Blair's blood pumped thick when she realized he was approaching her.

"Blair—what the hell was that?"

She didn't look at him.

"I just had to wake up your dad to see if you were home. He checked, and you weren't there. I've been texting you—"

He stopped himself, and Blair heard in his voice a mixture of concern and anger.

"Blair."

She refused to look up at him, no matter how firmly he said her name.

Blair quietly closed her book and slipped it into her backpack. Then she scooted her chair out, stood up, pushed it back in, and left the library.

Andrew followed her.

"Blair—" He grabbed her by the arm in the hallway, pulling her into him, then grabbed her by both upper arms.

She immediately flashed back to the time her father had slammed her into the fridge. Blair remembered now—she had taken the last cheese slice in the fridge for a sandwich.

"Blair—I'm sorry. You can't honestly be this upset about what happened yesterday."

Blair slowly brought her eyes up to look at him, her head as far back from him as it would go. Her eyes were filled with pure hatred.

"Get. Your. Hands. Off. Me."

Blair could see Andrew's terror as he realized how deeply he had messed up.

But he knew it was too late. They both did. Oh, was it ever too late.

If It All Fades Away

"Blair—no, no, no… Blair, please!" He tried to pull her into a hug. "Please don't do this. I'm sorry. I won't go to the study group. I promise. I love you. Please—"

Blair brought her hands up to his chest, resisting him with all of her strength, trying to create some distance between them. Andrew held her tightly; Blair could feel him shaking, his heart pounding into her hands. She *growled* into his chest, furious that he wasn't letting her go.

He brought his hand up to the back of her head, as he had done so many times to soothe her. "Please don't do this," he begged.

"Let go of me," she said through gritted teeth. "I mean it."

He pulled away to look at her.

"Blair—please—don't do this! I'm sorry. I love you. Please—no. This isn't who you are."

A deliciously wicked smile came across Blair's face. She chuckled softly, her eyes glazing to black.

"This is who I've always been, Stormant. You were just too *stupid* to see it."

There was enough space now, and Blair was only too glad to bring her hands up and rake her nails down the front of Andrew's face—*hard.*

He let out a cry of pain and let her go. Andrew looked nothing short of devastated with red marks striped down his face from her attack.

Blair took several steps backward, briefly examining Andrew's skin beneath her fingernails. Looking up once more with the eyes of a beast, clawed hands still held out before her, she turned and ran.

She was finally set free.

Chapter 33

A Taste

Blair ran to the girls' bathroom—the same one she had run to back when Andrew first told her about her eyes so long ago. Her hair was frazzled when she looked in the mirror, and her breath was heavy. She looked at her fingertips again, slightly in disbelief at seeing Andrew's skin there.

Rushing over to the sink, she washed her hands vigorously. Sure that she couldn't return to study hall, Blair managed to wait until second period. And then she went to her locker, grabbed her coat, and headed home—well, not home, exactly, but to the Hutchinson-Genesis Library.

By lunchtime, Rachel texted Blair, asking her if she was okay, since neither she nor Andrew was there. Blair explained what had happened. It made her sad that Andrew must have gone home, perhaps too humiliated to continue the rest of the day with half of his face scratched off.

Blair asked Rachel if she could pick up any of her assignments or review notes for their shared classes. Rachel agreed, noting that she would ask other classmates for notes for classes they didn't have together.

If It All Fades Away

Oddly enough, Blair's rage fueled her to want to prove Andrew wrong. Because deep down inside, she knew he thought she was too stupid to do well in school. Sure, he said she was smart, but it was only half true. Whatever intelligence he felt she had, it mattered little in comparison to her poor work ethic, which she was now determined to prove to him, herself, maybe her teachers, perhaps even her parents—that they were all wrong about her. One would think she would just say screw it and throw in the towel under such circumstances, but anger was a powerful tool, and dammit, was it ever delicious to lean into.

Rachel dropped by that Friday afternoon to give her the necessary notes. Blair would have invited her in, but she was too spent from the emotions of the last twenty-four hours. She thanked Rachel and hugged her. Blair didn't deserve her as a friend, but she was thankful for her during this period.

Blair did her usual household chores on Saturday and then studied all weekend. It was difficult, and she briefly considered what Andrew had previously mentioned about her having a learning disability. However, with frequent breaks and a few naps, Blair was able to power through.

She had never felt more confident about her midterm exams in her four years in high school than she did now.

* * *

On Monday, arriving at school on foot again, Blair felt like a year had passed between Friday and today. Putting her coat away and carefully pulling her books out of her locker, she set off for study hall.

Andrew was already there, in his usual spot, studying. Blair saw that all traces of any scratches she had left were almost gone, except for one that went down the right side of his face at a diagonal.

Jesus Christ, she thought in horror at the evidence she had left on him.

He looked up at her with expressionless eyes, then shifted his gaze back to his book.

Blair felt shame pang in her chest, but she shooed it away. Sitting in her usual spot, she opened her English book to read.

* * *

In gym class, Blair put on her new clothes that Aunt Natalie had purchased for her. Looking in the mirror at her crew-neck sweater and shorts, she had an idea.

Walking out to the gymnasium, head held high, Blair noticed a few boys glancing at her and pausing. As she went over to her usual stretching spot, Blair was only too glad to see Andrew stealing a glance and then freezing, looking away —only to steal another.

Hudson was practically drooling. He inched over to her.

"Hi, Blair."

They hadn't spoken to each other in a long time.

Blair stood up and gave him her best smile. "Oh, hi, Hudson. How's it going?"

Blair had come out in a tank top, pulled slightly lower so that her best features, her collarbones and shoulders, were completely exposed. Furthermore, she had rolled up the hems of her shorts so that they hiked up about two inches. The crease of her ass was just barely there—a *tease*—a *taste* of what was there.

Blair's stomach jumped joyfully, knowing she was

destroying Stormant from across the gym. She looked good, and she knew it.

All the boys in the class knew it, too, because Blair Simons had only ever worn shirts and sweaters that covered her up while she nervously pulled down the legs of her shorts as much as possible. Now, she was a walking advertisement: *I'm free and available.*

She and Stormant hadn't officially broken up, of course, but they might as well have. He had sent Blair a dozen texts over the weekend, all of which she ignored, until it finally reached the point where she had to turn her phone off.

She mindlessly chatted with Hudson, aware that Andrew was pacing in a corner. Julian and he were talking, and Blair was sure that Julian was filling him in on whatever he knew from Rachel.

After gym, Blair showered, letting the water run over her. She smiled into the stream, relishing the way she had commanded incredible power with a tease of her sexuality to all the boys in gym class—how they all, literally every single one of them, were a tad nicer. Even Julian had had a look of surprise in his eyes; she could practically hear him say, *"Okay, girl, I see you."*

It was hard to explain. She wasn't a man-stealer like Claire, but knew she was impossible to ignore. And the idea that Andrew had to sit and watch as all of the boys gawked at her made her feel *drunk* with superiority.

* * *

At lunch, Blair was only too excited to get in line. Only this time, instead of hearing Hudson shit-talking behind her, he was beside her.

"How's your studying for midterms going?" he asked.

And Blair realized he wasn't so bad. As she looked at him —*actually looked at him*—she suddenly realized just how attractive he was.

The next moment, his two cronies arrived, and for once, Blair remembered and committed their names to memory: Evan and Thomas.

They seemed bewildered at first, but Blair indirectly told them what was up with one flash of her best smile and speaking to them in her best voice. They all fell into step. It was as if this had always been the way things were, except that instead of Blair being an unwilling participant in their conversations, she was gladly part of them now.

Blair kept smiling, flirting with all three of the boys. And as they moved through the line, she wondered why she hadn't done this sooner, instead of acting like a scared and defensive little girl, making up such obvious crap about her banging Mr. Davis. Except now, all three of the boys knew Blair was sexually experienced. And none of them needed to tease her or talk about Mr. Davis, because the energy of her confidence with them said enough.

Blair's heart thudded as she approached the cashier, and once through the line, she let her eyes flick to her usual table with Andrew, Julian, and Rachel.

Then she looked at Hudson.

Once seated next to him, Evan, and Thomas, her table not far away, Blair felt she could have paid real money for the look on Andrew Stormant's face. His jaw was open, eyes wide. He was so shocked that he couldn't pretend to be otherwise.

Rachel and Julian saw it, and Blair kept smirking as they turned back to look at her. She didn't give a damn about any of them anymore. And Blair wondered why, oh, why she had fought against this so hard, for so long. Because there was comfort here.

Here. Exactly where she belonged.

Where she had *always* belonged.

Chapter 34

Barking Dog

Blair left school on Monday afternoon, still absolutely intoxicated with the high of making Andrew hurt as she had last week.

Come Tuesday, Blair decided to sit in the girl's bathroom near the library. Near a window above the stalls, above the heater, there was a ledge she liked to perch on sometimes. It was completely tucked away, and she enjoyed hanging out there when she wanted to skip classes.

Blair didn't want to endure study hall with Andrew a few tables before her. She couldn't stop staring at or being aware of him, even if she wanted to. And so, today, she would spare herself that pain. She pushed the window open, letting the cool January air hit her face as she quietly ate the chocolate muffin she'd purchased in the cafeteria before school.

Blair heard girls coming and going to use the bathroom. Luckily, she couldn't see anyone from the ledge at this height. She hadn't escaped to this spot in a long time, and just like the library, it welcomed her back so easily, as if to say, *"Where have you been? I've missed you."*

Sitting and enjoying the cloudy sky, finishing the last of

If It All Fades Away

her muffin, Blair heard a familiar voice come in. Two familiar voices.

Suddenly, she smelled cigarette smoke drifting up to the open windows. It was Claire Miller with Annabelle Peters. Blair stilled completely, barely breathing. They must have been skipping second period.

"Christ, I'm so sick of Dakota's shit," Annabelle muttered.

"She's so goddamn stupid," Claire agreed.

"Can I borrow your lighter?"

The flicking of a lighter followed.

Silence.

"You see Andrew's face?" Annabelle asked.

"I did," Claire said. "He missed our study group on Friday … and then all of a sudden, he has that big-ass scratch across his face."

"You don't think it was Simons, do you?"

"Please. Who the hell else could it be?"

"Wonder what happened?"

"It's obvious. He told her he was going to do something that didn't involve her, and she freaked out," Claire said.

Annabelle started laughing, then laughed some more.

"What?" Claire asked, laughter in her own voice.

Annabelle was almost hysterical at this point.

"Shut up, or we'll get caught! What the hell is so funny?"

Annabelle was wheezing now.

"Zane Johnson told me…" More laughter. "… that when Simons got into it with Mr. Banes her junior year—"

More cackling.

"Spit it out, you brat," Claire said, becoming less amused.

"I'm sorry…" Annabelle said with a breathless chuckle. "He said she *bit* Mr. Banes when he tried to pull her out of her desk, and that she started *barking* at him like a dog!"

Claire exploded with laughter. "WHAT?! How the hell did you not tell me this?" she asked, wheezing.

Annabelle rushed into a stall. "I gotta pee, I'm about to piss myself!"

Blair heard moments of streaming urine, followed by a bit more cackling—both girls' cackles, echoing off the cinder block walls.

"I gotta sit on the floor—" Claire howled, still laughing.

Blair felt hot tears slowly making their way down her cheeks. They were talking about the day that she was supposed to be expelled—a memory she tried to bury as deep as possible.

"How much—" Annabelle came out after flushing the toilet.

"Are you crawling on the floor?" Claire asked.

"Shut up!" Annabelle laughed. "I gotta—I gotta wash my hands—"

"Stupid bitch, hurry up," Claire said, then cackled some more. "I literally can't stop crying! How have you not told me about this sooner?"

Annabelle washed her hands, still laughing. "I don't know!"

Blair could tell they were near each other now, by the sinks.

"How much you wanna bet that she threatens to kill herself every time he wants to break up with her?" Annabelle laughed.

"STOP—" Claire wheezed.

Blair put her head in her hands, desperate for the sounds of their laughter to disappear. But they kept echoing and echoing through the space. Until finally, they subsided. A moment of silence—followed by more uncontrollable laughing. Their sounds told her they were lying on the floor, and she wondered if they were on something.

Then, it was silent again—unnervingly so.

"So, what's actually going on between you two?" Annabelle asked.

Blair heard Claire sigh.

"God... I don't even know. He helped me with some problems in calc a few times. He kept smiling at me, and I just really felt this connection between us."

"And?"

"I eventually worked up the courage to give him my number."

Blair wanted to throw up.

"You said you texted him a few times, right?"

"Yeah, while he was in the Bahamas with his family. I asked if he could send me a dick pic, but he just responded with a frowny face and said he was too drunk, and that he was pretty sure Blair wouldn't like that."

"Oh, fuck him," Annabelle said.

"But, I mean, he texted me back—so that has to mean something, right?"

"Totally," Annabelle said. There was a pause. "What do you plan to do?"

Blair could hear that Claire was taking a drag of a newly lit cigarette.

"I don't even know. If I could get him drunk at one of these study groups, it would be a lot easier to kiss him."

"Do you think they've banged yet?" Annabelle asked.

Claire scoffed. "Simons is so goddamn weird, she probably doesn't even know what a dick is. Stormant's probably just held hands with her anime-loving ass at best."

The girls laughed and laughed, and Blair could only choke back tears as she cried and cried.

Chapter 35

Stairwell Confessions

After Claire and Annabelle left, Blair was still crying.

She thought about the look Claire had given her when she moved tables with Rachel. Blair had known that one day, she would be repaid for pulling her best friend out from under her claws. She remembered thinking they were not the same breed of people—that Claire regarded her as a threat to be eliminated. Even though she had seen Blair kiss Andrew in the lunch line one day, she laughed with Annabelle about how she and Andrew probably only held hands.

Blair felt betrayed by Andrew, only for real this time. She hiccupped at the sheer ridiculousness of how she'd felt hurt and "betrayed" over him just watching a movie without her. She desperately wished she could go back to that being their biggest problem.

Blair didn't deserve Andrew. She had never felt like she did.

She remembered how sweet he looked, leaning over her and asking, "Can we be together?" The very first thought that had come to her was, why would he ever want to be with someone like her?

His voice, a memory now:

"Because ... I feel like I've known you my whole life already. Because you're funny, and kind. ... Because from the moment I first saw you through that window in the office, I knew I wanted to be closer to you.

"Because you're beautiful."

Blair was none of those things. She never had been. And she'd tried to tell him. She'd tried to warn him that she wasn't a good person. It was easy for him to say she was when it didn't involve her hurting him.

"You're a good person to me. And you're still young. You've been through a lot. It's not like you're an adult and still doing some of those things. And even if you were an adult —there's help out there. I think you're good. You've just been hurt a lot, that's all.

"You're so good."

Claire was a better fit for Andrew, really. She was smarter; she was even in AP Calculus with him. She had money and came from a normal family. Sure, she was a conniving bitch, but she would likely outgrow that someday ... maybe. He had been accepted to many colleges; he could follow her wherever she went. Blair, however, only had a half-baked dream of living in Chicago with Andrew and Natalie. She could almost laugh now at how stupid that dream was, at how naively hopeful she'd felt when she submitted her application.

Living with Natalie was the only thing that gave her some hope now ... but even that seemed so far-fetched. It was only January, and school didn't start until the end of August. She wouldn't graduate until the beginning of June. Blair wasn't sure she could make it until then. Bit by bit, piece by piece, she was being taken apart.

Blair imagined Claire in Andrew's bed. Him making love to her, like he did with Blair. He was a considerate partner, always worrying about Blair's pleasure. She had overheard some girls talking at their lockers the one day—how one's boyfriend didn't care about her, he just came, and that was that. He never went down on her, either.

Blair had no concept of such behavior. That was a thing? She had secretly counted her blessings, because that was not Andrew at all.

* * *

Blair wanted to skip second and third period, but couldn't, because she had her midterm exams. By fourth period, however, when she would typically have gym, Blair spent it sleeping in the corner of the library at the far tables in the back, behind some bookcases.

At lunch, Blair tried to stay chipper with Hudson and the boys, but she dreaded seeing Andrew. Sitting down with her tray, she did her best to just eat and try not to look at the back of his head. He had taken to having his back turned to her now.

Rachel had texted Blair a WTF yesterday when she was sitting with Hudson. Blair replied that she needed some space. Rachel and Julian were now seated where Andrew and she usually would be.

When her food continued to taste like sand, Blair finally decided to text Andrew.

Meet me in the stairwell.

She saw him pull out his phone, quickly shoot off a text, then put it back in his pocket.

My mom wants me to stay away from you.

Blair's heart dropped at reading that. It hurt. But then again, she'd never belonged in the Stormants' lives anyway. She was a feral animal that Andrew had been stupid enough to try to tame, and he'd eventually gotten scratched up because of it.

She's not wrong. It'll only take a few minutes.

Blair watched as Andrew pulled his phone out again and gave pause. He must not have been expecting that reaction, because she saw him turn to look at her. He hesitated for a moment, then stood up with his tray to throw it out. Blair waited until he was out in the hallway to follow, emptying her tray on her way out, too.

Eventually, they both were in the stairwell. Blair immediately took notice of Andrew's closed-off body language. She decided to keep a respectable distance. She said nothing at first.

Andrew gave her a look, then put his hands out. "Well?"

Blair sighed with a shudder. "I figured we could talk this out before I make any more rash decisions."

"… Okay."

Blair couldn't help but get slightly sarcastic as she spoke, if only to keep from crying. She looked down at her Mary Janes.

"I just overheard a rather interesting conversation this morning in the girls' bathroom. Between Claire Miller and Annabelle Peters, no less."

Andrew's demeanor remained unchanged.

"There's a little spot I like to sit in when skipping class. I can't see anyone, and they can't see me, but I can hear them."

"Okay."

"So, Claire said she gave you her number at some point … and was texting you while you were in the Bahamas. Is that true?" Blair felt weird, calmly channeling all the times she'd sat in the courtroom with her mother as a child, watching that prick she barely remembered at the time cross-examining someone.

Andrew closed his eyes, then put his hand to his face.

"Fuck."

"Mmm. Fuck, indeed," Blair said. "And here I was, thinking—and being made to believe—that I'm just the crazy psycho jealous bitch of a girlfriend."

Andrew sighed deeply, his back against the wall as he looked up into the stairwell.

A long moment of silence.

"Yeah, what was that you said to me? 'I think you're being irrational and jealous for no reason right now.' Was that it?"

Andrew still wasn't looking at Blair.

"I'm asking an actual question here, Andrew."

"Yes, that's what I said."

"Okay—so, assuming I'm still your girlfriend right now, and you're still my boyfriend, I don't suppose I have any right to ask what you guys texted about?" Blair crossed her arms.

"She initially texted me some questions about calc. I didn't think anything of it and just responded. It was the night after you and I sexted … and I missed you. So, after my parents went to bed, I had some of their alcohol. Which was a mistake, because I got super messed up."

"That is a bit unusual for you, I must say, Stormant," Blair said.

"Yeah, well, I missed you."

"And?"

"So, before I knew it, she asked me how the vacation was

going. And I told her. She said some stupid crap about how she wished she was there."

"Oh, I'm sure she did," Blair said, hands trembling on her crossed arms. "Then what happened?"

"I was getting ready to pass out ... and then she sent me another text ... asking for—for—"

Blair could almost smirk at how nice it was to see Andrew admitting to what she'd just heard. "Spit it out, Stormant."

"She wanted a dick pic."

Blair started clapping softly, and the sound echoed upwards. Andrew looked over to her in surprise.

She smiled. "There you go. Good job. See? It wasn't that hard to admit that your girlfriend *wasn't* being a paranoid bitch, now, was it?"

"This isn't funny, Blair," Andrew said, his eyes dark.

"Does it look like I'm laughing?" Blair retorted. "So, then what happened?"

Andrew was looking at his feet now. "I just told her I didn't think you would like it if I did that."

"Which was super shitty to say, by the way—you could have said nothing, but instead, you threw *me* under the bus like some jealous freak."

"I didn't want to be rude and not respond," he mumbled.

Blair's eyes widened. "My God, you really *are* this stupid, aren't you?"

"Sorry, I don't just fucking *ignore* people, Simons."

"Simons." He had never called her by her last name during their entire relationship.

"I mean, imagine if Hudson asked me for a picture of my pussy while I was away on vacation, drunk, and then I just replied that I didn't think *you'd* like that?"

She saw Andrew's nostrils flare, because suddenly, with it

put into that context, he seemed to realize the gravity of the situation.

"Speaking of which, real cute, you sitting with him, by the way," he snapped.

Blair turned her chin up at him. "Why? Does that bother you? It shouldn't. I could say I think you're just being 'irrationally jealous for no reason.' Because last I checked, I didn't like him either—yet here we are."

This was the third time that Blair had seen Andrew visibly angry.

"You're really something else, you know that?"

"I am," Blair said, only too proud. "But now I also know that I'm not just a crazy bitch imagining things. You *lied* to me. Maybe not directly, but by omission."

"No, you're right," Andrew said. "You're right, Simons. I *did* lie by omission, because I don't like the girl. I never have, and I never will. And what boyfriend is going to say, 'Oh, hey, babe, after we sexted, I got a text from that girl you hate, asking for a picture of my cock'?"

"An honest one."

Andrew's mouth opened.

"What did you think it meant when she asked you?"

"You want to know the truth?" Andrew asked, standing up straighter.

Blair swallowed.

"I thought she was drunk too and just being stupid."

Blair snorted.

"No, I'm fucking serious, Simons! No girl has *ever* liked me before. Ever."

Blair was a bit stunned now, her eyes were wide.

"I mean it. And if they did, then I was too stupid to be able to tell, just like you said. I've always just—just focused on my schoolwork."

Blair could see his eyes getting glassy, which made hers get a bit wet, too.

"So, imagine how caught off guard I was when you practically made it your job to start messing with me. And all I could think was, 'Wow, she's beautiful—and kinda funny for fucking with me.' But I still just kept focusing on school, because I was new here, and I was nervous. And then, I smash my head on your locker door—which, by the way, hurt like hell..." Andrew took a moment to breathe. "And while my head was throbbing like I might have actually been hurt, all I could hear was you cackling like a goddamn witch. My only thought, even after trying to be nice to you that day, was, 'Who on Earth hurt this girl for her to act like this?'"

Blair let her tears escape her.

"And it was weird, because when I stood up after slamming your door, you looked terrified, and you suddenly hit me. My thought then was, you were scared, and you didn't know what you needed, except maybe attention. It was just ... natural for me to hug you."

Andrew was crying now.

"You know what the saddest part of all of that was to me?"

Blair's lip trembled.

"It was that you would have been *happy* if I'd hit you back."

Blair looked down, the tears trailing down her cheeks softly.

"What kind of life have you lived that the way for you to get attention is to *want* to be physically abused?" Andrew sniffled and wiped his nose on his sweater. Blair rubbed her eyes with her palms. "You so obviously just needed someone to love you. And I just ... I loved you from the moment I first saw you. How is that? How is it that we both were immediately interested at the same time?"

Blair choked slightly. "I don't know."

Andrew inhaled and exhaled deeply. He looked at his phone.

"I have to go. But ... I do think we should ... take a break or something. My mom was really upset when I came home on Friday. I did my best to explain stuff to her, but she was pretty adamant."

"Andrew..." Blair said, looking up now, suddenly very calm. "You deserve better." She laughed slightly. "Trust you to still try to find some middle ground by suggesting a break ... but ... I think it's best if we just ... break up now."

"Blair—"

"It's for the best, Andrew."

His eyes looked pained, but he didn't argue.

"Okay," he said softly.

He walked to the double doors, looked back at Blair, and quietly left.

Chapter 36

Playing With Fire

During Thursday Mass, Blair sat next to Hudson, Evan, and Thomas.

Hudson was well aware now that she and Andrew had broken up. And he was only too eager to have her taking an active interest in him. He also had to have known that Blair had initially done it to make Andrew jealous. Except now, Blair felt this was truly where she belonged. While Rachel had understood her motives initially, Blair could tell they were growing further apart because of Julian and Andrew. All four of them had been friends, and now, Blair was not only giving a giant screw-you to Andrew, she was giving it to all of them.

The moment of provoking Andrew's jealousy and insecurity had since passed. However, Blair found herself only too comfortable with the boys who had tormented her for four years. Eventually, she defaulted to her bullying ways with them. Instead of her being the target this time, it was other people. It felt powerful to have a malicious little snide crew to roll with.

At lunch that day, Hudson had dared Thomas that he

wouldn't launch a tray full of ice cubes over his head. Blair drank the last of her pop and poured her contents onto the tray before Thomas.

"Dude, just freakin' do it." Evan cackled.

Blair buried her head in her arms, laughing as well. She peeked up exaggeratedly, at which Hudson and Thomas laughed.

"One, two, three—go!" Blair said.

Thomas brought his tray FULL of all of their ice from their beverages up and over his head. Blair saw how high and far all the cubes went, and she laughed so hard, she thought she was going to pee herself. They all were in stitches as some sophomore and junior girls shrieked in horror as the ice cubes rained down. Blair had tears running down her face when she vaguely caught her old table looking at her. Andrew was furious as he glared at her. Blair didn't give a damn anymore—least of all about good little rich boy Andrew Stormant.

Their laughs were so loud and disruptive—especially Hudson's, whose octave was especially obnoxious—that it drew the attention of almost all the tables around them. They laughed and laughed. Blair couldn't breathe. And then—she saw Ms. Holland walk by with a sandwich and drink in hand. She paused, giving an inquisitive look to Blair, then her eyes tracked to Andrew—then back to Blair.

Blair paid her no mind as she cackled and cackled, too amused by the chaos and shenanigans she, Hudson, and the boys created each and every day. It was fun. It was too much fun, and Blair again wondered why she hadn't joined them sooner.

After their laughs had finally subsided, they all composed themselves enough to speak again.

"Oh…" Hudson breathed.

If It All Fades Away

A moment of silence managed to greet their table.

"Say, Simons," he said.

"Yeah?" She was still laughing, her lungs hurting in the best way possible.

"There's a thing tomorrow night at one of my buddy's houses from St. John's. You wanna go?"

Blair felt a shiver run through her entire body.

"What time does it start?"

"Eight or so. He's having a bonfire. There'll be booze. Should be a good time."

Blair looked over to her old table and noticed that Andrew was gone.

"Yeah, I'll go," she said.

Hudson lit up. "Really?"

"Yeah." Blair smiled. "But—I'll need a ride."

Hudson laughed. "Are you asking me to pick you up, Simons?"

"Yes, Bentley, I am asking you to pick me up."

Something about her calling him "Bentley" for the first time must have done something to him, because suddenly he perked up, realizing that truly, there was something different developing between them.

"It's not a problem," he said, with the most serious face Blair had ever seen on him.

Blair knew she was playing with fire. But she didn't care anymore—she couldn't.

She just hoped she would catch fire and burn alive.

Chapter 37

Holland's Sacrifice

On Friday, Ms. Holland stopped Blair on her way out of English class.

"Blair, can I see you after school for a few minutes today?"

Blair stood awkwardly, one hand on her backpack strap. Ms. Holland had never asked to see her after school before. It was always Blair and her hanging out and chatting, so this was about something in particular.

"Yeah, sure," Blair said dismissively, then left.

* * *

Later that day, Blair's stomach was in knots as she approached Ms. Holland's room.

"You wanted to see me?" she asked uncertainly in the doorway.

Ms. Holland looked up from her desk. "I did. Please close the door."

In all the times Blair had talked with Ms. Holland, she'd

If It All Fades Away

never asked her to close the door. She grabbed the knob and pulled the heavy wooden door shut.

"Have a seat, please."

It was also the first time she'd told Blair what to do.

Blair dropped her book bag and sat in the front seat, which she had always occupied.

"I ... wasn't going to say anything initially, but given that it's been a week now, I wanted to talk."

Blair said nothing.

"I assume you know what I'm talking about?"

"No, I don't," Blair lied.

"You, sitting at lunch with Bentley Hudson?"

"And?"

"Well…" Ms. Holland drawled as if saying, *"if you want to play this game…"* "Considering that earlier this year, you got suspended for punching him in the face, and just last week, you and Andrew were sitting together ... I can't imagine what would have happened to make you go from sitting with Stormant to sitting with someone who could have charged you with assault."

Blair's eyes fluttered in anger. She wasn't going to budge. Not now.

"We're having a disagreement, that's all," she said, crossing her arms defiantly.

Ms. Holland nodded her head. "Right… Right."

Silence.

"I mean, it's just very strange, because I essentially had to negotiate with Bentley's mother to have him agree to stay away from you. Not to mention, getting you Church Duty on Wednesdays after failing to pull you from gym class."

"And no one asked you to do that," Blair spat before she could even catch herself.

Ms. Holland's eyes widened, and her mouth opened.

"No. No one did. It's just… I'm concerned about you, is all."

"Well, don't be. I'm not a charity case."

Ms. Holland let a quiet noise of disbelief escape her.

Blair was not like this with her usually. But she didn't care anymore—not about her or anyone.

And to drive the knife in a little further, Blair added, "Also, I don't think what I'm doing outside of your class is any of your business."

Ms. Holland was stunned. Blair liked how powerful she felt lately, just essentially telling anyone and everyone to get fucked.

"No. You're right. It's none of my business," Ms. Holland said.

"Can I go now?" Blair asked. She uncrossed her arms and sat up, ready to leave the desk.

Ms. Holland lowered her head. Blair could tell that she was affecting her, maybe even hurting her.

Good.

"You can go. But before you do…" Ms. Holland said, lifting her head high and proud, despite being obviously hurt. "I just have to tell you, in the fifteen years that I've been teaching here, and for the last four that I've been fighting for you—I gotta say, my least favorite moment of my entire career was when your mother threatened to come after my job."

Blair's eyes widened.

"Yeah." Ms. Holland leaned back in her chair, crossing her arms and looking at the ceiling. "In fact, if memory serves me correctly, it came after an especially exhausting and emotional day of fighting with my boss and speaking with you present in front of your parents. Only to go home after

If It All Fades Away

and get a call several hours later from your mother, telling me…"

Ms. Holland paused for effect. She had Blair's full attention now.

"… and I quote: 'You're nothing but an unqualified, childless lesbian, and if you ever suggest that my daughter needs medication or professional help again, I'll have your *fucking* head on a platter'—end quote."

Blair had never heard Ms. Holland swear. And she knew that was her mother coming through her, no question. "Horrified" did not begin to describe Blair's emotion at that moment.

Ms. Holland continued, in a slightly more upbeat but sarcastic tone, "She then proceeded to mention the very powerful and successful prosecutor she works for, noting that I wouldn't stand a chance in court."

Blair put her hand to her forehead and closed her eyes. She was rendered speechless. Ms. Holland knew what to say to keep her seated, and it worked.

"Just … you know … for your information," Ms. Holland said, almost casually. "I mean, it's not like us teachers are people with lives or feelings or anything."

With both hands at her head, pushing her hair back, Blair spoke less defensively this time. Ms. Holland had cracked her first layer of defense—an easy feat when mentioning her mother.

"What else did she say?" Blair asked quietly, observing how the lights above highlighted the various scratches in the laminated desk below.

"Oh, I think that pretty much covers it. She didn't have much ground to stand on after you did what you did." Ms. Holland was saying all of this as if Blair could forget. "She knew deep down inside that we were doing you a favor by not expelling you then."

Blair closed her eyes in shame, the memory gripping her now.

* * *

It was her junior year. She was on the third floor, and Mr. Banes was teaching trigonometry. Blair had already been in trouble for cheating on his previous year's geometry exam. She looked out the window on this particular day, wishing she were anywhere but there. She wasn't thinking about anything in particular, just how clear and cloudless the sky looked. A large brick corner was visible from where she sat, and she imagined the men laying the brick in the mid-eighties when the school was built. What would life have been like then? Who were the men who built it on that particular day? What were their lives like? Where were they now? Had some of them died since then?

"Blair," Mr. Banes snapped.

She startled and turned to the front.

"The final exam is in two weeks, and you, of all people, should be paying attention."

A few students snickered.

Mr. Banes turned and sighed.

Blair was so over everything. She could imagine herself on that brick ledge, jumping off of it...

"Really?" she taunted, but she was also upset that he had to embarrass her like that.

"Well..." he said, taking the bait. "Considering you got caught *cheating* last year, it would behoove you to pay attention and try to learn something."

A few audible gasps could be heard. An odd laugh of

If It All Fades Away

discomfort also sounded. No one had known about that until that moment. Mr. Banes had spared her the humiliation at the time, waiting until later to confront her privately—but apparently, he wasn't going to do that now.

Blair looked down and twiddled with her book.

"You know…" she said, so casually, so cool. "The only reason I cheated was because the content was so fucking boring."

More audible gasps at her swearing. Then, some jeering.

"Quiet!"

"I mean … if you had given us geometry problems about the *size* … *shape* … and *length* of how small your penis is relative to other, larger penises, then that—THAT would have interested me enough to study *harder*… You know what I mean?"

The whole class burst out laughing, and a few guys clapped. Someone was doubled over at their desk.

Mr. Banes came over and grabbed Blair just above her elbow.

"Hey! You're not allowed to touch me!" Blair snarled.

"Get up," Mr. Banes demanded.

Before she could help herself—because there was always something about anyone grabbing Blair by her upper arms—she lunged forward and sank her teeth into Mr. Bane's forearm.

The man screamed in pain.

Like a dog, Blair started barking at him to mess with him.

There were more gasps, then riotous laughing, and then sheer and total chaos. The room was a clamor of noises, indistinguishable.

"Someone, go get another teacher!" one student shouted.

Another student ran off to do so.

"Damn, he's going to have to get a rabies shot now," another classmate said.

Mr. Banes was holding his forearm in agony, hunched over, stumbling away.

"SIMONS, GET THE FUCK OUT OF MY CLASSROOM NOW!"

Dead silence. There was nothing funny about it now.

However, Blair started laughing while shoving her book into her backpack and getting up to leave.

"You taste fucking disgusting, by the way," she said to him in passing, with a sneer.

Someone barked a laugh, then quickly silenced it.

At that moment, another teacher was at the door with a look of shock on their face.

"Take her to Davis," Mr. Banes snapped. "She won't be coming back here, if I have anything to say about it."

* * *

"Blair," Ms. Holland said, snapping her back to the present. Blair hadn't realized large tear droplets had fallen onto the desk.

"Andrew and I broke up," she said through her tears.

Ms. Holland waited for a moment. "I know."

"You do?"

"I spoke with him yesterday after I saw you sitting with Hudson. I noticed that large scratch down his face. He tried really hard to tell me it wasn't you."

"God, I'm a fucking mess." Blair sobbed.

"I don't suppose I need to tell you that what you did to him was assault—and abuse."

Blair just choked at that. Ms. Holland came over with a box of Kleenex and started rubbing her back.

"I see you, Blair," she said. "I've always seen you. In the way that only people like us can see each other."

Blair was gritting her teeth, shoving down the sounds that were trying to escape her throat as hard as she could. Her tears were thick and hot. Ms. Holland rubbed her back in gentle circles, then pulled away, taking her place leaning up against her desk in front of Blair.

"It's not easy growing up. Being different... Not to mention knowing you've liked girls since you were seven."

It was Ms. Holland's first actual admission that she was a lesbian. Blair took a breath and looked up through her tears, blowing her nose and drying her eyes somewhat.

"And then you grow older, and you feel like everyone can just see it written all over you. *Terrified* that you're going to be outed at any moment. So, you spend a lot of time alone, already being a strange child, and then add a queer orientation onto that... It makes for a pretty awful combination."

Ms. Holland could lose her job by openly admitting she was a lesbian teaching at a Catholic school. The weight of what she had just shared with Blair was not lost on her. Blair noticed the rings on her fingers clutching the edges of her desk—all except a wedding ring. Ms. Holland had made no mention of a partner, and if she had one, there was no evidence of it—couldn't be any evidence of it.

"You've obviously grown up very lonely, Blair. Probably even had an imaginary friend or two?"

Blair looked down again, nodding her head. Ms. Holland was trying to destroy every barrier she had created—and it was working.

"Mine were 'Lena' and 'Skip.' Did yours have names?"

"'Timothy,'" Blair said quietly. She didn't tell Ms. Holland it was Timothy, Mrs. Brisby's son from *The Secret of NIMH*.

There was a very long silence between them, the hum of the fluorescent lights and the subtle buzzing of the wall clock filling the space between them.

Finally, Ms. Holland broke the silence.

"One other thing I wanted to mention to you. That *1984* assignment I gave you and Andrew—"

Blair looked up with curious, puffy eyes.

"His paper was ... average. About what I would expect from an AP student. But yours? Yours was exceptional. You had analysis in there that I had to look up online to see if it had been discovered already. Of course, I shouldn't have doubted you, but I was truly blown away, Blair."

Blair started crying softly again.

"You're smarter than Andrew in many ways—and he knows that. It's part of why I think he likes you. Loves you, too, obviously. Among many other reasons."

Blair tried to choke out what had happened. She wanted to tell her about Claire, about all of it. But she shoved it back down. What was left unsaid was saying more than anything she could explain.

Another moment of silence.

"Whatever he did wrong, I just hope you know how deeply you've embedded yourself into that boy's soul, as he's done with yours. Don't let a high school misunderstanding ruin what you two have."

Ms. Holland glanced at her wall clock and then stood up.

"I really hate leaving you like this. But I must get home and eat before heading out for my night classes."

Blair started shifting and wiping her nose, moving quickly. "Yeah—no, no—I'm sorry to keep you. I should get going, too."

"Take your time." Ms. Holland came over and put her hand on Blair's shoulder. "I'll lock the door on my way out, so make sure you take your stuff when you go. Otherwise, you won't be able to get back in."

Blair nodded, still trying to clean up her face. She couldn't look at Ms. Holland; she just let her touch her shoulder. The woman had already defeated her, and anything more than a back rub and shoulder squeeze would send her to her grave.

Ms. Holland gave her a final pat, then released her reassuring touch.

"Have a good night, Blair."

"G'night," Blair mumbled, her head still lowered.

"Make sure to turn these lights off when you leave, will ya?"

"I will."

"Thanks."

She heard the clicking of the door and Ms. Holland turning the lock, followed by her footsteps down the hall.

Chapter 38

Prayers

Blair eventually composed herself and left Ms. Holland's room, turning the lights off.

The halls were especially empty, it being a Friday afternoon. Blair hadn't realized how long she had been there from start to finish. There might have been some faculty left somewhere, but in the senior hall, it was completely dead, the fluorescent lights half off.

Arriving at her locker, Blair put away some books she didn't need. She was still slightly lost in her head, thinking of everything Ms. Holland had said to her.

A thought occurred to her as she stood there, head down. She looked left and right, certain she was alone, but just to be sure, she placed a few books on the floor. That way, it wouldn't look so weird that she was kneeling if someone came by.

Once lowered, Blair steadied her hands on Andrew's locker below hers. She leaned into the upper air vents, closed her eyes, and inhaled deeply. She could smell him instantly. It was dark in the locker, but Blair was sure he had a spare green wool sweater in there. Being that close to him again, the smell of *him*—she pulled away and put a hand to her mouth, suffocating any cries she might make.

Was she just torturing herself after the Ms. Holland conversation, where she had cried a lot already? Or did she just need to feel close to Andrew again—to know he was still nearby somehow? It was one thing to conceptually know he still existed, seeing him in passing at their lockers, study hall, gym, and lunch. But it was quite another to *smell* him. All she could smell were the best memories of her life, however short-lived they may have been.

Blair cried for a good minute, shuddering. She needed to get home to cry it out, so she wouldn't have to try so hard to silence herself.

* * *

At home, Blair turned off her phone. She didn't want to deal with Hudson texting her about the bonfire. She didn't want to deal with anyone. She just needed to sleep. Sleep was her escape at the moment. It was the only place she could find a brief pause from the chaos.

On Saturday, Blair completed her chores, as usual. Her father was home, sleeping and lounging about. Her mother dropped by briefly and then was gone just as quickly.

The next day, Blair felt a bit funny, and she wasn't sure why she would put herself through it, but she decided to go to Sunday Mass. Maybe it was because of loneliness—or because there was a good chance Andrew would be there. Blair didn't know, but she set out on foot anyway.

Once there, Blair realized she hadn't attended a Sunday service at St. Michael's for a long time. She had gone sporadically as a child with her parents, which eventually stopped altogether. She wasn't complaining; she was usually bored to tears. But deciding to go by herself today gave her a weird sense of accomplishment. Even though she dreaded possibly seeing Andrew and his parents, Blair was hopeful to see him, too. There was also something familiar and comforting about being someplace other than her bedroom all weekend.

Walking in with the other parishioners, Blair tried her best not to feel like an imposter who didn't belong. Making her way up the steps in the front entrance, she bristled once out of the cold. Anxiously looking around, she didn't see Andrew or his parents anywhere. An elderly woman who entered behind Blair touched her arm; she turned with wide eyes. Blair had no idea who she was, but hearing her compliment her reading for Christmas Mass was nice. Blair bowed her head and thanked her politely.

Unsure of where to sit, Blair took her place in one of the back pews, the same as Thursday Mass.

And then, Blair's heart dropped into her stomach as out of the corner of her eye, she immediately recognized Andrew with his dark head of hair passing by. Lily and Henry were with him. Blair saw Andrew pause momentarily, startled—and then he kept walking. Blair put her head down, desperate not to see the expression on Lily's face. The Stormants sat in the middle pew area. Blair knew she would do nothing but stare at the back of Andrew's head the entire service.

During Communion, when Blair went up, Father Donovan looked at her with surprise and approval as he handed her her wafer. Something about that made her feel really good, happy that he seemed proud and pleased to see her.

Once seated again, looking at the back of Andrew's head of black hair, Blair felt a physical *ache* in her chest. It felt strange to be so far away from him, knowing how close she had once been to him. She admired how the sun through the

If It All Fades Away

stained glass looked in his dark tresses. She remembered how his strands felt between her fingers, how warm his breath felt against her cheeks and ears, and the way his eyes looked when he was about to kiss her.

Blair desperately wanted to talk to Andrew and apologize to him and his parents, especially Lily. She had warmly welcomed Blair into her home more than once, fed her, and put her up for the night—two actually, although she wasn't sure if Lily knew about the second time—only for Blair to hurt and humiliate her son.

Blair bowed her head during the rest of Communion as the music played, letting Sister Eugene's fingers on the piano soothe her as she prayed.

Blair hated that she was one of those people Father Donovan talked about, who only prayed when they needed something. He said you should pray for others, pray in thanks and glory—pray always.

When Blair had prayed before, it was aimless and stupid, like asking for new clothes or toys. Now, however, she felt like she had something real to pray for.

Blair prayed for a few things—more than a few, actually.

She prayed not to feel the pain in her heart anymore.

She prayed to *get her shit together*—to not act like a damn cat caught in a trash bag at the first sign of conflict, literally scratching, biting, punching, and cursing people out.

She prayed for help. That something could happen so she could go to counseling again and maybe get on medication, as Ms. Holland had suggested to her parents last year. Maybe Natalie could help her. She just had to get through the rest of her senior year and summer.

Blair prayed that she could continue living in her parents' house without incident, without any fights or conflicts, and that her parents would be tolerable until she could move out.

The last thing Blair prayed for, what she wanted most of all: she prayed to have Andrew back in her life.

She asked God to help her get better and be a better person. That perhaps if she did, Andrew could forgive her and give her another chance. The same was true for Lily. Father Donovan said that God's timing was perfect and never wrong.

Blair squeezed her eyes shut, hoping, praying, wishing that God's timing to help her reunite with Andrew would be perfect. Before it was too late—before he decided to go someplace else for college and they drifted apart forever.

Blair ended her prayer, made the sign of the cross, and then quietly left. Not necessarily the best etiquette to leave right after Communion, but at least she had showed up. That had to count for something.

Chapter 39

Safe

Arriving at school on Monday morning, Blair felt more optimistic about the future. She had hope and ambition and had felt some release during her prayers to God during Sunday Mass. She wasn't sure if they were heard or not, but she had to believe they were—somewhere in the universe.

Blair had all but forgotten about Hudson and the boys until she decided to turn her phone back on at her locker. She had let it die completely during the weekend, charged it that morning, and finally worked up the courage to turn it on.

She had thirteen missed calls and messages from Hudson. Something about that made Blair sick to her stomach. The messages started friendly enough, but then they quickly devolved into anger, and then what appeared to be outright rage, calling her a "selfish bitch."

Blair started shaking. She had to have known this would result from her bailing on him on Friday night. She desperately wanted to turn back, to run home. But she had to keep going—for herself and her future—if she had any hope of having a chance with Andrew again. Or any hope to get herself out of this wretched city, away from her parents.

Meandering to study hall very slowly, Blair was shaking uncontrollably. She felt a fear that was all too real and didn't know what to do. Her stomach was turning and twisting with a sickening feeling she couldn't shake.

Blair saw Andrew briefly and then, probably looking like an old woman, hobbled her way over to her old spot. She sat carefully and laid her head in her arms. She couldn't soothe herself. Something visceral had been triggered by Hudson's furious messages. Somewhere in her memory, she heard Andrew's voice:

"He's a dangerous idiot, Blair."

But was he really? What was the worst he could do to her for standing him up? She hadn't said anything mean to him, she'd just … had her phone turned off all weekend. She had needed the time, space, and quiet to herself.

Blair tried to steady her breathing. It wasn't working. Her legs shook horribly. She felt hot and cold all at once. She didn't know what she would do about gym or lunch. She could try to lie to him, but somehow, she knew that no matter what she said, it wouldn't be good enough.

Blair suddenly began dry heaving into her lap in the library. She quickly brought her hand to her mouth. But it was no use; the sensations were those of anxiety, not a stomach sickness. The only way to stop them was to remove the threat.

Hudson, living in her mind, sitting around angrily texting her as the night went on, filled her with dread. If she hadn't felt so ill, she might be capable of crying. Instead, she just felt awful.

"Are you okay?"

Blair closed her eyes.

"I'm fine," she said.

"You don't look fine."

Blair said nothing. But Andrew's voice, his tone of genuine concern—it always did something to her. Softened her. Weakened her. Even though she had scratched his face, flaunted herself to all the boys in gym class, sat with Hudson and his friends to make Andrew jealous, started bullying people again, ignored him, belittled him, and name-called him—he still had it in him to care.

Blair had never deserved him. She knew that. And yet, he still loved her anyway. Still cared even though they weren't together anymore. A testament to the authenticity of his truly good character.

Blair swallowed hard as Andrew pulled out a chair in front of her. She couldn't bear to look at him.

"Blair, what's wrong?" he asked.

She choked, head still in her arms.

"I was stupid," she garbled.

She felt his hand reach over and touch her forearm. His touch destroyed her instantly. He rested his hand there to reassure her, as he had always done.

"I was supposed to go with Hudson to this thing on Friday, and I didn't go," she said.

"Let's go outside."

Still keeping her head down, Blair wordlessly followed him. She managed to steal a glance at Andrew in the space between the double doors that they had been in once before. The scratch on the right side of his face was completely gone, thank God.

"What's going on?" he asked again.

"I ... I was supposed to go to this stupid thing with

Hudson on Friday—" Blair choked out again. "But I didn't. I just… I couldn't."

Andrew was keeping his distance. That crushed Blair. But she knew it was a natural consequence of her violence and them not being together anymore. He was listening as a friend, and something about that broke Blair's heart even more. He wasn't saying anything from a place of judgment; he just listened.

"I … I had my phone off all weekend. I just … didn't want to deal with him or anyone else. And I … I turned it on finally, this morning."

Blair sat down on the floor, shuddering from anxiety and cold. Andrew came to sit next to her, right up against the heater, where they would be warmer. She could feel him looking at her.

"He sent me all these really mean text messages."

Out of the corner of her eye, where Andrew's arms were crossed over his knees, she saw him clench one of his fists. But he said nothing.

"I'm so stupid," Blair said, putting her head on her knees.

"You're not stupid, Blair," Andrew said quietly, as he had done many times before.

She wished that Andrew would touch her somehow. But why would he? He had no reason to.

Blair remembered how good it had felt to ask God for help the day before. Andrew was still a dear friend, even if she didn't know what would happen with them—a friend she most definitely didn't deserve, but still needed. A friend who still cared, no matter what.

"Can you…" Blair choked. "Can you just hold me?"

"Of course," Andrew said.

And before Blair knew it, she was in Andrew Stormant's arms again.

If It All Fades Away

It was simultaneously the best and worst feeling in the world. Because once again, Blair was safe. Safe in the arms of Andrew Stormant.

Chapter 40

Admit It

"I don't want to live like this anymore, Andrew," Blair said.

She leaned against the heater with her legs stretched out on the floor, staring despondently at her feet.

"I'm just so ... so very tired." Blair closed her eyes. "It's a tiredness that even sleep can't help."

"What would you like to be different?" Andrew asked.

Blair scoffed. "Everything. I'd want everything to be different." She began to pick at a loose thread on her skirt. "I wish I could get back into counseling... I went last year, after I was supposed to be expelled. Ms. Holland had suggested medication—"

"You were supposed to be expelled?" Andrew asked quietly.

Blair turned to look at him. "You didn't know that?"

"You ... you never said anything."

Blair looked forward again. "Yeah. In addition to overhearing how Claire wanted you to send her a dick pic, I got to hear her and Annabelle laugh hysterically about when I was supposed to be expelled." Blair's brow was furrowed.

If It All Fades Away

The memory of them laughing was both painful and angering.

"Can I ask what happened?"

"Does it really matter?" Blair muttered. "I'm trash, Andrew." She paused. "Anyway, my parents came, and Ms. Holland really went to bat for me. I ended up just getting suspended and had to do six counseling sessions to avoid expulsion. You can imagine how pleased my parents were at that."

"What about the school counselor?"

Blair was becoming irritated with Andrew's lack of knowledge, which seemed like redundant old news. But she tried to be patient, because he didn't even know half the trouble she'd gotten into over the years.

"The guy's an idiot. That's why Ms. Holland suggested private counseling. My parents were kinda backed into a corner. So ... my mom had me do it, and then that was that." Blair laughed to herself. "She was so mad. She smacked me on the back of the head as soon as we got in the car." She just shook her head and looked away from Andrew completely, cursing under her breath.

The bell rang. First period was over.

Blair stood up immediately. Andrew did likewise, a little more slowly, given his tall frame.

"What about Hudson?" Andrew asked.

Blair dusted herself off. "What about him?"

"It's just ... he's harassing you. That's not okay."

Blair sighed. "I'm not telling on him. It's not worth it."

"But this is concrete proof that he's saying inappropriate stuff to you."

"And what am I going to say to Mr. Davis? 'He was supposed to avoid me as much as possible, and now he's mad because I didn't go with him to a party, like I said I would'?"

Andrew grimaced.

"I gotta get to class," Blair said, opening one of the large double doors.

Andrew wordlessly followed behind her. They retrieved their backpacks from the library and went their separate ways.

* * *

Gym was upon Blair before she knew it. She still felt anxiety in the pit of her stomach. She shook as she changed clothes, wearing long sweatpants and a crew-neck T-shirt. Exiting the locker room, Blair went to the gym on shaking legs.

Andrew was stretching with Julian. Hudson was in a corner with a few guys. Blair went to a corner all by herself and started stretching her quads, looking at the floor. She heard Hudson's obnoxious laughing and felt his eyes on her out of her periphery. She felt safe with Andrew there, but also somewhat foolish for the stark contrast of her recently wearing more revealing clothes and now suddenly covering back up.

Mr. Parks came in and began talking. To Blair's horror, it was dodgeball today—and, of course, she was assigned to the opposite team of Andrew and Hudson. Luckily, Julian was on her team.

She did her best to aim at others that weren't the two of them. She noticed Andrew was doing the same. Hudson, however, wore a shit-eating grin and began mercilessly chucking the ball at Blair. She was his sole target. She successfully blocked a few times with her own ball, jumping out of the way during other attacks, but he got her legs a few times, forcing her out. Julian noticed Hudson's attacks and got him out during at least one round.

If It All Fades Away

In the final round, as Blair was dodging an attack from someone else, she turned—and was hit square in the face with a ball from Hudson, who was laughing hysterically and red in the face.

Andrew looked furious and started saying something indiscernible to Hudson. Blair blinked through the mortified wetness forming in her eyes. She walked off the court, not staying around to deal with any further assaults.

"Blair, is everything okay?" Mr. Parks called out to her.

"Blair," Julian called.

She ignored them both and went to the girls' locker room. After showering and changing back into her uniform, Blair decided what she needed to do.

Exiting the locker rooms, she was surprised to see Andrew leaning against the wall, waiting for her.

"I'm fine," she said.

"He's such an asshole," Andrew breathed. "I'm going to go talk to Ms. Holland after this."

"Don't," Blair said. "I got this."

"Blair, please don't do anything rash."

"No, I won't. I just want to talk to him—"

Andrew stood up straighter as Hudson exited the boys' locker room. Hudson walked past the two of them, talking to Christopher Moore as if they weren't even there. Blair started to follow him. Andrew opened his mouth to protest.

"Stay here. I promise if something goes down, you'll hear it."

Andrew did as she said, staying put, but he didn't look too pleased.

"Hey, Hudson," Blair called. She was now around the corner from Andrew.

Hudson kept walking.

"You want to tell me why you can't just admit you like me?" she said a bit louder.

Hudson stopped. She knew he would. Christopher Moore turned first, then Hudson.

"What?" He laughed.

"You heard me."

"Simons, don't flatter yourself. Your tits are too small, and you have big teeth."

Blair winced, but she remained undeterred.

"That hasn't stopped you from harassing the absolute shit out of me for four years. Not to mention the dozens of text messages you sent like a jerk this weekend."

Christopher began to look uncomfortable.

Blair saw Hudson's jaw working. He muttered something to Christopher, essentially dismissing him. Christopher walked down the hallway and turned out of sight, looking only too happy to get out of there.

"You and Stormant back together?" he asked. "Is that why you have him hiding around the corner? What, is he too much of a pussy to fight me?"

"We can go someplace else if you want," Blair said, chin held high.

Hudson came up to her. They were close together now.

"We can talk where no one will hear us," she added.

Hudson looked like he was contemplating it. "Okay."

Blair could sense Andrew's tension around the corner. Even though she couldn't see him, she knew it was there.

Blair led Hudson to a corner near another exit by the concession stands. Hudson turned to regard her. "What'd you bring me here for? Wanna suck my dick behind the counter?"

"Stop talking like that," Blair snapped. She could feel how cross her face was.

Hudson sighed, then laughed. "I liked you better last

week … when you showed off those small tits and had your shorts hiked up your ass."

"You know, Hudson," Blair said, unfazed and unafraid of him for the first time ever. "If you hadn't been such a prick to me ever since freshmen year, I might have actually *like*-liked you."

Hudson's mouth opened slightly, surprised. "What?"

"Just admit it," Blair said. "You torment me because you like me."

Hudson looked down and away.

Blair continued, "And I could have liked you back … if you hadn't hurt me so much."

Hudson looked up at her, eyes completely serious through the strands of his red hair.

"Yeah—you win, *Bentley Hudson*," Blair said, putting her hands out. "You've hurt me. A lot. Are you happy now?"

Hudson's face had softened.

Blair looked down, not wanting to cry. She saw that he wasn't a total monster. Not yet, anyway. He was a bastard for his bullshit, but if she was ever going to try to get through to him, she might as well do it when she just couldn't fight anymore.

"I just took you, Evan, and Thomas's crap—all this time—and I thought, 'If I just play along, they'll leave me alone. If I just ignore it, they'll leave me alone. If I just punch you, you'll all leave me alone.'"

"So, why sit with us, then?" Hudson asked, eyes narrowing.

"Because I was pissed off at Stormant," Blair said immediately. "Come on, now, don't act stupid—you know the game."

Hudson shifted his weight, and Blair moved back slightly,

staying a safe distance away. He looked a bit angry, but he dropped the joker act.

"I've done literally everything I could think of," Blair said. "Hoping eventually you guys would just freakin' leave me alone. And then this weekend, I had my phone off because I haven't…"

"Haven't what?" Hudson asked, impatient.

Blair swallowed. "I haven't … felt good … lately." She kept her head lowered. "I'm … I'm sorry if you felt … like something more was developing between us. But I'm … I'm not okay right now. And it's not even just Stormant. I'm just going through a lot."

Silence. Blair saw Hudson's feet shifting back and forth, apparently a self-soothing technique. Everyone would be at lunch now. It was just the two of them.

"I couldn't," Hudson said.

Blair looked up. "Couldn't what?"

"Couldn't admit it," Hudson said, barely audible, then quietly added, "I've always liked you, Blair."

Blair's breath caught in her throat. "Then why … why'd you have to be so *mean* to me?" The desperation and hurt were surely evident in her voice. "Why couldn't you just fucking *talk* to me like a normal human being?"

Hudson's head was hung in shame. He was twisting his foot in a small circle now. "I don't know," he said. "I thought you'd laugh at me if I told you."

"And that's the worst thing that could have happened?" Blair asked, still hurt, her anger coming through somewhat. "Instead, you had to call me a 'dirty little slut' that liked to bang Mr. Davis? You snapped my bra strap in basketball. You called me a 'selfish bitch' this weekend. You attacked me with dodgeballs in gym today. And you literally just said, not even ten minutes ago, that I have small tits and big teeth.

If It All Fades Away

How the hell did you think I was ever going to respond to any of that?"

Hudson looked up at her, his eyes fluttering. "I thought what happened last week would be what would happen eventually."

Blair's eyes were wide. She could feel her mouth hanging open, stunned.

"And then what? I go to the bonfire and get smashed-ass drunk, and you weren't going to take advantage of me?"

"What?" Hudson said. "No!"

"Oh my God," Blair said, hands over her face. "I should've known."

"Known what, Simons?" Hudson demanded, angry, but not threatening.

"Here I was, just making shit up in my head," Blair said. "God, even Ms. Holland believed it. And I let your big-ass mouth scare me all this time, but it's so obvious."

Hudson's lips pursed, and his nostrils flared.

"Have you—have you ever had a girlfriend before?" she asked.

Blair and he both knew what she was really asking.

"No," he said flatly. His eyes were dark.

Blair looked down. He had still snapped her bra strap that time. He had said so many awful things to her. He had legitimately tormented her at various points throughout high school. He had never actually gotten to know her. He *still* didn't know her.

Blair straightened up. There was a strange moment when they were just staring at each other.

"If you … if you still care about me at all," Blair said, her voice uneven, "please just let me finish this year in peace."

Hudson's throat bobbed. "Okay."

"I ... uh, I can't sit with you anymore," Blair said. "I'm really sorry, but—"

"Stormant," he muttered. "I got it."

"We're actually not back together," Blair corrected him.

"What?" Hudson said, perking up.

"It's ... just... Whatever, we need to get to lunch. We've got, like, fifteen minutes left now."

Blair started to walk down the hallway, and Hudson followed her.

She couldn't wrap her head around the conversation they'd just had. She still didn't entirely trust Hudson. But with any luck, she may have just disarmed him some. Another part of Blair wondered if he would continue to be on his best behavior because he still felt like he had a chance.

Whatever the case, Blair would do her best to remain cordial with Hudson, but keep a safe distance from him. Unpredictable. That was how she looked at him now. It was hard for her to see which way he would turn in time, but she just had to manage him as best she could for five more months.

For now, she just wanted to get some food in her.

Chapter 41

Worth Fighting For

Blair didn't sit with anyone at lunch. She grabbed a sandwich as she had done many times before and quickly scurried off, eating it in the hallway.

Walking home that afternoon, she felt a familiar prickle on the back of her neck.

"It's really cold out, you know," a familiar voice said.

"I'm okay," Blair called.

"It's not that hard to just get in and let me take you home," Andrew said.

Blair closed her eyes and inhaled deeply. "I'm fine, Stormant."

She continued to walk.

"Please?" Andrew asked.

Blair turned to look at him. She couldn't deny his puppy-dog eyes. And it *was* cold out.

Once inside his vehicle, Blair said nothing.

"Did everything go okay earlier?" Andrew asked.

"It went fine."

"So ... he's going to leave you alone, or do I still need to talk to Ms. Holland?"

"He agreed to leave me alone."

"Good," Andrew said. But he sounded a little too firm when he said it.

They were on Blair's street now.

"Is your mom home today?" Andrew asked.

Blair turned to look at him. "No."

"Okay."

Once they were in her driveway, Blair spoke.

"Andrew, what is actually going on here?"

"What?" He glanced at her. "You're the one who broke up with me, remember?"

"So ... are you asking to get back together?" Blair asked. They had broken up last Tuesday, and it was now Monday.

"I just want to be with you. However that needs to happen," Andrew said quietly.

"I'm a goddamn mess, Andrew."

"I know. You've said that numerous times now."

"You want the truth?"

Andrew turned to regard her, confused.

"I don't care what we are to each other now. I just want you to fuck my brains out," she admitted.

Andrew laughed while looking down, his face a mixture of amusement and sadness.

* * *

Ten minutes later, Blair clung to Andrew as he slowly thrust into her. Warm tingles of pleasure radiated inside of her.

There was an animalistic nature to their sex this time. The first time had been sweet and clumsy, with Andrew confessing he wanted to spend the rest of his life with her. The second time, he had been worn out from traveling, though it was good sex because they'd missed each other. But this time... This time felt entirely different—heavier, darker, forbidden, even. They weren't back together in the official sense of the word, because nothing had been properly talked about or resolved. But in this way, they were together again.

When they were finished, Blair rolled away to face the wall.

Andrew's smell, his body, his voice—all of him. He was here, with her again, his big arm wrapped around her tiny middle. He kissed the back of her head, then inhaled deeply. "Ah, I've missed this."

Blair didn't want him to see her soft tears as he brushed her hair away repeatedly.

"I love you," he said.

Blair's throat caught—a frog in it for sure. "I love you, too," she managed quietly.

She felt Andrew still, but he didn't press it, even though he could tell she was weeping.

They stayed together quietly until both fell asleep.

* * *

Blair awoke a few hours later. Andrew was still sleeping, his mouth open slightly, his eyes and brows completely relaxed. She watched him, his slow and steady breathing. He was right there, had just inside been her ... and yet, he still felt so far away. Although the light from outside was practically gone, Blair could make out his features from the streetlights glowing on the ceiling.

She searched and searched his face, looking for any remains of her violence. The memory alone twisted her stomach in shame.

His mother wouldn't want them back together; she knew that. Andrew didn't want to be with her, realistically—not after what had happened. And truth be told, she still didn't trust him entirely. He had hurt her—even though he'd said he never would when he first asked if they could be together. He'd lied to her, made her think everything with Claire was all in her head, until she confronted him with the truth.

Blair wondered how someone as good, kind, and handsome as Andrew had gone his whole life being overlooked by girls. It was utterly absurd. He had to have simply not noticed.

And yet, he had ended up with her. She wasn't worthy of him; she had known that since day one.

Blair had worked harder to be a better student since they got together, studying, completing all her assignments, even doing Ms. Holland's extra credit. She wanted to impress Andrew, wanted to make sure her last semester of high school wasn't a complete disaster grade-wise.

Andrew began to stir. He smiled at her with bleary eyes. "Hi."

"Hi." She smiled back softly.

He rolled slightly. "What time is it?"

"Almost six."

That seemed to wake him up a bit more. "Are you hungry?"

Blair hesitated. "I am."

"We should go somewhere to eat."

"No, I really shouldn't."

Andrew looked confused. Something about how Blair said it tripped him up, and he seemed at a loss for words.

Blair didn't want to ask, but she couldn't help it. She couldn't go out to eat or do any couple things—not like this.

"Andrew?"

"Yes?"

"What's going on with us?"

If It All Fades Away

"What do you mean?"

"I mean this," she said, gesturing to them lying together.

"I don't know. I was hoping you could tell me. Since you said earlier that you just wanted to have sex."

"I didn't say that," Blair weakly protested.

"You did."

Blair opened her mouth, then closed it. He was right; she had said that.

"You're right. I'm sorry."

"What *is* going on with us, Blair?"

"I don't know," she said softly. "I want us to be together again, but—I can't… Not after I scratched up your face. And your mom hates me now, and—"

"My mom doesn't *hate* you," Andrew cut in, almost offended.

"You said yourself that she wants me to stay away from you. And that she was really upset."

"She was. But that doesn't mean she *hates* you."

"She hates me now, I'm sure of it."

"Blair, she does not."

"You don't know how women work," Blair said defiantly.

Andrew seemed to be getting defensive, but she could tell he was trying to keep it under control.

"You don't know how I work, or how Claire works, or how your mother works," Blair said, looking at his chest rising and falling rapidly. "I keep thinking I'm the only problem here. But then I remember … you just don't want to see people for who they really are. Or I should say, how *women* are. You think everyone is virtuous and good by nature, like you. But you're wrong."

"I don't know what you're saying, exactly."

"I told you I wasn't good, but you didn't believe me. I told you Claire wasn't good, and you didn't believe me. I'm telling you your mom hates me now, and you don't believe me."

"I might not know exactly how girls my age work," Andrew said. "But I do know that my mother doesn't hate you. She was just worried about me."

"But did she worry about *me*?"

"Yes," Andrew said instantly. "She was worried about you before any of this stupid shit happened."

"I wouldn't call it 'stupid shit,' exactly, Andrew. Seemed pretty valid to me."

"You know what I mean. She was distraught after we saw you and your mother at Christmas."

Blair's eyes shimmered. She had almost forgotten.

"She saw how full of crap your mother is. And it was all she could talk about on the way home. I know they aren't psychologists or anything, but they did have to study it as a part of medicine, and both my mom and dad think your mother is a narcissist."

Blair looked up at Andrew with wide eyes.

"I should have seen it, too. It wasn't obvious from everything I'd read, until my mom started pointing out stuff she saw right away."

"Like what?"

Andrew sighed, obviously a bit worked up. "She said your mother wanted to take credit for all the good things you did. Whenever my mom tried to talk about you, Angela redirected the conversation to something about herself or made up a lie. Like that shit about you guys dress shopping. I couldn't believe she was so comfortable telling such a bald-faced lie, when she knew I had to come and pick you up from the mall. Knew you'd stayed the night at my place." Andrew lay on his back, Blair still curled in his arm. He ran a hand through his hair. "Maybe she thinks my mom and I don't talk

If It All Fades Away

or something. Or maybe she didn't care that we knew she was full of it."

"She'd do anything to save face," Blair said quietly.

"Yeah, and that part where she was grabbing you by the back of the neck… My mom said that's a common thing she's seen as a nurse, when abusers are subtly controlling their victims."

"Thought she was going to leave bruises on me."

"I was really upset after we left church. We all were. So … when I tell you that my mom doesn't hate you, believe that, as a mother, she was shocked at seeing my face, and then realized how badly things must be at home for you to act out like that."

"I'm really sorry, Andrew," Blair murmured, her voice tight.

Andrew rolled back to her, pulling her into his chest. "I know," he said confidently. "I know who you are, Blair. Please—just—let me help you."

"How?" Blair asked.

"I don't know. Just … don't push me out. Let's talk when something bad happens. I'm sorry for how I mishandled everything with Claire. I was an idiot—I know that now. But I promise you, I don't like her."

"I want you to stay away from her," Blair said. "If I say stay away from a conniving bitch, you'd better listen to me."

"Anything," Andrew said, raising her chin to look at him. "I'm yours, Blair. Just say the word, and I'll do it. I love you so much. I don't care if people think you're controlling me. I know who I am, and I know who you are. You're just wounded, and you haven't been given the chance to heal."

Blair sniffled into him, her hands at his chest. He smelled so good.

"I want to get better, Andrew, I do."

"I know. Which is why I'll talk to my parents tonight to see if we can help you somehow."

"What?" Blair asked, looking up.

"If your worthless parents won't do it, then I will."

"I don't think… I can't—can't do anything without their permission. I don't turn eighteen until March."

That gave Andrew pause.

"Have you thought about trying to be emancipated before?"

"I looked into it. Once," Blair said. "It's really not that bad here, Andrew. My parents aren't even around half the time. But I'm provided with food, housing, education, and medical care. Angela's … narcissism … or whatever you want to call it, doesn't affect me that much. And my dad's a professional drunk who just works when he isn't drinking."

Andrew sighed. "They do affect you, though. They've eroded your self-confidence into dust. And it's not your fault, but it's been hell trying to help you see your own worth."

"I'd rather just try to make it until graduation, and then hopefully make it out to my aunt's."

Andrew was silent at the mention of Chicago. Then he said tentatively, "Would you … would you still be interested if I wanted to be a part of that?"

"Yes." Blair smiled.

Andrew kissed her deeply, hand on her cheek. "I told you, we're going to get through this. I've never wanted to stop trying for one second. Just—please don't shut me out again, Blair. I'd do anything to keep you in my life."

Blair's lip quivered. "I don't know how you can keep saying that when I've hurt you so much, and I'm … a broken mess, all the time—"

"Blair, look at me."

Blair's eyes met his magnetic gaze.

"It's because we're meant to be together." Andrew laughed under his breath. "I feel it in my soul. And that's a feeling worth fighting for."

Blair kissed Andrew desperately, their hands tangling in each other's hair until they were making love once more.

Chapter 42

Tart

Blair went to sleep that night, the smell of Andrew still all over her and her bed. She felt so good, so warm again.

They were back together.

Thursday would be two weeks to the day since she'd confronted Andrew in his car about Claire. It seemed much longer. Blair was glad it hadn't lasted any longer than it did. Her emotions had been pure hell in the time she and Andrew were apart.

She drifted into a deep sleep and slept better than she had for the last two weeks.

* * *

The next day, Blair and Andrew made their way to their lockers together as they used to, talking and laughing. As they rounded the corner, they slowed. Hudson was at his locker, and there was a moment of recognition, his eyes wide before they narrowed. Blair could tell he had been waiting for her ... and then realized she was back with Stormant. She

If It All Fades Away

kept her head down and put her stuff away. Then she and Andrew made their way to first period.

Come gym time, Blair was on her way down the small enclosed hallway to the girls' locker room when she stopped, awash with terror instantly. Hudson stood by the door, leaning against the wall, arms crossed, waiting for her.

"H—hi," she said, her voice shaky.

"Go on in," he said, gesturing with his head.

"What?"

"I won't tell you again, Simons."

Blair should have turned and run, but Hudson grabbed her by her upper arm before she could. It instantly put her into fight mode.

No! Don't do it. Think of your future. Think of Andrew!

Blair allowed him to hold her as he pushed the door open. He locked it behind him.

She tried to maintain her cool composure. She was trapped. The door was locked. Only someone with a key could get in.

"Wha—what's going on?" Blair stammered.

"I thought about what you said yesterday," Hudson said.

Blair's whole body was shaking, her hands especially.

"About how you could have liked me if I wasn't such a prick. And then I realized—*you* are a selfish bitch."

Blair felt her face fall. "Hudson—"

"You just used me to make Stormant jealous. And then, here you are, back with him today."

"I—I told you that, though. You seemed fine with it yesterday. Why are you being like this now?" Blair demanded.

"Because I told you how I felt after you slutted it out of me."

"I just—I was just telling you the truth, Hudson. I could

have liked you." Her heart hammered in her chest, and she clenched her fists to stop the shaking.

"You were never going to give me a chance. You just said that crap so I'd leave you alone. So you'd get Stormant to get back with you. And don't say you're not; I saw you two this morning."

Blair felt an icy dread come over her.

"So … so if I hadn't been with him this morning, then what?"

Hudson laughed. "Doesn't matter now."

Blair felt her throat close up. She had felt a glimmer of hope yesterday that maybe Hudson wasn't so bad. She remembered thinking that the trajectory of his life wasn't set yet—that he could choose what type of a man he would become one day. But he had no reason to change. His mother got him out of everything. They had money. He was set to go anywhere in the country for college. He wasn't used to earning anything; he just took it as he wanted. And if things didn't go exactly his way, there was a price to pay.

"You wouldn't have been happy if I'd said no to you this morning."

"You're right, I wouldn't have … which is why I realized it didn't matter either way."

In that moment, Blair knew what would happen, but didn't want to believe or acknowledge it.

"I thought you said you've never had a girlfriend," she said.

"I haven't. But that doesn't mean I haven't been with girls before."

Blair closed her eyes as she saw him start to unzip his pants.

No, no, no, no… God, Ms. Holland was right. Andrew

If It All Fades Away

was right. Blair's gut instincts were right. He'd never had a girlfriend—but he'd taken advantage of girls before.

"What do you want from me?" Blair choked out.

"You suck Stormant off?" he asked casually.

Blair lowered her head.

"Yes?"

She nodded.

"You're going to show me how you do it to him."

"Oh, God…" Blair breathed.

"You're screwed anyway, Simons. You were supposed to stay away from me. Ms. Holland won't be able to help you now. And as soon as Mr. Davis hears that you've been sitting with me at lunch and Mass, no one will believe you didn't want this."

Hudson began to push his pants down and leaned up against the door.

"Get over here," he demanded.

Blair couldn't look at him as she approached. He grabbed a fistful of her hair, jerking her hard, then shoving her to the floor. She could smell him. He had his own unique scent. Not anything that she would find instinctively attractive. He smelled too much of laundry detergent and some sort of bar soap.

Blair should bite his dick. Should punch him in the nuts. Should do any number of things.

No. Don't do anything stupid.
Think of your future.
Think of Andrew.
Just imagine it's Andrew.
This is only temporary.
This isn't real.

Blair tried desperately to imagine that Andrew was in

front of her and that none of it was real. Her mind disassociated as much as possible.

Hudson reached into his pants and freed himself.

He began to pull her head closer. Blair closed her eyes. *God, this isn't happening...* She would just get through this, and everything would be alright.

Then, a loud knock came on the door.

"Blair, are you in there?"

"ANDREW!" Blair screamed, eyes snapping open.

"Shit," Hudson muttered, shoving himself back into his pants.

"HUDSON is in here!"

"Shut up!" Hudson backhanded Blair across the face. It felt like a wound-up tree branch had just smacked her. God, did it hurt.

"Blair!" Andrew began pounding on the door. "Hudson, you piece of shit! I swear to God, as soon as I get this door open, you're leaving here on a stretcher!"

"Fuck you!" Hudson yelled.

"Mr. Parks!" Andrew yelled.

Hudson tried to run and hide in a corner, but it was useless. Very shortly, the sound of the door unlocking was the last thing Blair heard before she was crying hysterically.

"Stormant!" Mr. Parks called. Julian and two other boys were there.

Blair's last image before Julian pulled her up by her arms and asked her frantically if she was okay was Andrew leaping over her, rushing to where Hudson was, out of sight. She heard scuffling and blows landing, shouting.

Julian led Blair away.

"That bastard," Julian said, looking at her face. "Let's get you out of here, Blair. I gotta take a picture of this when we get out into the light, before the mark is gone."

"How did Andrew know—"

"What?"

"How did Andrew know to come and knock?"

"I—uh… I don't know. I guess we were all sorta coming into the gym, and suddenly he looked like he'd seen a ghost and ran."

In the gymnasium, making it past the other boys who were gawking, Blair let Julian take quick photos of her face. She couldn't stop shaking. She had to sit down.

"Whoa, whoa, whoa, you're alright, Blair… You're alright," Julian said, guiding her to the floor.

* * *

"We can't have this again!" Mr. Davis yelled. Blair heard his fist pound his desk.

"No, *you* can't have this again!" Ms. Holland shouted. "Never mind that we've known he was a threat for a long time!"

"What? Your unfounded rumors again? His family is practically St. Michael's royalty!"

"You think I give a *shit*?!" Ms. Holland snapped back.

Blair and Andrew were sitting together outside of Mr. Davis's office. Blair kept touching her face, although there were no marks left, but the memory of Hudson's strike was forever embedded in her body's memory now.

Andrew had an ice pack on his knuckles. He sat slouched, brow furrowed, fuming.

"You know who her mother works for?" Ms. Holland asked.

Blair laughed to herself. *Yes, let's put Angela's side piece to good use for once.*

Mr. Davis could be heard groaning loudly, the sound of his chair going around in a circle.

"Yeah, you want John J. Turner to get a hold of this? It'll be all over the news. You'll be reliving two years ago all over again."

"Where is he now?" Mr. Davis asked regarding Hudson.

"Home. Not that he was going to stick around, but he practically ran after Nick managed to break him and Stormant up with some help. Do you realize we have Title IX obligations to uphold? The police are supposed to be notified—"

"Don't even think about it."

"Brad—" Ms. Holland said firmly. "This needs to be reported."

Silence.

"You're really willing to throw it all away for this tart?" he asked, almost smugly.

Mrs. Welsh looked over, concerned as Andrew stood up.

"Don't," Blair said, grabbing him by his arm. "Please don't."

Ms. Holland opened the door. "Blair."

"Yes?"

"Call your mother."

Chapter 43

Sic 'Em

"Andrew," Ms. Holland said. "You might want to call your mother as well."

Blair's stomach was in knots as she dialed her mother's phone number. Andrew grimaced as he stepped out and called his mother as well. For once, Blair agonized more over seeing Lily than she did Angela.

Ms. Holland allowed Blair and Andrew to go to lunch to grab a bite. However, Blair could hardly eat, even though Andrew encouraged her.

Ms. Holland then moved them to a conference room while waiting for Lily and Angela. Blair kept her head in her arms. Ms. Holland paced and spoke with Andrew intermittently.

"I'm very sorry, Blair," she said.

"It's fine," Blair mumbled into her arms.

Andrew rubbed her back.

Finally, Angela arrived, and Ms. Holland stepped out to explain the situation to her. Lily came shortly after, and Blair couldn't bring herself to look up.

Andrew removed himself to go and speak with his mother.

Then Angela quietly entered.

"Blair," she said.

Blair sat upright, unable to look at her.

"I'm told you punched this boy at the start of this year," her mother said.

Blair closed her eyes. "He's been harassing me for four years, Mom." She was so tired. So, so very tired.

"Well … it's about to get interesting now."

Blair didn't know what her mother meant by that.

Eventually, Lily and Andrew entered the room, along with Ms. Holland, shortly after Mr. Davis came out from his office.

Mr. Davis began to lay out Blair's long history of misbehavior at St. Michael's. They all sat and listened. Blair was sure she would die of shame as Andrew had to hear every retelling, including her biting Mr. Banes and barking at him like a dog. The humiliation was too great to bear, and Blair buried her face in her hands. Andrew rubbed her shoulders, reassuring her.

"Are you finished?" Angela asked Mr. Davis. "Because all I heard was how you let this boy torment my daughter for four straight years. And apparently, you didn't bother to call me after the incident between them at the beginning of the year."

Mr. Davis squirmed slightly. "She … she begged me not to."

A tense silence settled in the room.

"And yet, you still failed to uphold your responsibilities."

"She's seventeen. She's practically an adult," Mr. Davis protested.

If It All Fades Away

Angela inhaled deeply. Then she set to performing.

"Let me tell you how this will go," she began.

Blair glanced over and saw a smirk on Ms. Holland's face. It was as if she had known precisely when the right moment was to sic her mother on Mr. Davis.

Blair couldn't determine whether Angela was actually on her side or just reveling in her moment to shine at what she did best: busting balls and abusing people. Blair hoped she wouldn't hear about what a slut she was later. She hoped that her mother could be on her side for once. Whatever her reasoning, the room's energy quickly became tense as Angela Simons set out to give Brad Davis the dressing-down of his life.

"You're going to expel this boy, or I'm going to have John J. Turner take this case on. We'll find other victims, with the help of Ms. Holland. We'll get the press involved—"

"Your daughter has been a problem since day one."

"My daughter is the *victim* of a crime here, *sir*. And you failed to protect her."

"She's hardly a victim. I saw them sitting together at lunch."

"And? What if they had been dating? What then?!"

Blair stole a look at Andrew and Lily at one point, their eyes wide as they watched Angela stand up, yelling and pointing. Ms. Holland seemed relatively unfazed—maybe a bit too glad it wasn't her on the receiving end of Angela's abuse this time. Mr. Davis looked so utterly worn down, exhausted. Angela had spent so much time in the courtroom assisting John—weeks on end for some cases—that she was used to things dragging out, going on and on. Mr. Davis, however, was always quick to put things to rest as soon as possible.

"If something isn't done about this boy, *immediately*, I'll make sure this whole thing drags on for as long and as painfully as possible. You'll be forced to resign." Nearing the end of her tirade, Angela glanced over to Lily, as if to ask if she had anything to add.

"The boy seems like a genuine problem," Lily said, wrapping her arm around Andrew's shoulders. "Andrew's never hit anyone in his life. And I'm deeply disturbed that this was allowed to escalate to this point. Should Andrew become involved in any of this, we would have to involve our attorney as well."

Mr. Davis sighed, pinching the bridge of his nose. "I need to talk to my boss—and the board. We'll have an answer for you as soon as possible."

"Great," Angela said, with a disturbingly genuine smile. But this was her realm, her world—conflict like this. She lived for it. Thrived on it. Leaving the room, Angela seemed energized—*alive*—while everyone else was drained and exhausted.

Blair stood with her mother as she watched Lily, Andrew, and Ms. Holland speaking together as Mr. Davis walked past them, unable to get away fast enough. Angela wrapped her arm around Blair while looking on, waiting for the others to turn and see them—to see what a loving and wonderful mother she was.

Andrew walked over to Blair.

"Blair's so lucky to have you, Andrew," Angela said.

He nodded. "I'm lucky to have her."

Angela blinked momentarily, as if the idea that Blair was the catch for *him*, and not the other way around, was bewildering.

"Um, if it's alright with you, Mrs. Simons, can Blair and I please go out to lunch together, and I can bring her home?"

If It All Fades Away

Lily and Ms. Holland weren't far behind Andrew.

"Of course," she said.

Blair began to walk away with Andrew, looking back to see the three women talking together.

Chapter 44

Trapped

Andrew and Blair ate in silence at a local fast food restaurant. Blair was starved at that point, as she hadn't eaten a proper lunch. Andrew ordered a milkshake as she hastily wolfed down French fries and chicken tenders.

When Andrew drove them back to her house, Blair was surprised to see a car she didn't recognize in the driveway. Entering the front door with Andrew, Blair tensed slightly, but did her best to relax. John J. Turner was sitting in the living room with her mother. Blair glanced at the wall clock. She had completely lost track of time. Her father had left for work a little while ago. She had no idea where the hours had gone, between Hudson, Mr. Davis's office, trying to eat lunch, the meeting, and then Blair *actually* eating with Andrew.

"Hi, Blair," John said, standing up.

"Hi," she said, a bit uneasy.

"This must be Andrew." He strode over and shook his hand.

Andrew didn't know about what had happened at

Christmas Mass—that Blair had realized Angela and John were screwing, or that he had given Blair his business card, assuring her he would "help" her should she ever need it.

John returned to her father's recliner. Her mother was sitting in the other one. Blair and Andrew hesitantly sat on the couch.

"So, uh… Wow, what a day you two had, huh?"

Blair simply nodded.

"Well, your mother has filled me in on everything that happened. She mentioned that she told your… What is he again?" John turned to ask Angela.

"Vice principal. But he's basically the principal. The actual principal doesn't do anything there. He's in another building doing … who knows what."

"Right, right. Well, your mother mentioned that your VP wants this situation to go away as quickly as possible. Now, she said she told this Davis guy that if something isn't done immediately, she would be bringing charges against him, the school, and this Bentley Hudson boy."

John leaned forward, a mannerism that seemed so natural for his profession.

"Now, I know you've had some difficulties at the school. However, despite that, they should legally be reporting this to the police and doing their own investigation based on Title IX rules, regardless of whether a report is filed. Your mother and I discussed this, and you're so close to the end of your senior year. Do you really want to move forward with this? Because the boy's family does have quite a bit of money. I would be representing you as a friend, of course, so no fees incurred by you or your mother. However, this could potentially be drawn out and made very public. You could potentially face a lot of harassment and backlash. Unless we were to find other victims who would come forward—"

"I don't want to file a report or press charges or anything," Blair interrupted.

"Blair..." Andrew said softly.

"I just want him to go away. I've always wanted him to just ... go away and leave me alone," Blair said.

John swallowed, looking at Angela and then back at Blair. "Unfortunately, sometimes not moving forward is the better option in situations like these."

"And he gets to go on like nothing happened? Potentially raping other girls out there?" Andrew demanded.

Blair spun her head to him, a bit shocked.

"Yes, son. I'm afraid that's how it works sometimes," John said slowly. "If Blair doesn't want to move forward, it stops here. Unfortunately, even if that English teacher could find other victims, they might back out eventually, too. Things like this can get very nasty very quickly, and fall apart just as quickly. I'd give it everything I had, but this case would be tough with Blair's past and ... her sitting with the boy recently."

"He didn't even really do anything to me," Blair said quietly.

Andrew abruptly stood up and stormed to the front door, wordlessly opening it and exiting. Blair turned to see him through the window, pacing back and forth on the front porch.

"We're waiting on the phone call from Vice Principal Davis," John continued. "With what your mother told him earlier, I believe if he and the board are smart, they'll have this boy removed."

"And what if they don't?"

"I'd take care of it," John said. "Make sure they get it done."

Blair felt relieved for once. She knew she should have felt

angry that Hudson wouldn't have to face any further accountability for what he had done—not just to her, but to others as well, according to Ms. Holland. But Blair just wanted it all to go away, to get on with her life at St. Michael's, to just get through the rest of the year.

"You want another coffee, John?" Angela asked.

He pulled back from where his forearms were on his knees, looking at his cup. "Oh—uh, sure."

Blair watched with disgust as her mother leapt to her feet and dutifully retrieved John's coffee mug, like the perfect wife she wasn't. She came back with it filled, the steam wafting up.

"Andrew seems like a nice young man," John mused, sipping his coffee.

All three turned to look at Andrew, still pacing back and forth.

"He's going to be a doctor," Angela offered, beaming.

"Is that right?" John turned to look at her. He then regarded his cup of coffee, eyes down, letting a small sneer form at the corner of his lips. "Where's he going to school?"

Blair fisted her skirt down, feeling itchy. She and her mother hadn't spoken of Chicago, Natalie, or her plans with Andrew. And it disturbed her still that Angela had not asked after Christmas Mass.

"He's ... he's not sure yet," Blair said. "He's been accepted to a few places."

"Mm. And you're still going to Chi-town?"

Blair could feel her mother's grip on her neck again, even if it wasn't really there.

"I-I don't know yet. I haven't been accepted to the school I want to attend."

"Columbia, right?"

Blair was shaking. Her mother's eyes were dark with

contempt and unpredictability. She seemed angry that John knew about Chicago in addition to Andrew's parents—everyone except her.

"Y-yes," Blair said faintly.

"You didn't tell me what you were studying last we spoke."

Angela sprang to her feet.

"Well, I think it's about time we head back to the office and wait for the call, don't you think, John? Plus, we've got the Pratmoore case files to look over."

John looked up at her, mildly surprised. "Oh. Oh, right." He stood up, smoothing his slacks and buttoning his suit jacket.

Blair remained seated.

"Well, Blair, I'm very sorry about all of this, but things should be better for you from here on out. And as your beautiful mother knows, I'm happy to help you ladies any time."

Angela beamed at the praise, and Blair could have barfed at how obvious they were. Further still, Angela had clearly picked up on John lurching for Blair, but instead of being disgusted, she'd decided to compete for his attention.

"I'm, uh… I'm exhausted," Blair said, standing. "Is it okay if I go lie down?"

"Yes, of course, dear." Angela smiled.

"Is … is it okay if Andrew stays for a bit?"

"You know he's welcome here anytime."

Blair scurried to the front door quickly, all too aware of John and Angela's eyes on her.

"They're, uh, they're leaving," Blair informed Andrew, who had stopped pacing, his back to her. "My mom says you're welcome to stay. She's heading back to the office with John right now."

If It All Fades Away

Andrew didn't turn to look at her, his breath visible in the winter air as he spoke. "Okay."

Blair waited, then closed the door. John and Angela were packing up their things. Blair didn't speak to either of them as she bounded up the stairs to her room.

"It was nice seeing you, Blair," John called.

"Yeah, you, too," she called back, her voice high, tripping at the top step as she rushed to her bedroom.

Once inside, she ran to her bed and threw herself onto it. Through the heater vent, she heard the commotion of them leaving, Andrew's voice for a bit, and then the front door closing.

Rolling over, Blair saw John's card staring back at her, resting where it had been propped against her TV for over a month. She grabbed it and shoved it under her mattress, close to her vibrator. She didn't want to see him staring at her, even if it was only his name.

Blair knew she was so screwed later. Angela was sure to lay into her about Chicago now, and Blair had no plan for how she would manage or explain herself during that conversation.

Andrew quietly entered her bedroom, closing the door behind him. Blair looked up at him, still shaking. He wasn't looking at her as he approached her bed, sitting at the end where her feet were. Blair didn't like how he looked—almost as if he were disappointed in her.

"Are you... Are you mad at me?" Blair asked.

Andrew inhaled deeply, then exhaled, looking straight ahead to where her closet was across the room.

"I just can't believe this is happening."

Blair sat up slightly. "What would you want to see happen instead?"

Andrew sighed, pausing before he spoke, still not looking at her.

"He's going to get away with all of this—all of the things he's done—and he's going to get to go off to university and abuse and rape women there, too."

Blair let her eyes fall. The room was becoming dark with the winter sun setting.

Andrew turned to regard Blair. "That doesn't bother you?"

Blair looked up with her mouth open. "What?"

"He's going to get away with this, Blair."

"And what am I supposed to do, huh? Put myself through a whole-ass court case so I can sit up there and say he *almost* assaulted me, but didn't?"

Andrew turned away again, a scowl on his face. "I didn't mean it like that, Blair. I just... I'm so angry, and I wish..."

"You wish what?"

"Please don't think I'm blaming you. But I wish you wouldn't have..."

"You wish I hadn't sat with him?"

Andrew kept his head lowered. "I hate him. I was so angry ... so jealous when I saw you two together. I hated how genuinely happy you looked—"

"I wasn't happy, Andrew."

"I felt like I really didn't know you. But I still loved you ... still wanted us to be together. And I wanted to hit him whenever I saw you two laughing together. I was so mad that I've never been able to make you laugh as much as he could."

Blair said nothing. And she felt sick that she had genuinely laughed with Hudson. A lot. She had enjoyed herself more than a few times for the brief time she and those boys were together.

If It All Fades Away

"I'm a sick person, Andrew," she said. "I'm sorry I don't laugh enough with you."

"So, it was real ... the few times that you looked like you were dying of laughter with him?" he asked, looking at her.

"Yes."

Andrew rested his head in his hands.

"But that doesn't matter," Blair said, trying to move closer.

"You're not a guy. You don't understand."

Blair wanted to touch him, but decided to hold back, in case he rejected her. "W-what do you mean?"

"To a guy, making a girl laugh is everything, sometimes."

"You ... you have made me laugh, though. A lot."

"I know. It's just ... we're in this mess now. And I just—I'm struggling." Andrew wiped his nose and his eyes. "Because none of this—this situation with Hudson... None of it was necessary."

Blair retreated from Andrew and rolled over to face the wall. He moved to come behind her. He wrapped his arms around her, snuggling up to her. She felt a strange desperation in Andrew's embrace. Something was different. He tried to rock her over to him, but she wouldn't budge. Andrew rested his chin on her as best he could, but she wasn't turning to look at him.

"Can I just hold you right now?" Andrew asked.

"You are," Blair said flatly.

"I mean, *hold* you, hold you."

Blair inhaled deeply, her body lifting Andrew's head weight slightly.

"What do you mean, none of this with Hudson was necessary?"

There was a moment before Andrew spoke. "I just wish none of this had happened, is all. I—"

"You mean, had you not said I was being 'irrational and jealous for no reason' about Claire, none of this would have happened? Yeah, that's how I feel, too."

Andrew sighed deeply. "A lot of this is my fault. And not just the Claire crap, but Hudson, too."

Blair's breathing was ragged and uneven. She waited for him to continue.

"I should have made it clearer how dangerous he really was. Instead, I just … got mad about you guys sitting together, because I was hurt. But I really should have tried to warn you better."

"How?" Blair croaked.

"It's not just how he looked at you all the time, which I've always noticed even when he didn't think people were watching him. It's the other stuff he said when I sat with him."

Blair waited with bated breath. "Are you… Are you going to tell me now?"

"I never wanted to repeat it. He said…" Andrew's breath caught in his throat. "He said you probably liked being chained up and raped by Mr. Davis. Said some shit about how all the times you've missed class through the years—which is creepy that's he's kept track of it—it was because Mr. Davis was secretly raping you in the school basement."

Blair rolled over to face Andrew.

"Who even says that about a classmate?" he asked with his eyes closed. "And those fucking idiots he hung out with—they just laughed and laughed. It's almost all they could talk about. We're eating, and they're all laughing and getting hard at the idea of a grown-ass man sexually assaulting you."

Blair's eyes were forlorn as she brushed Andrew's dark hair back. He put his hand over his eyes. "I should have told you. God, I hate him. My only source of comfort was punching him in the face repeatedly. That's the only justice that bastard will face for all this."

"I'm really sorry, Andrew."

"It's not your fault," he said, stilling himself. "None of this is your fault. I just... I didn't protect you. I didn't warn you. I didn't do more. And I was an idiot about Claire, and I drove you right into his path."

Unexpectedly, Andrew removed his hand from his face and grabbed Blair's with both hands, her eyes wide. "This is all my fault, you understand me? All of it. I was an idiot. I—I didn't believe you about Claire—"

"Andrew, I didn't believe you about Hudson," Blair interrupted. "I don't know that I would have, even if you had told me that stuff. He's always talked about me like that—not that stuff about the basement and chains, but—"

Andrew kissed Blair suddenly, silencing her. His eyes were closed as he pressed his lips to hers. It was desperate, terrified kissing, as if Andrew was worried that Blair would disappear at any moment.

"Andrew," she breathed.

"I won't let anything like this happen to you again. Claire, Hudson, anyone that comes between us—the first sign of someone trying to do something to you, or if you're unhappy, I'll end it immediately."

Blair's hands gripped Andrew's sweater. "You can't protect me from everything. I'm... Even here—I'm not completely safe here."

"I know." Andrew buried his head under Blair's chin now, a strange and awkward position for him. He curled into her as much as possible, for someone as large as he was. "I talked to my parents last night, which feels like a hundred years ago. And they said what you said—that it would be hard to get you out of here. That waiting until you turn eighteen is the best choice."

"We're so close to the end, Andrew. That's why I don't want to deal with this Hudson stuff any more than I have to. Also..." Blair swallowed. "You forget that my mother would find a way to make this all about how she saved me 'that time.'"

"Oh, God," Andrew said, suddenly realizing Blair was right. "Why are people so *wicked*?"

Blair raised her hand to the back of his head, petting him the way she liked to be pet. The only other time she had done so for him was the night they'd first had sex.

"I've never felt so helpless in all my life," Andrew finally whispered, his voice nearly gone.

There was a very long moment of silence. Blair heard her rattling heater kick on. It was completely dark in the room, save for the orange glow of the streetlights illuminating the ceiling.

"I've always felt this way," Blair said softly. "It only feels awful when you get a taste of freedom and realize just how trapped you've actually been your whole life."

Chapter 45

His Name Is Andrew

Blair awoke in the middle of the night and checked her phone. There was a message from her mother:

The boy was expelled. You won't have to see him ever again.

Blair rolled over and fell back asleep, feeling a little lighter, but not completely relaxed.

The next morning, Blair and Andrew walked down the long hallway to the senior hall. A few people stopped and stared, then resumed their conversations. Blair tensed at that. Eventually, they were both at their lockers. Blair spotted Claire with Annabelle, some girls from their former lunch table surrounding her.

"I mean, it's not like she couldn't just bite his dick... She's pretty good at biting people," Claire joked.

Annabelle laughed while the others snickered.

Blair felt her head lurch forward. She closed her eyes.

Just ignore it. Just ignore it...

They must not have seen her and Andrew among the throng of other students.

"I mean, she was literally sitting with him last week, and now she wants to cry 'rape'?" Annabelle said. *"Please."*

A small group of students between Andrew and Blair and the corner where Claire and her little crew was dispersed. The girls looked startled to see them. Blair kept her head down and removed some books from her locker, and Andrew did likewise.

"Blair!" Claire called.

Blair glanced over to her briefly, then resumed what she was doing.

The group of girls came over to her, with Claire and Annabelle leading. "We're so sorry to hear what happened yesterday," Claire said, hand on her heart. It was a mannerism Blair hated.

"Seriously, he was a creep," Annabelle said.

Claire kept glancing down at Andrew and apparently didn't get the memo that he and Blair were back together. Blair anxiously waited for Andrew, and he eventually stood up.

"Hi, Andrew," Claire said, but he didn't meet her eyes. Blair saw her glance at her and then back to Andrew.

"Are you sure about that?" Andrew asked, bringing his eyes to meet hers.

"What?" Claire said, taken aback.

"Are you sure you're sorry about what happened to Blair yesterday?"

Claire scoffed slightly. "I mean, yeah—Hudson was scary."

"Really? Because you do realize we both just overheard you two saying Blair should have bitten his dick, and that she was 'crying rape'?"

Annabelle began to back away as their other little followers quickly dismissed themselves.

If It All Fades Away

"Wha— I didn't—"

"You did," Andrew said firmly. "Also, don't talk to me anymore. Ever."

Claire opened her mouth to protest, and Blair's eyes widened as she stood behind Andrew slightly. Now that Claire knew the hunt was over, she immediately turned mean.

"Pfft. And here I was beginning to think you were cool, Stormant."

"I don't care what you think of me," he said flatly. "You're a parasite that latches onto vulnerable people and feeds on their pain. What happened to Blair was sexual assault, and here you are laughing at her. It's disgusting."

Claire waved her hand as she walked past the two of them. "Whatever, Stormant."

"It's *Andrew*."

"What?" she turned to snap.

"My name is *Andrew*. Stop calling me 'Stormant.' You don't know me like that."

Claire turned red, thoroughly humiliated as she stormed off. "Okay—whatever, *Andrew*. Fuck you and your ugly-ass little … *girlfriend* … or whatever she is," she muttered.

Andrew's eyes, dark and unwavering, followed her as she rounded the corner and left. He turned to regard Blair, his eyes shifting at the sight of her to something wonderful and kind. Blair was speechless. The hall had been long empty after the second bell rang for first hour.

"There, I think that pretty well takes care of that, don't you?" Andrew asked.

Blair slammed her locker shut and threw her arms around Andrew's neck, drawing him in for a kiss.

"Thank you," she breathed.

* * *

It was Wednesday, which typically meant Church Duty. Blair realized with horror that now that Hudson was gone, she might be pulled out of it. She tepidly went to Ms. Holland's room after third period, the next class shuffling in.

"Oh, hi, Blair. How are you?" Ms. Holland asked at the door. She looked happy to see her, but also weary from the day before.

"Um, I'm good," she said. "All things considered."

Ms. Holland gave her a small smile. "Is there something I can do for you?"

"Do I, uh… Do I still have Church Duty today? Now that … Hudson is … gone?" Blair asked.

Ms. Holland paused momentarily, as if the thought hadn't occurred to her. "Do you still *want* Church Duty?"

"Oh, I mean," Blair responded quickly, not realizing how her question may have come across. "Um, yes, if it's okay with Mr. Parks and all, and with you. I just … I just wasn't sure."

Ms. Holland smiled. "It shouldn't be a problem. Besides, I'm told you do an excellent job there."

Blair turned to leave, giving her thanks.

"If you and Andrew have time today," she added, "maybe you can stop by here in the afternoon?"

Blair nodded. No doubt Ms. Holland wanted to debrief them about what had happened with Hudson.

Come Church Duty, Blair checked the pews for litter, then took a bucket of watered-down Pine-Sol and a washcloth and wiped them down one by one.

"You can always be counted on to go above and beyond, Ms. Simons," Father Donovan called, his voice echoing slightly.

Blair glanced up at him, giving him a nod in acknowledgement. He came down the altar steps to where she was.

If It All Fades Away

"I heard about your classmate and what happened yesterday. I'm very sorry to hear you went through that. Are you okay?"

Blair swallowed and nodded.

"You know," he said, gesturing for her to sit in one of the pews. Blair set her cleaning supplies down to sit. He leaned against another pew on the other side of the one in front of her. "When they first asked me about you doing Church Duty, I thought it strange that they didn't try to get that boy help—maybe send him to me for confession or something, at least once. But instead, they sent you my way. And I'm very grateful for that, because you've grown well here."

Father Donovan paused and adjusted his white clerical collar, his shirt and pants all black. "Have you found your time here to be helpful?"

Blair was worried he was trying to kick her out, now that she was no longer needed. "Yes, sir. Very much," she said, nodding fervently.

"I thought so." He smiled. "You know, Blair, I'm very proud of you."

Her throat caught, and her eyes were immediately glassy.

"And not just me, but Sister Eugene, and Amelia Holland. You've taken your work here very seriously, and it hasn't been missed by any of us."

She said nothing. She didn't know what to say.

"I don't know what that boy's future holds." Father Donovan looked down, sighing deeply. "But I'll continue to pray for him."

Blair admired the idea of praying for Hudson, even though she could not bring herself to do it. The thought had never occurred to her—where he fit in the eyes of God in all of this, where she fit. Father Donovan didn't look like he knew, either, but he would diligently uphold his promise to the Lord to pray for all of His children, the sinners and their sins.

"You only have a few more months here," he said, almost melancholy. "Do you have college plans?"

"I, uh... I plan to go to Columbia College ... in Chicago." She fisted her skirt down. "For ... for screenwriting."

He smiled at her. "I know we discussed it before, but I didn't miss seeing you in church here on Sunday. Would you be opposed to reading once a month ... until it's time for you to leave?"

Blair couldn't say no, even if she wanted to. The adrenaline rush and crash of reading, followed by individual praise afterward, were too compelling to resist. She knew she was supposed to just be a conduit for God's word, but that was impossible to feel entirely when people she knew and strangers alike were praising her.

"I can do it," she said shyly.

"Great. You did such a great job at Christmas, and I've been meaning to ask you if you were interested in doing it again, but it just kept slipping my mind. I'll get the schedule to you this Sunday," he said, moving to leave.

Blair bristled at the idea that she was now roped into attending Sunday Mass regularly. Then she instantly remembered that Andrew had also attended Sunday Mass, and maybe, just maybe, she could sit with him—or they could somehow spend more time together afterward. Because she had so easily forgotten, Blair's stomach dropped at the thought of Lily. She still had yet to properly apologize to her for hurting Andrew. Blair had wanted the floor to swallow her whole when Lily and Andrew had to listen to Mr. Davis outline her four years of troublemaking.

By the time she was done using Pine-Sol on the pews, Blair was sweating. Not taking a moment for a break, she immediately began cleaning the main entrance area of the church. As usual, it was much colder in this area than in the central part of the church. Blair always tried to go as quickly as possible, sweeping and such. Today, however, thoroughly exhausted from everything that had occurred in the last twenty-four hours, she sat on the winding steps that led upstairs. Blair had always thought the cold draft was coming from the doors, but sitting where she was, she finally noticed the small window at the base of the landing. It was held in place at the frame by duct tape. Old, rotten wood had given way, and there was nothing except the tape to hold the window in place. For all the money coming in and out of St. Michael's Catholic School and Church, the idea that they couldn't fix a small window baffled her. Maybe next week, she would bring her own duct tape and do a better job of sealing it up, since the current maintenance people didn't care any more than the next person.

Finishing her tasks for the day, Blair returned all of her cleaning equipment to the designated closet in the cry room (where parents took their babies and children to avoid disrupting Mass). Blair was hungry for lunch. She hoped returning to her old lunch table would be okay. Even though she knew it would be, Blair sighed at the realization that she owed an apology to Julian and Rachel, too, for how she had behaved.

* * *

Julian and Rachel accepted Blair's apology. Julian immediately understood after bearing witness to the events of the day before, but Rachel took a moment longer to accept. Blair wished she had first apologized to her privately, but it was what it was. She resolved to buy Rachel a nice gift or something as an additional component of her apology.

Sitting and watching Rachel, Julian, and Andrew laugh, as they all used to before everything with Hudson had happened, Blair realized she didn't deserve any of them as friends, but she was grateful to have them, nonetheless—more than they would ever know.

Chapter 46

Little Mouse

Andrew and Blair spoke with Ms. Holland after school. It was brief. She told them that Hudson would be transferring to another school—St. John's—for the remainder of the year. Blair remembered that he'd mentioned that was where his friend went—the one who had hosted the bonfire she didn't go to.

Ms. Holland asked how they were doing and reassured them that they could use the school's counseling services or come to her if they needed to.

Leaving school that afternoon, Blair checked her phone. Natalie had sent her a message, checking in. It was too upbeat for her to know about what had happened with Hudson, and of course, Angela wouldn't have told her—although she should have.

Blair didn't feel like rehashing the details to her, so she just responded with a funny picture.

Natalie: *Anything from Columbia yet?*

Blair: *Not yet.*
Natalie: *And what about Andrew?*
Blair: *Same.*
Natalie: *Okay. Keep me posted. I love and miss you both.*

Blair smiled at Natalie saying that. It was unsurprising that she said she loved Andrew, but it was still heartwarming.

Once they were in her driveway, Blair began to gather her things. Andrew reached for the ignition, but stopped.

"Your … your parents aren't home, are they?"

Blair blinked over at Andrew. He had been here the previous two days. On Monday, they'd had makeup sex and gotten back together, and yesterday, he had stayed after John and Angela left, talking and snuggling.

"My mom has a big case they're working on, so she said she won't be home all week."

Andrew's hand rested on his thigh, and he lowered his head, as if waiting. Through the haze and drama of all that had happened, Blair realized that while it had only been two days since they were back together, Andrew was breaking his rule of not seeing her until Friday afternoons. She didn't know what to make of that.

"Don't you have homework to do?" she asked.

"I can do it later," he said.

"Are you… Do you want to come in?"

"If it's okay," he said, looking over at her.

* * *

After sex, Blair and Andrew decided to take a shower together.

If It All Fades Away

"You sure your mom isn't going to come home randomly?" Andrew asked, standing by as the water ran hot.

"Well, I mean, I suppose she could come home at any time, but why would she? She's got that apartment in the city I've never seen, plus she's fucking that John guy." Blair held her hand out to the shower's streaming water to test its temperature.

"Wait—*what*?"

Blair told Andrew about all that she had put together, plus John being creepy towards her at Christmas Mass while giving her his business card.

Andrew's pupils narrowed as he shook his head.

"It's ready," Blair said, stepping into the shower. "You can get in."

Andrew put one foot forward, his muscular thigh flexing as he did. They rinsed off together, allowing hot water to pour over them. As Blair began shampooing her hair, Andrew's mouth found the curve of her neck from behind.

"Stop," she giggled, curling into him.

"I can't," he said. "You taste too good."

"You don't taste shampoo?"

"No," Andrew said. "Just you."

Blair turned her head towards Andrew, their mouths meeting. Andrew removed the showerhead nozzle and rinsed Blair's hair. She aided his efforts by running her fingers through until all the shampoo was gone.

When Andrew started shampooing his own hair, Blair let out a surprised gasp.

"What?" Andrew asked.

"Your ears!"

Andrew instantly became self-conscious, slapping both hands to his ears.

"No, don't," Blair said, pulling his hands away. "I love them! You look like a little mouse. *My* little mouse." She stood on her tiptoes and kissed him.

Andrew smiled and stepped into the stream, washing the shampoo away.

After they finished, Blair towel-dried her hair and sifted through the clothes in her closet. Andrew came up behind her, towel wrapped around his waist. He put his arms around her.

"I can't wait for prom," he said, looking at her Winter Wonderland dress.

"Oh… Yeah, gosh, I forgot about that." Blair's face fell slightly. "I'll need a dress for that, too, I guess."

"I want to take you to this dress shop in Detroit," he said.

"What?" Blair turned to look at him.

"It's a bigger store than Carmen's. I thought it would be fun to make a day out of it. Go to Somerset Mall."

"Oh my gosh, I've never been!" Blair brought her hand to her mouth. "Rachel kinda brags about it now and again when she visits her grandma down there, and I've always been a bit jealous that I could never go."

Andrew scooped Blair up and kissed her as she shrieked and giggled.

* * *

After dinner, Andrew and Blair went to a movie. Even though it was a Wednesday night, he insisted on taking her, and Blair was happy about that. It was much easier to "sneak away" on a weeknight than to try to go on a weekend date.

During the movie, Andrew reached over and interlaced his fingers with Blair's. She turned and smiled at him as he brought her hand up to kiss the back of it.

Blair couldn't wait until she graduated, couldn't wait to

If It All Fades Away

move out. They were at the end of January now. As she felt Andrew's fingers linked with her own, she thought maybe, just maybe, they could find a place together after graduation. Before, the thought of moving in together had seemed like it needed to wait until college, but maybe he wouldn't be opposed to the idea now that things had shifted with him.

On their way back to her house, Blair broached the topic.

"Do you think…" she began. "What are your thoughts on us moving in together after we graduate?"

Andrew glanced at her, then back to the road. "You mean like an apartment?"

"Yeah."

Andrew sighed deeply, his grip tightening on the steering wheel. "I had asked my parents about you moving in with us, actually."

"You did?"

"Yeah. And I mean, technically, there isn't anything stopping you, because you're seventeen. There's a weird loophole in Michigan law that allows seventeen-year-old kids to move out, but at the same time, their parents are still financially responsible and obligated to them until they're eighteen. If you run away or something though—not saying you would do that—"

"Trust me, I've thought about it," Blair huffed.

"If you ran away… It would depend on the police officer if your parents called, but technically, they can't force you to go back home. So … either way, moving out is almost a non-issue, from what I've read."

Blair sat with her hands in her lap like a child. "What did your parents say?" Andrew was quiet. "They said…"

Andrew's jaw worked. "They said it would be hard to get you out of here now—that if you did want to leave, waiting until you turned eighteen would be the best choice. Less …

messy. And you could sign legal documents and whatnot as an adult."

Andrew paused momentarily, as if he were leaving something heavy unsaid.

"What is it?" Blair asked.

"I got mad at them," he said quietly. "Because we could easily have you come and live with us, and they just ... said you needed to have a job, still needed your driver's license, that you should pay rent—"

Blair knew all of those things to be true, even if it stung—that she was practically useless as far as *actually* trying to become an adult went.

"Let's, uh ... let's just say I didn't handle hearing that very well."

Blair's eyes became heavy. She was both hurt and embarrassed that his parents were speaking the truth about what she already knew—what Andrew logically knew—but it was still painful to hear.

"They're not wrong. I can't do shit on my own. And I do need my driver's license."

Andrew pulled into the parking lot of a small liquor store near her house. "Sorry, I can't talk about important stuff like this while driving, and we're close to your house already."

"It's fine," Blair mumbled.

"You shouldn't have to pay rent at our house, Blair," Andrew said. "That's absolutely ridiculous. And they know it. I mean, look at where we live. My mom has old money from her great-grandfather, for God's sake."

"I wouldn't feel good if I was just freeloading off of you guys anyway, though."

"You wouldn't be." Andrew turned the heater up slightly.

"I would. And I should get a job. I don't want handouts. I just ... I just want to get the hell out of my parents' house. I should have been working since I turned sixteen, but I was too chickenshit to go and apply for a job."

"And why wouldn't you be?" Andrew turned his body toward her. "Your parents have neglected you most of your life, and hurt you, too—and your self-image is dog shit—no offense…" Andrew gestured over to her, taking a breath. "So, why on Earth would you, or anyone else, expect you to have the courage to go out and put yourself in unknown and vulnerable situations that require transportation, people skills, and the ability to juggle a work and school schedule?"

Blair's eyes spilled over.

"You're too hard on yourself, Blair. No one should ask you to do anything you've been ill-prepared to do. That's why I got so mad at my mom and dad. They think you can just go out there and do it, and they don't realize how goddamned privileged that is."

Andrew stopped himself to catch his breath. He was visibly worked up. "The job thing… God, it made me mad—"

"Andrew," Blair said, as if to soothe him. "There're people who have it way worse than I do, who have to do it and don't have a choice."

"But you *do* have a choice." Andrew's hands shot out in desperation in front of him, his way of speaking when passionate about something. "You have me. You have a choice."

"Imagine the people who aren't so lucky, Andrew," Blair said. "I'll… It's fine. I can make it until I graduate. It's not that big of a deal. My parents really aren't that bad."

"*Yes*, they are!" Andrew shouted. Blair flinched. "I'm sorry." He stopped himself, closing his eyes and taking steadying breaths. Blair watched as a few cars came and went.

"We have the *means*, we have the *money*—and yet, they still don't want to help you."

Blair wasn't going to counter Andrew anymore. She could tell how upset he was getting, how helpless he was starting to feel yet again. She didn't like seeing him like this.

Chapter 47

Tick-Tock

On Thursday and Friday, Andrew was at Blair's again in the afternoon. They watched movies, had sex, and snuggled. On Friday evening, Andrew made breakfast for dinner for her.

It was pure bliss.

"I'll see you at Mass?" Blair asked Andrew at the door afterward.

"Yeah," he said, leaning down to kiss her.

Saturday, Blair did her usual chores. Her father was watching TV and drinking beer as she timidly worked around him.

Doing laundry in the basement, Blair glanced over to the stack of boxes in the corner. Her name was written in permanent marker, waving at her. The findings were still itching at the back of her mind.

Blair was a bit anxious, as she hadn't seen Angela all week—not since the Hudson incident on Tuesday. She also hadn't texted Blair anything else except to inform her that he had been expelled. Blair worried that she was receiving an

Angela Silent Treatment—either because of Hudson, or it had something to do with John knowing about Chicago.

Andrew had been a welcome distraction, but now that it was the weekend, her anxiety about her mother was really beginning to set in. Typically, her mother came home on the weekends.

Blair brought the folded laundry upstairs in a basket. She paused, debating whether or not to ask.

"Do you…" She hesitated. "Do you know if Mom is coming home today?"

At first, her father remained expressionless in front of the television. Blair opened her mouth to speak again.

"She's got that big case." He paused, taking a drink. "That's all I know." Another moment of silence, the television the only sound. "She's probably off slamming martinis with that prick in his thousand-dollar suit somewhere."

Blair bristled at the mention of John.

So, he knew. Her father absolutely *knew*—and he more or less didn't care.

Blair said nothing as she took the basket to her bedroom, put her clothes away first, and then went to her parents' room. She wondered why they even bothered. Why stay together if they were so miserable? Angela wasn't even visible at church anymore, and Blair wasn't with her in the courtroom, either. Their attendance at Christmas Mass was the first family function they had attended together in a long time.

She thought of the pictures she had seen of her parents when they were younger—how handsome her father looked, and how undeniably smoking hot Angela was. They both were stupidly good-looking. But they had been forced to marry when they got pregnant, and her father later inherited the house. Angela, refusing to be a knocked-up failure—always the golden child compared to Natalie—had gone on to

If It All Fades Away

complete her paralegal degree. Blair figured Angela would mold herself to whatever narrative earned her the most praise. She could still wear a wedding ring, boasting of her daughter and husband when it served her, casting them off when they didn't—which it seemed was most of the time.

* * *

Blair went to Mass on Sunday and physically cringed, head turned away, shoulders up to her ears when Andrew's parents walked in. He spoke to his parents briefly and then left them to sit with her as they continued to their usual pew.

So, they did hate her.

Andrew smiled at her as he sat in a back-row pew beside her. His smile was an apparent attempt to cover for his parents' discontent with her. It made Blair physically ill. The fact that they didn't think she was worthy of Andrew was only further confirmation that she wasn't—not after what she had done. Blair noted the energy from Lily as she glanced at her; she clearly felt some type of way about Blair, that perhaps Andrew was being influenced or corrupted by her, and she disapproved. But Andrew had already long since fallen for Blair. Yet she didn't want him to become alienated from his parents. If anything, she wanted to be a part of their family.

Andrew's departure from them to sit with Blair, however, was a welcome yet somber statement to them that he would choose her, should it come down to it.

At the end of Mass, Blair went to the main entrance to leave. She hugged Andrew off to the side a bit, so his parents wouldn't see. Blair shivered and glanced over to the window in the corner. "Christ, they really need to fix that window," she remarked, putting her coat on.

Andrew glanced over to the duct-taped window. "Wow... That's not exactly sealed up well, is it?"

"All this big money they have, and yet they can't fix a window that could let a homeless person or serial killer in at any time."

Andrew laughed. He leaned in to give her a final hug as the young ushers came to open the large wooden doors.

"I'll see you tomorrow," he said with a stolen peck on her cheek.

"I love you," Blair said.

Andrew smiled. "I love you, too."

* * *

On Monday, Blair felt awkward at lunch. She had noticed that Rachel remained polite with her, but not friendly—not like a best friend should be. She could tell by her body language and the way she gave a closed-lipped smile. Rachel mainly spoke with Andrew and Julian, but ultimately avoided responding to Blair's jokes and conversation starters.

When the bell rang to signal the end of lunch, Blair's stomach tightened as Rachel quickly got up and went over to empty her tray with Julian. Andrew was behind her.

"I'll catch up with you later. I have to talk to Rachel," she told a quizzical Andrew. He nodded.

Rachel had already grabbed her backpack from the backpack mountain and was down the hallway with Julian.

"Rachel!" Blair called.

Rachel and Julian turned to look; she had interrupted their conversation. Rachel tried to keep walking, but Julian stopped completely. Blair caught up to them.

"Hey, can I talk to you for a second?" she asked.

Rachel's eyes shifted. Blair glanced at Julian, and he got the hint to leave.

"Sure," Rachel said, her voice cold.

Blair pulled her aside, in a corner near the sophomore lockers. She exhaled an uneven breath.

"I just want to say…" Blair began. She was breathing heavily from the anxiety and rushing up to Rachel and Julian. "This is heavy," she mumbled, removing her backpack. Rachel clutched both straps of hers.

Blair swallowed and stood up straight, looking at her friend now. "Rachel, I just want to say, I'm very sorry for how I've treated you recently."

Rachel, sensitive and sweet, changed in demeanor almost instantly.

"I'm sorry I ignored your texts, and for being a bitch and sitting with Hudson even though it was stressful for you—and Julian and Andrew—and I just—"

Blair felt her eyes getting watery. She looked away when she saw that Rachel's eyes were also glassy. "I was going through a tough time with the Claire shit and Andrew, but I know that's not an excuse for shutting you out and ignoring you. And I'm—" Blair's voice cracked as she looked down. "I'm very sorry."

She couldn't look up—not yet.

Silence.

Rachel was a simple person. She didn't hold grudges if you sincerely apologized, and she didn't get mean with people. She just … became distant. Her parents, Vietnamese refugees who'd had her when they were a bit older, spoke plainly and directly—a trait that Rachel had been raised with.

"I accept your apology," Rachel said.

Blair wasn't good at hugs. The last time she'd hugged Rachel was in the bathroom during Mass before she decided to get them both away from Claire. She wanted to hug Rachel, though. It was a strange feeling, but one she was becoming used to from all of Andrew's hugs. It felt right, and Blair was confident she wouldn't be rejected as she moved in to embrace Rachel. The two cried silently together.

"I'm a shitty friend, but I love you," Blair said.

Rachel shuddered. The sophomores trickling away from their lockers for fifth period were starting to stare at them, but Blair didn't care.

"You're not a shitty friend, Blair," Rachel said.

The two held each other for a long moment, and then Blair made a joke.

"For all the problems he's caused us, I probably should have bitten Hudson's dick off though, don't you think?" Blair mused.

Rachel laughed as they pulled apart. "You forgot about Claire, too."

"I wish you were there to see her face when Andrew told her to go screw herself."

The stories of Hudson and Claire had been rehashed at least two to three times at their lunch table, but Rachel had remained unmoved until now, in the context of Blair not apologizing to her. The energy was lighter now, and Blair felt relieved to see her best friend from childhood forgive her. She may not have earned it entirely, but she was genuinely sorry, and Rachel had always been a little too quick to forgive people in general. But they also both knew, deep down inside, that Blair was the only person who did not exploit that about her character. If Blair was sorry, she was genuinely sorry; if Rachel forgave, she had truly forgiven.

All was right in Blair's world at that moment.

After that, Blair told Rachel what Andrew had said about going to Detroit to shop for prom dresses. Soon, the two were plotting a double date for shopping, dinner, and dress selection.

* * *

Blair came home a little later that afternoon, as she and Andrew had hung out in Ms. Holland's room for at least an hour, talking and laughing. They joked about what a piece of crap rich prick Hudson was. Blair didn't realize just how late it was until the winter sun had begun to set behind the school building. She had largely kept the conversation going, not wanting to go home.

Blair's stomach clenched. She still hadn't heard from her mother in almost a week. Her text messages on Saturday and Sunday went unanswered. And that was how Blair knew for sure that she was getting the silent treatment—but for what, exactly, she couldn't pinpoint. And it made her sick to her stomach with anxiety now.

Blair waved to Andrew, feeling that he shouldn't be over today—not with Angela gone for so long. She could unpredictably be home on Mondays, and perhaps could be there this afternoon. Blair inhaled deeply, closing her eyes as she turned her house key in the tumbler and slowly opened the door.

The wall clock was the first thing she heard.

Tick...

Tock...

Tick...

Tock...

Tick...

Tock...

As Blair came past the door, the blinds were closed in the

living room, giving the illusion that no one was there. However, Blair saw that someone was.

Angela Simons.

She wasn't sitting on the couch as usual, sipping coffee. And she wasn't sitting in her designated recliner. She was sitting, arms on both armrests, in Blair's father's recliner. She never sat in her father's recliner. Ever.

Blair knew then that something awful awaited her.

Chapter 48

Mother

Blair closed the door, removed her shoes, and turned on the light switch for the lamps in the living room. She removed her bag from her shoulders and set it near the door, shaking, aware that her mother was watching her every move. When Blair was finished, she stood facing her mother at the edge of the living room.

Blair went to speak, but before she could, her mother grabbed a Ziploc bag that had been sitting tucked between her leg and the recliner. Blair couldn't make out what it was immediately, but as her mother strode over to her, holding it out, she realized with mounting terror that it was her vibrator placed inside—like some dangerous specimen not to be handled.

"You want to explain this?" her mother demanded.

"... It's a vibrator?" she said, confused. Surely this wasn't what Angela was sitting and seething over in the dark.

"Where did you get it?" Angela asked, still holding the bag out in front of Blair's face.

"With Andrew and Natalie when she came to visit," Blair

said before she could catch herself. Her mother didn't know that Andrew had met up with them at the mall.

Angela's arm lowered slightly. "Uh-huh. So, you guys met up to plot your escape to Chicago?"

Blair knew to tread lightly. "Aunt Natalie just said we should invite him out for lunch."

"When were you going to tell me you applied to Columbia?" her mother snapped.

Blair then noticed that her mother's other hand was holding something else as she crossed her arms.

"I..." Blair swallowed. "I wanted to wait until I got accepted. I ... I didn't want you to be disappointed if I didn't get in."

Blair thought that maybe that sounded believable. And maybe it was half true—she didn't want her mother to weaponize it against her if she didn't get in, reminding her of how stupid she was and what a failure she was when others weren't around for Angela to pretend otherwise. Blair's hands trembled.

Her mother twisted her lip, arms still crossed, until she held out the other item she had been holding.

It was John J. Turner's business card.

"And you want to explain how you got this, and why it was next to your *vibrator* under your mattress?"

Blair hadn't used her vibrator since she'd stuffed John's card into her bed on the day of the Hudson incident. She didn't want to see his name staring back at her.

"He gave it to me at Christmas Mass," Blair admitted. She didn't know what came over her, but she couldn't help but laugh a little. Her mother's interrogation was suddenly weirdly absurd and funny, with Blair's vibrator dangling in her hand like a contaminated specimen.

If It All Fades Away

It was funny until Angela dropped the bag to the floor and smacked Blair across the face—hard.

It was the hardest Blair had ever been hit by her. Her cheek stung, and her ear started to ring, and ring, and *ring*.

As the ringing dissipated, Blair instinctively brought her hand up to her face, flinching away from her mother.

"I'm sorry," Angela said, *ever* so sweetly. "Do you want to try that again?" Her head followed where Blair had shifted to look—anywhere but at her mother's face.

"I don't—" Blair choked out. "I don't know what you mean."

Her mother held out the card again. "*When* did he give this to you?"

"I … I just told you," Blair said, her voice incredibly small.

"You think I'm stupid, don't you?" Angela growled.

"He gave it to me while you were talking to his wife."

Blair looked at her mother with pleading eyes, hoping she would realize she was telling the truth. But they only narrowed further, and she looked *furious* at the realization that John had slipped Blair his business card right under her nose.

"What did he say to you?"

Blair lowered her hand, trying to stand up straighter to speak. She cleared her throat. "He … he just asked me where I planned to go to college, and said he has a friend who lives in Chicago. And then … he—he—"

Blair couldn't speak, her heart pounding and pounding. Her hands were shaking—her whole *body* was shaking. Her ear and the side of her head hurt from the strike.

She was trying. She was really trying. Trying to find the right words. Trying to ensure that she didn't mess up what she said or didn't say. Trying to be careful. Trying not to infuriate her mother further.

"Spit it out," Angela said. "*What* did he *say* to you when he gave this to you?"

"He just said to let him know if I needed any legal help in the future."

Blair couldn't understand what was wrong with that. She had given the right answer, and it still didn't matter—because Angela struck her again, even harder.

"You fucking *whore*," her mother spat.

"That's all he said to me, I swear!" Blair cried, falling to the floor.

"You little bitch. You're a *whore*, and you always have been. You think I gave a shit about you getting on birth control so you could screw your boyfriend, who's obviously too good for you? I did it so you wouldn't get knocked up and make a fool out of me—and yet here you are, whoring yourself out some more."

"I'm *sorry*! I didn't do anything—I didn't call him or anything!"

Angela grabbed Blair by her hair, jerking her head back.

"You've taken so much from me. It's too bad you didn't die like you were supposed to when you were a baby—"

Blair's neck hurt. Everything hurt. "Mom, I'm *sorry*!" she cried, her voice pleading.

"You want to keep taking from me? I can take from you just as easily," Angela said, pushing Blair back by the hold of her hair. With the imbalance, she fell backward.

"*Conniving whore,*" her mother breathed, storming off to the kitchen.

Blair heard her rummaging around in the junk drawer. She curled up into a ball on the floor. She would stay there

If It All Fades Away

and do whatever her mother wanted her to do to get her to stop. She could be a good ball. She could.

Blair curled up as tightly as possible as she heard her mother stomp back over to her. Blair covered her head with both arms, knees to chest. Angela was going upstairs, and when Blair opened her eyes to watch her mother ascend, she saw a pair of scissors in her hand.

Blair realized with utter horror where her mother was going.

No.

No, no, no...

It was the reason she had kept it at Andrew's. It was the reason she had then kept it at Rachel's. It was the reason she had that weird feeling, that pit in her stomach, that *knowing* that she should not have kept it at home.

Her dress.

That was where Angela was heading now.

And then, something inside Blair snapped.

She charged up the stairs.

No.

Angela wasn't going to ruin her favorite memory with Andrew. Everything about that night had been perfect. Them dancing together under the lights, there with friends. Andrew confessing that he loved her and wanted to spend the rest of his life with her, and then them losing their virginity together in the most beautiful way possible.

"No!" Blair bawled, stumbling up the steps as Angela rounded the corner to stalk down the hallway.

Her mother was there before she could stop her. Blair rushed to her room and saw her opening the closet door, jerking the string to turn the light on.

Blair grabbed her arm.

Angela turned with fury and surprise. She was at Blair's

throat immediately with one hand, the scissors held high in the other.

She was fast. Frighteningly fast.

Angela shoved Blair up against the bedroom door by her throat, slamming it shut with the force and weight of Blair's body.

"I'll fucking *kill you* if you touch me again," Angela breathed.

Blair brought both hands up to her throat. She knew that Angela meant it.

With the scissors still raised, Blair felt constricting pressure on her trachea, Angela's manicured nails stabbing into her neck like tiny knives. She couldn't breathe.

When Angela saw that Blair understood, she released her grip. Blair slumped to the floor, coughing and choking.

Angela turned back to the closet and jerked the dress from its hanger. Standing there rigid, she *ripped* the fabric bag open with her bare hands, angrily snatching the sparkling blue dress from its protective sheath. She started trying to cut it up, but the scissors weren't made for fabric. She swore under her breath, then threw the scissors down and ripped the dress apart at its weaker points.

It was the most awful sound Blair had ever heard in her entire life. At that moment, she wished she couldn't even hear —wished that her ears could be spared the reality of such awfulness.

"Conniving whore," her mother repeated. "And this harlot dress you had him buy for you, like the *prostitute* that you are—"

Fabric ripped mercilessly, and sparkles were now floating through the air. Blair looked up at her mother, the bun in her hair now sagging. Angela didn't even appear human as she continued her assault. Maybe she never had been.

If It All Fades Away

The only thing Blair knew now was that whatever her mother was, she had to run. Run for her life. Because there was no telling what Angela was going to do next.

Blair scrambled to her feet and swung her bedroom door open as fast as possible. Running down the hallway, she slipped in her stockings on the hardwood floor. Her phone clattered out of her skirt pocket. And just as she turned back to try to grab it, Angela came after her.

"You're not going *anywhere*!" she shouted.

Blair practically tumbled down the stairs, Angela stomping down after her.

When Blair reached the base of the steps, she swiped up her Mary Janes and fumbled to open the front door, cursing herself for locking it behind her out of habit when she'd entered the house.

The winter air hit her like another slap in the face. Blair ran, and then ran some more.

"You won't get far!" Angela called, her voice echoing off the porch walls and garage door. "I'm calling the cops right now!"

Blair felt terror at the thought of the police coming to get her. She remembered what Andrew had said: technically, they couldn't force her to return home. But in her line of work, Angela was chummy with many local police, so she could probably get them to do anything.

Blair couldn't think about that now—not as her feet stomped across the snow-covered grass and ice-slick concrete down the street.

Not as she ran for her life.

Chapter 49

Waiting

Andrew was eating dinner when he felt a sudden, excruciating pain in his chest and stomach.

"Are you okay, dear?" Lily asked immediately.

Andrew's ears were ringing, painfully. He could barely hear her.

"What?" he asked, almost annoyed.

Lily frowned. "Is everything okay? You look pale."

Andrew swallowed. "Fine," he lied. "Can I save this for later? I'm still full from lunch."

His mother gave a half-convinced smile. "Of course, dear."

Andrew put his food away in a glass container and quietly exited the kitchen. Things had been tense at the Stormant household. Ever since he had tried to convince his parents to let Blair move in with them. Ever since he had come home with scratch marks on his face.

Upstairs, Andrew lay on his bed, gazing at the ceiling. He still felt the pain in his chest and gut, his left ear still ringing—and he thought about the saying that if your ears were ringing, it meant someone was talking about you—except he knew that wasn't what was happening here. He knew that something was happening with Blair. It was the same feeling he had felt when she went to talk to Hudson alone. And then the next day, it had intensified into a blazing white light, a feeling beyond reason, that something awful was taking place in the girls' locker room. When his brain made the connection (apart from the obvious clues that it must have been Hudson), he took off running, sprinting the short distance across the gymnasium.

It was *that* feeling again. Only this was the worst of them.

Andrew rolled over and texted Blair, hoping he would get a response sooner rather than later. He became anxious when he didn't hear from her after a while. He tried to call her, but it just went straight to voicemail. Andrew was half tempted to go back to her house, to see if she was alright, but he didn't want to upset Lily any more than he already had. She had remained silently upset over the past week that he was going to Blair's after school now (and not telling her) and wasn't coming home to dutifully finish his homework and work on extra credit projects as he usually did.

Andrew was tired of being good, if he had to admit it. He was tired of constantly studying, reading, and writing, of going above and beyond when he was so close to the end of high school. There would be tons more work in medical school, and Andrew wondered if he had what it took to endure it, if he was already feeling this burnt out at eighteen.

One of his teachers had joked that he could literally fail the midterm exam or not take it and still get an A in the class. His classmates laughed, but not in a teasing way. Andrew liked that praise, yet he wanted to tell them he *couldn't* fail—that his anxiety over doing well meant failing wasn't an option. Ever.

Things had begun to shift for him when Blair tried to tell

him that the *1984* assignment wasn't that serious. He had struggled with the assignment, finding information online with analysis that was so obvious, he knew he couldn't use it. He'd wanted to ask Blair what she thought, but he would have had to admit that he watched the movie without her—which he'd instantly regretted. It was a lonely experience, watching it on their giant flatscreen TV in the entertainment room that weekend, wishing she were there. Wishing he could snuggle with her, smell her hair, and maybe even mess around a bit.

Andrew's mind began to race. The physical sensations had waned a bit, but now he was suddenly very cold, his feet especially. He crawled under his thick blankets and began rubbing them together. He checked the remote near his bed for temperature controls and increased the heat.

Andrew closed his eyes, shivering and worried, his mind turning over and over. He tried not to replay his argument with his parents last week, how Lily and Henry's eyes had widened at hearing him swear and raise his voice. He knew he'd scared them a little, but he couldn't help it. He loved Blair; he wanted to get her out of that hell she was living in, to come live with them. Andrew had snapped when he heard Lily start rattling on about Blair needing to get a job and pay rent. His father then firmly told him to get it together.

It had ultimately culminated in Andrew storming off.

Andrew refused to apologize to either of them, only validated further the next day when he saw Lily's eyes fill with genuine fear as they watched Angela dig into Mr. Davis—taunting him, mocking him, laying out how she would destroy his reputation, possibly even get him charged for knowingly allowing a sexual predator to stay enrolled at St. Michael's.

Andrew's feet eventually began to warm up, and he hoped

If It All Fades Away

that whatever was happening with Blair, she was okay. He had not stopped staring at his phone, hoping and praying for a response.

But it never came. Not within the next hour, or two, or three. As the night darkened, Andrew got ready for bed, feeling completely sick with worry.

All he could do was wait.

Chapter 50

Rumination

Blair's feet were soaked from the snow and hurt from running on concrete. It was also icy in some parts. About four houses down, she shakily put her Mary Janes on, red fingers numb from the cold. She had left her coat on the arm of the sofa; she just had her skirt, blouse, and green school sweater on. Blair was thankful it was wool, likely the only thing keeping her warm. Once her shoes were on, she continued to run. She kept glancing behind her, sure that her mother might chase after her. Blair didn't have her phone, didn't have a coat—she didn't have anything but the clothes on her back.

As she rounded the curve of their subdivision, Blair tried to think of where she would go. Andrew lived twenty minutes away by car, and with how cold it was outside—cold enough to see her breath, feet now soaked from the snow—she wouldn't make it very far, just like her mother had said.

The panic of the police coming to fetch her and taking her back home, only for her mother to manage an elaborate and believable lie, was enough to make Blair run faster. She had to get out of their subdivision. At the end of the street, where

If It All Fades Away

it met a main road, Blair ran across, taking to another side street. Running also kept her as warm as possible.

Blair remembered from a documentary how you could go for about two weeks without food, and three days without water, but without heat, you could die very quickly. Becoming wet in the cold was a death sentence if it wasn't remedied immediately.

Rachel lived farther away than Andrew did, about thirty minutes, on the outskirts of town. Blair had nowhere to go. Where could she go? She couldn't go to the local liquor and grocery store. If she did and tried to call for help, she'd probably just sound hysterical. There was no telling what the police officer would do. She couldn't risk it.

The closest place she was familiar with was St. Michael's.
St. Michael's...

The realization flooded her with both hope and fear.

The window. The one that hadn't been fixed. She could enter that way. She could stay there until she could gather her thoughts and try to figure out a way to contact Andrew. She could get warm and take her stockings off to dry, at least.

Blair ran faster now that she had a place to go.

She arrived at the church and school. It was dark, except for a light illuminating the church's steps. The busted window was a little off the ground, but not impossible to get to. Blair felt like a creep, scurrying across the snow and then making her way to the side of the brick building. She came to the window and hesitated, but didn't have time to think. A car drove by on the road, causing Blair to duck down. She touched the rotting wood of the window frame, dug her fingernails into the side, and then pulled out slightly. Worried she might be making too much noise, she went slowly. Her fingers, however, had no feeling and demanded that she go faster. She had to hurry. As she pulled up with one swift motion, some of the wood fell away, and the duct tape made a weird peeling noise. Blair hoisted herself up and through the opening.

She went slowly over the threshold, her eyes transfixed on the inside of the church. It was completely dark, except for a soft light emanating from underneath the second double doors, no doubt from the altar, illuminating the cross.

Blair steadied her hands on the stair landing, bringing her legs through. She paused, waiting for any sound to alert someone that she had just broken into the church.

Father Donovan and Sister Eugene lived in the rectory, attached beyond the reception area in the back of the church. Surely, neither of them could hear her.

Why didn't she ring at the reception area? Blair felt stupid for crawling through a window, but there was no turning back now. She just needed to get warm. She was cold. So cold. Frozen.

She did her best with red, numb fingers to draw the window back in, the top hanging by its old hinge. She replaced the less-than-sticky duct tape around the edges. Blair removed her shoes on the landing, then her socks. She carried them in her hand and slowly crept to the second entrance of the church. She hesitated, then carefully opened one of the double doors, just enough to slide through.

The cross was illuminated, just as she had thought.

Blair paused, considering her options. There was no telephone inside the church, and she knew the doors to the reception area behind the altar would be locked.

Looking to her left, she saw the cry room. It was her only hope. She prayed the door wouldn't be locked. Padding over with bare feet on the tiled floor, she exhaled, then gave the door a timid pull, not expecting much. But to her surprise, it was unlocked. Her mind had a moment of triumphant joy.

If It All Fades Away

Blair inched her way through the opening, then paused once inside. She looked around. She had no idea what she was thinking when she ran away from home. She wasn't thinking at all, just running, escaping. Now here she was. It had already been dark when she left. She glanced at the wall clock up above. She would have a long night if she planned to stay here. But with no way to contact Andrew, she had no choice but to wait until morning.

How on earth was she going to sleep in here? She immediately inched over to the old wall heater and sat, putting her feet to it, warming up. It felt amazing, though it almost hurt, since she had been so frigid.

Blair gently placed her Mary Janes in front of the heater, draping her completely soaked stockings over the foot openings to dry. After some time, now that she was warm and her adrenaline had subsided, Blair's body registered that she was thirsty, hungry, and had to pee. She went to the small bathroom attached to the cry room. Blair took a drink of water from the sink after she washed her hands, noting how eerie it was to be in the dark. She always cleaned this bathroom in the daylight.

Blair considered her options. She'd have to wait until morning to see Andrew or Ms. Holland. As much as she liked Father Donovan, she wasn't comfortable having him be privy to the situation with her mother. Not when he wasn't already familiar.

Blair ultimately decided to sleep, to pass the time. It was going to be a very long night.

She went over to an old cupboard and found two small blankets, no doubt meant for babies to play on. She grabbed them and a few stuffed animals, then crawled under one of the two pews in the room. It was dark and lonely, but Blair felt safe for the first time since escaping her house. She used the stuffed animals as pillows and covered up with the small blankets as much as possible. Finally settled, Blair stared out at the wooden wall in front of her, the light of the altar shining through the glass window above.

The shock and absurdity of what had occurred finally hit her. She was lying with some stuffed animals and baby blankets under a pew in the cry room of St. Michael's, where she had just broken in through a busted window, because her mother had threatened to kill her with a pair of scissors while strangling her.

Jesus.

Blair closed her eyes, still a little puffy from all the crying with her mother, and as exhausted as she felt, she was thankful that sleep came quickly.

* * *

Andrew slept like shit. He awoke a few hours later, a little past midnight, immediately checking his phone.

Still nothing from Blair.

Andrew stared at her name in his messages. He decided to pass the time by deleting old messages, hoping by chance that he would finally get one from Blair. He went through the shortlist of names in his message box. *Claire Miller* was about four or five names down.

Andrew paused. He clicked on the bar containing their exchange; he hadn't looked at it since he was in the Bahamas.

It started innocently enough. Claire said, *Sorry to bother you, but I had a question about this equation and was wondering if you could help me.*

Andrew took a look. The solution was easy. He suspected now that she had already known the answer. He remembered

If It All Fades Away

feeling confused about why she was messaging him instead of others in their calc group.

Claire: *Omg thx so much :) Ur such a big help*
    Andrew: *No prob*
    Claire: *So, what are you up to? :)*
    Andrew: *Just on vacation with my parents*
    Claire: *O rly? Where at?*
    Andrew: *Bahamas*
    Claire: *Ugh, I'm so jealous. I've always wanted to go, but we usually just go to Cancun.*
    Claire: *wish I was there ;)*
    Andrew: *It's not anything special, really*
    Claire: *Really? Why not?*
    Andrew: *It's just me and my parents*
    Claire: *Oh... Blair couldn't go?*
    Claire: *So how r u going to pass the time?*
    Andrew: *drinking*
    Claire: *wait, u drink?!*
    Andrew: *occasionally*
    Claire: *r u drinking now? I bet the Bahamas has some amazing cocktails like Cancun does*
    Andrew: *sure*
    Claire: *I'm drinking right now too ;)*
    Andrew: *cool*
    Claire: *hey can I ask u something?*
    Andrew: *shoot*
    Claire: *Can u send me a pic of ... well u know*
    Andrew: *??*
    Claire: *Oh come on, don't play dumb*
    Claire: *fine, if ur going to make me spell it out & beg*

Andrew: *sorry i'm kinda fucked up right now :(i don't know what u mean*

Claire: *a dick pic, Stormant. Geez*

Andrew: *:(i'm too drunk and i don't think Blair would like that*

Claire: *r u saying u *wouldn't* be opposed to sending me one if u weren't drunk & if she wasn't ur gf?*

Claire: *She wouldn't have to know ;) I *promise* I won't share with anyone. It'd be just between u & me :P*

Claire: *Well, suit yourself, Stormant. I had fun chatting ;) have a good night xoxo*

Andrew felt awash with shame, both for being an idiot *and* a bad boyfriend for ever letting the conversation with Claire get that far in the first place. He was also somewhat horrified that he had no memory of her saying that Blair didn't have to know. He must have blacked out not long after.

He felt ashamed of everything that had happened afterwards, too. He had acted like a total asshole when Blair was brave enough to voice her anxieties about Claire's interest in him. Fucking Claire, whom he had no allegiance to whatsoever, and he was sitting on proof that she was precisely the kind of person Blair accused her of being—someone who had no conscience about casually soliciting dick pics from a disinterested classmate, another girl's boyfriend. HIM—Blair's actual boyfriend.

Andrew knew he had been trying to avoid conflict, but he could now see that some part of him had felt guilty. He didn't want to share and protect secrets with people like Claire—a bully, a true one. Someone who was probably just as dangerous as Hudson. Someone who had lived their whole spoiled-rotten life going unchallenged for their transgressions.

Andrew could take some small solace in the fact that he'd essentially told her to go fuck herself. He could also hope that just maybe there was some cosmic scale out there, a balance to be made—and perhaps Claire Miller was another person who'd had their spoiled scale tipped over after messing with Blair Simons.

Even though he and Blair were technically past it, everything made a little lap around in Andrew's head again, reminding him that he'd messed up. He caught himself ruminating. That was what his therapist said it was called when he got like this. He was rehashing events, conversations, and sometimes test answers he'd gotten wrong over and over again, as if thinking about them enough would somehow change the past, even though he knew that it couldn't.

Andrew tried to calm himself and use some techniques his therapist had taught him about a year ago—how to challenge unhealthy thought patterns, ask questions, and take situations as far as they logically could go. If this happened, then what? And after that, then what? What was the worst that could happen? What was the best that could happen?

Andrew deleted the messages with Claire without a second thought. He didn't like Claire. Never had. Never would. Not only was she not his type, in any sense of the word, she just ... wasn't Blair. No one was, or ever could be.

Blair.

Still sick with worry about her, Andrew tried to use the same therapy techniques he had learned to help manage his anxiety and rumination. What was the worst thing that could be happening to her right now? What was the best thing that could be happening to her right now?

Try as he might, Andrew could only focus on the worst.
He clicked his phone off and rolled over in bed.
Andrew would toss and turn all night, thinking of nothing and no one but Blair.

Chapter 51

Rooted

"Blair?" a voice said.

Blair jolted awake immediately. It was still early—that much she could tell by the light coming into the cry room.

"Blair, what on Earth are you doing here?" Father Donovan asked. "Is everything alright?"

Blair scrambled out from under the pew, her words a babbled mess as she tried to explain herself. She sat on the wooden structure, as if the stuffed animals and baby blankets underneath weren't evidence of her trespassing.

"I'm so sorry, Father, I—I—"

Father Donovan sat next to her. He placed a hand on her shoulder, reassuring her. Something about seeing a kind face she could trust, after the hatred and homicidal look she had seen in her mother's eyes, sent Blair spiraling. She started sobbing, spilling out the events of the night before. How she had gotten into the church. That she was so sorry for bothering him, that she was going to fix the window, that she should have gone to reception, that she—

"Blair," Father Donovan interrupted. "Just breathe. It's alright. *Breathe.* You're safe now. *You're safe here.*"

Blair was hyperventilating, but trying to do as he said. She took a deep, deep breath, shuddered, then started crying again. Father Donovan left briefly to fetch her some toilet paper to use as Kleenex. Then he just sat with her. He didn't touch her again, and that was fine by her. He had a good sense of what she needed, which was comforting. Blair imagined he'd seen a lot as a priest—giving people their last rites, praying with them, baptizing babies, visiting the sick, and washing feet as Jesus did.

When Blair was eventually able to compose herself, Father Donovan spoke again.

"I'm very sorry this has happened to you, Blair. But I want you to know that I'm pleased you felt like the church was a safe place to come."

That was nice to hear. Blair sniffled and blotted her eyes, then looked up at the clock. It was a quarter after seven.

She looked out at the church, the empty pews.

"How did you—"

"I open the doors every morning at seven," he told her with a smile.

Blair smiled back, then laughed at the irony of her crying in the cry room. Father Donovan didn't laugh, but kept his forever-kind smile.

"Oh, what a mess I've gotten myself into..." Blair breathed.

"Is there anyone I can call for you?" he asked.

Blair turned to look at him. "Andrew?" she said. "I left without grabbing my phone. He usually picks me up before school, and I definitely don't want him to go to my house right now."

If It All Fades Away

"We have a list of phone numbers in the rectory for all the families. Why don't we go there now?"

Blair felt her heart leap for the first time since this wretched experience began.

Father Donovan led her to the main office, where Sister Eugene was. She was just getting the day started, as Father Donovan had been, her eyes wide at seeing a disheveled Blair. Father Donovan asked if she could find the Stormant family's phone number; no verbal confirmation was needed that he would explain everything later. Once she had located the information, Sister Eugene asked if Blair wanted to call, but Blair shook her head. Sister Eugene didn't seem bothered by that.

Blair's heart thumped in her chest as Sister Eugene held the phone to her ear.

"It's ringing," she informed Blair. Tense, awkward silence, then a look of success. "Hello, Mrs. Stormant? Good morning. This is Sister Eugene from St. Michael's Church. How are you doing?"

Father Donovan suddenly took the phone, sparing Blair the disaster that surely would have come had she herself tried to speak with Lily.

"Hi, Lily. How are you?" he asked, his voice smooth as silk. "I hate to bother you this early in the morning, but there's a bit of a situation, and I was hoping you could help us out."

Blair wanted to cry at that—how Father Donovan had the authority to address Mrs. Stormant by her first name, conveying there was a situation that required her help, calling upon her to act. Sister Eugene motioned for Blair to sit in one of the chairs in front of her desk, which she did gladly. She rested her head in her hand, utterly exhausted, then noticed the small crystal dish of caramel candies. She was starving.

One glance at Sister Eugene, and her smile told Blair to help herself. The salty-sweet taste on her tongue was so welcome after the worst night of her life and not eating for so long.

Father Donovan kept the conversation upbeat and light, almost playful, acting as if anytime Lily could stop by to see him would be great. He said that Blair needed some help, and that he would happily explain everything in person should she stop by today.

Blair was shocked that Father Donovan never asked for Andrew. Something about his voice and how he spoke with Lily seemed familiar. It was as if he had known her for years, even though realistically, it had only been a little less than three months. Blair wondered if perhaps Lily had come to him previously with her concerns. Did Lily go to confession? Did she confess that she hated Blair, that she was worried the devil was polluting her son? Blair's mind played through a variety of scripts.

At the end of the conversation, Father Donovan looked at Blair.

"Yes, Blair is here now. Tell Andrew he has nothing to worry about. She's in good hands. Yeah, alright. Okay. See you soon, Lily."

Father Donovan hung up the phone with a smile. "Andrew and his mother are on their way."

"Oh, God…" Blair said, sick to her stomach again.

"It's going to be fine," Father Donovan reassured her, coming over and placing both hands on her shoulders to steady her. "Sister Eugene, would you mind taking Blair to the lounge and seeing what we have to eat? I imagine she's very hungry."

Feed the poor and the hungry. Of course.

If Blair hadn't been sure about her belief in God before, she was sure of it now—and maybe not entirely in him, her, *it*, whatever, but she could be sure of the people who did believe with all their might. She could believe in his most faithful servants.

And even if God didn't exist, Father Donovan and Sister Eugene had dedicated their entire lives to serving him, his people, his children. If ever there was a moment Blair when felt deeply rooted in and connected to her faith, it was now.

That had to count for something.

Chapter 52

Never Again

Andrew couldn't get to St. Michael's fast enough. He had seen how his mother looked and responded with Father Donovan on the phone, somehow confirming his worst fears without any details.

His mother followed behind him in her car, so she could leave for work afterward. Typically at this time, Andrew would be picking Blair up at home. But not today.

Lily had ended her cell phone call with a look of concern and confusion. She informed Andrew that Father Donovan said there was a situation with Blair that he needed her help with, but he would not discuss it over the phone. Andrew knew without a doubt that it had to do with her parents.

Pulling into the church parking lot, Andrew was annoyed that Lily was taking her sweet time parking. He couldn't get to Blair fast enough.

As Lily locked her car doors, Andrew was speed-walking to the rectory reception area, then broke into a run. He didn't have time to wait for Lily as he swung the doors open.

Oddly, Father Donovan was sitting where Sister Eugene usually sat.

If It All Fades Away

"Andrew," he greeted him, standing up.

Andrew couldn't focus on anything but the absence of Blair.

"Blair is getting something to eat with Sister Eugene," Father Donovan said, noticing his tension and frantic scanning of the empty room. Just then, Lily came in through the double doors. Father Donovan gave her a warm smile and a nod. "Why don't you both have a seat?" he offered.

Lily seemed put off at first, not that that would be obvious to anyone but Andrew; he knew when she didn't like to be inconvenienced. Still, she was putting on her best face for Father Donovan.

Once Andrew and Lily were seated, Father Donovan opened again with polite formalities, asking how they were. Andrew didn't have the patience for that. It took all of him not to scream, *"Shut up and just tell me what's going on!"*

As Father Donovan's usual warm smile faded, he began to explain the sight he had come upon that morning, and what Blair had told him.

To say Andrew was devastated would have been an understatement. He was—but most of all, he was *furious*. But not just with Angela. No, he was furious with his mother, too. Because deep down inside, Andrew had known it could eventually come to something like this, but neither Lily nor Henry would hear anything of it.

Andrew gritted his teeth, palming his slacks when he heard that Blair had run for her life.

Father Donovan must have picked up on all of this.

"Andrew, why don't you go down to the lounge? I'm sure Blair would be more than happy to see you. It'll give your mother and me time to speak in private."

Andrew practically leapt out of his chair.

"Down the very end of the hall, to your right," Father Donovan directed.

Andrew couldn't look at Lily—refused to look at her. His worst fears of what could happen to Blair had come full circle —just as he'd suspected, or at least agonized they would. And yet, his mother had ignored his pleas for them to help her. Andrew took off, feeling more rage than satisfaction at knowing he had been right.

Making his way down the carpeted hallway with many closed doors, Andrew was elated to see Blair sitting with a paper plate in front of her, speaking with Sister Eugene.

And when Blair saw him—Blair, who had tried to bully him at first; Blair, who had cried in his arms more times than he could count; Blair, whom he lost his virginity to—that Blair, all of her... When that Blair saw him, the look of relief, shock, and revelation on her face that Andrew was there for her—he wished he could bottle it up and keep it forever, despite the awful circumstances. Because even though he always and forever knew who she was, in that moment, after the worst night of his life, and what he imagined might have been the worst of hers, the look she wore, so many emotions all at once—there were no words. Her face cracked open like a porcelain doll's, the same way it had cracked the first time he told her she was beautiful and asked if they could be together. It was that face, all over again—a homecoming of sorts.

As Blair ran to him with a broken face full of tears, he welcomed her with every fiber of his being, scooping her up in his arms in one swift motion. Andrew couldn't help the tears that spilled from his eyes as he received his Blair. She was here; she was *alive*. Angela hadn't killed her. She was still breathing; she was still here.

She is still with me.

"Andrew!" she cried as he lifted her clean off her feet.

"I know," he cried, breathing life and love into her neck and hair.

Andrew vaguely felt Sister Eugene turning around in her seat, smiling gently.

Andrew rocked Blair in his arms, her feet still dangling as she cried, and he cried with her.

"I'll give you two kids a moment," Sister Eugene said with a smile as she walked past them.

Andrew took in all of Blair, her hair and body scent, how she felt against him, and how light she was. The moment he heard the door close behind him, he couldn't help it—he started sobbing himself.

Together, he and Blair sobbed as he guided them to the floor. And there, in the rectory lunch lounge, Andrew and Blair cried, a mess of tears and hugs and kisses on the white tiled floor.

"Andrew," Blair sobbed.

"I got you," he said, pushing her hair back while she lay on top of him. "I've always got you." *I've always had you.*

He felt Blair's whole body shudder as she sobbed into his embrace once more. Andrew wrapped his arms around her even harder, squeezing tighter, letting her know that no matter what, he would never let her go. Never again would he let her slip away.

Not for as long as he lived.

Chapter 53

Psychosomatic

When Andrew and Blair came out of the rectory lounge and back down to the reception area, Sister Eugene was sitting at her desk. Father Donovan and Lily were now speaking privately in his office.

Sister Eugene made small talk with them for a while. She called the school office to tell them where Blair and Andrew were. And then she resumed typing up whatever she was working on, scuffling around here and there, talking to herself rather humorously, occasionally answering the phone. A mailman came to deliver a package at one point.

Finally, Lily and Father Donovan emerged from his office. Andrew could tell she had been crying. It was evident from how she was wiping her nose, her eyes still a bit red.

"How are you, dear?" Lily asked Blair.

Blair looked up from beneath long lashes. "I'm fine," she said shyly.

Andrew could tell something had dramatically shifted during Lily's time with Father Donovan.

"Andrew, are you planning on going to school today?"

If It All Fades Away

Lily asked. "Or did you want to take Blair back home to our place? I imagine she's exhausted and would like to take a shower and get some sleep in an actual bed."

Lily surely had to have known the obvious answer to her question, but Andrew tried to hide his wide eyes when she offered to let him skip school to be with Blair.

"I'll take her home," Andrew said, standing up.

Blair stood, too, head lowered. Andrew could tell she still wasn't comfortable with Lily, but her shoulders had relaxed somewhat.

"We'll inform the office and let them know the circumstances of your absences for the day," Father Donovan said with a smile. "I'll contact Amelia Holland for you both, too. I understand she's been of great help recently."

Andrew nodded.

"Thank you very much," Blair said to Sister Eugene and Father Donovan. "For everything."

"Of course, dear," Sister Eugene said, smiling. "Go and get some rest."

Lily walked over to Andrew and hugged him. So much was communicated in it. "I have to head into work after this, but text me when you get home, okay?"

"Okay," Andrew said, hugging her more firmly in return.

She understood. She was committed to helping.

Lily sniffled and straightened herself as he pulled away, turning to regard Blair.

"Blair, dear, I'm very, very sorry for everything that's happened to you. And I just want you to know, we will do everything we can to help you. I understand you're close with your aunt Natalie?"

Blair nodded.

"We would like to be in touch with her, to try to help

figure out what our next steps should be. But in the meantime, you're welcome to stay with us."

Blair swallowed, and Andrew felt his own throat get tight. Lily then wrapped her arms around Blair, who softly returned the embrace.

"I don't have my phone," Blair said quietly. "I'll have to message her online."

"Don't worry about contacting her right now, just get some rest, okay?" Lily stroked Blair's face.

Then she gave Andrew a final hug. "I love you," she said.

"I love you, too, Mom."

Walking to the reception doors, Andrew gave Blair his coat. As they were making their way out, Andrew held the door open for Blair, and he looked back to see Father Donovan put his hand on Lily's shoulder.

"It's going to be alright," he said.

Andrew saw his mother look down, bringing her hand to her mouth as her face crinkled with tears.

Andrew felt his eyes droop at seeing his mother so vulnerable. Then he felt guilty, because it all had to have been a lot lately—the move, her new job, Dad's new job, Andrew at a new school, the situation with Blair that had steadily escalated over time. It was then that Andrew realized his mother must attend confession, based on how close she and Father Donovan seemed.

"Andrew...?" Blair asked.

Andrew turned his head and let the door go. He would have time to talk to his mother later that evening. "I'm coming."

The sun was shining, melting the snow. Andrew got into the car with Blair. He turned to look at her, then reached over and grabbed her face with both hands, kissing her deeply again.

If It All Fades Away

Blair smiled with glassy eyes, her cheeks smooshed.

* * *

Blair felt like a new person after she showered, washing the night before off of herself. She looked in the mirror and grimaced at the bruises left behind from where Angela had strangled her and dug her manicured nails into her neck.

Wrapping herself in a towel, she stepped out into the guest room.

Andrew was lying atop the bed.

"You feel better?" he asked.

"A lot better."

She looked over to the dresser where she had gotten pajamas once before. "May I?" she asked.

"Of course."

Blair opened the drawers and pulled out a top and a pair of shorts, just like she had done before. She glanced over her shoulder at Andrew, then dropped her towel.

Andrew looked visibly unnerved.

Blair slowly slid on the top she'd picked out, not bothering to button it, then sensually slipped on the shorts she had worn once before. Crawling into the bed, Blair was on Andrew before he had time to contemplate what was happening.

Clothes were off with little effort, and before Blair knew it, Andrew was kissing her lips, her bruised neck, her collarbone—all of her.

They made love in the best way possible.

Together, they were crying again, just as they had done earlier.

"I love you so, so much," Andrew sobbed into her shoulder.

"I love you, too," Blair replied, her voice cracking. Only then did it hit her: she was *finally* free and safe. "I love you so much," she sobbed.

Together, they lay there—crying, kissing, clinging to each other.

Shortly after, they fell asleep.

Blair had never felt so safe, so relieved in her life. Now she knew that she was finally, *finally* free of Angela Simons.

* * *

Andrew awoke around 2:00 p.m. with Blair still beside him.

He sat up, completely disoriented to all that had occurred. He had forgotten to text Lily. He reached over to the bedside table opposite Blair's. There were a few texts from her. Andrew immediately messaged with apologies and said that everything was fine.

There was an email from Ms. Holland, offering condolences and the like. He saw that Blair had been CCed on the same emails, even though she had no way to access them yet.

Andrew looked over to Blair, who was still sleeping soundly. Suddenly, his stomach growled. It was well past lunchtime. He leaned over, kissed Blair's forehead, and crawled out of bed.

Andrew made himself something to eat. Unsure of what to do with himself when he was supposed to be in school, he also fixed Blair's lunch. However, when he brought it up to her, she batted him away and rolled over. He decided to put it in a container and save it for later.

Andrew was downstairs, doing homework from one of his books, until he heard a strange noise. He went to investigate immediately.

"Blair?" he called.

If It All Fades Away

She was throwing up in the guest room toilet. He rushed to her side immediately. "Blair!" Andrew shouted in shock.

"Don't touch me," she barked, then lurched, throwing up what little she must have eaten with Sister Eugene.

"Blair…" Andrew said again, softly.

"I'm fine," she said, then vomited some more. "I'm *fine*."

* * *

When Lily came home early to see Blair, she ran all of her usual nursing diagnostics.

"Andrew," she said to him.

He left the room with his mother. She looked nothing short of exhausted.

"Everything she's experiencing is psychosomatic," she informed him.

Andrew shook his head, as if he hearing that term for the first time.

"She's going to be fine," Lily said, pulling him into an unexpected hug. "She's safe now, you hear me?" Andrew's throat caught. "She's just purging all that shit she's been holding in all this time."

Andrew nodded.

"I'll be downstairs. Your father will be home soon," she informed him.

"No…" Andrew protested.

"You don't have to worry about any of that," Lily said sharply into his shoulder. "Everything's going to be okay, you hear me?"

Andrew and his mother rocked together in the hallway.

"Okay," he said.

Pulling away, Lily looked up at Andrew. "I do have one

request, though," she said. "Is there any way we can contact her aunt, Natalie?"

Natalie.

Of course. Andrew was friends with her on social media. He could reach out to her—the only real family Blair had that was worth a damn.

Chapter 54

One Day

"Hey, cauliflower," a voice said.

Blair rolled over and could hardly believe her eyes. It was Natalie.

The room was dark, but the hallway lights of the Stormant residence were enough to illuminate everything. Blair sat up and threw her arms around her aunt.

"What time is it?" she asked.

"Almost ten. I left as soon as Andrew and his mother got a hold of me."

"He told you what happened?"

"His mother did when she called me. I… I'm so sorry, Blair. There's—there's not enough words to describe how I'm feeling at the moment."

"Where is Andrew now?" Blair asked.

"He's downstairs with his mom and dad."

"I can't go back there," Blair said immediately, shaking her head. "I can't!"

"No one in their right mind would expect that. I know you don't feel the greatest, but we'll sort this out. Luckily, I have flexibility with my job to be here for at least a few days."

"God, I don't even know how it all happened! She just—lost her mind about that pervert John that's she's been screwing. I didn't even do anything wrong," Blair muttered.

Natalie looked down into her lap.

Blair looked up at her. "So, you knew?"

"They've been a thing since you were a baby, unfortunately. I didn't talk to her for almost a year when I found out."

"What about the other time?" Blair asked, a little too quickly.

Natalie sighed. "There's actually been a few times. But the last one was when we got into a fight about how she 'disciplined' you. We can talk about it more another time. For now, I need to speak with Andrew's parents. I'll come back up to see you when we're done." There was a pause as Natalie looked around. "Quite the place they got here, eh?"

Blair laughed softly. "Yeah."

"They showed me where I'll be sleeping, and I tried not to laugh."

Blair smiled. "It's obscene."

"I'll be back, but I'm going to talk to them now, okay?" Natalie said.

"Can you let Andrew know I'd like to see him?" Blair asked.

"Of course," Natalie said, kissing her forehead. "I planned on sending him up anyway."

* * *

When Natalie came downstairs, Andrew was sitting at the kitchen table with Henry and Lily.

"Andrew," she said at the kitchen entrance. "Blair asked to see you."

"How's she feeling?" he asked.

"She's exhausted. Do you have something like Vernor's or Sprite to give her to drink? That always helped when she was younger."

Andrew stood to get Blair a drink. Natalie was at the table now.

"Oh, and Andrew?"

"Yeah?"

"I'll need some time alone with your parents, if you don't mind."

"Yeah, no problem," Andrew said. He filled a glass with ice and then scurried off.

At the top of the stairs, he held the can of Sprite in one hand and the glass in the other. He paused, debating whether he should just mind his own damn business, or eavesdrop. He wanted to know what his parents and Natalie were going to discuss. He hoped it wouldn't be Blair leaving with her. God, he hoped not. He worried that that was what his parents were going to suggest. His heart thudded. He could just make out what was being said, the voices carrying through the formal dining room. He carefully sat down, then placed the can and glass far enough behind him that he wouldn't accidentally knock them over.

"I'm terribly sorry to hear about Blair's behavior towards Andrew," Natalie said.

Andrew's stomach sank. He had messaged Natalie online, but Lily had spoken to her on the phone in her bedroom. Andrew hadn't thought anything of it, but now he realized that his mother had told Natalie *everything* that had happened, not just the situation with Angela.

"I almost screamed when I saw him," Lily said. "I was so angry at her, but... I—*we* ... we just didn't want Andrew to get in over his head and lose focus on his priorities."

"No, of course not," Natalie said. "He's a very bright and wonderful young man."

"Thank you," Lily said humbly.

"I haven't talked to Blair yet, but I'm not quite ready for her to come to Chicago. I'm still remodeling the spare bedroom and trying to get it ready for her. Plus, with her so close to graduating, it really doesn't make sense for her to transfer now."

"We know how hard that can be," Henry said, his deeper voice more easily heard. "Andrew has always been resilient, but it was a huge transition for him to leave so close to the end of school when Lily accepted her job here with the university."

"Last I heard from Blair, she hasn't gotten any word from Columbia. I imagine Andrew's acceptance may take a little longer than hers, correct?"

"Yes, though he's already been accepted to a few other universities," Lily said, reminding Natalie that he had options.

Andrew only had one option in his mind, as far as he was concerned, and it involved Blair.

The conversation carried on. Henry and Lily mentioned how torn Andrew had been for a while about what he wanted to do. Natalie noted that Blair had always enjoyed writing and movies. They then discussed Chicago. Natalie reiterated the conversation she'd had with Andrew and Blair during their Black Friday lunch.

"Well, I plan to let Blair stay with me, but should Andrew need someplace while he searches for an apartment, I do have a pull-out couch." Natalie laughed.

"That's very kind of you to offer," Lily said. "Andrew would have to apartment-hunt anyway, so it may save him

If It All Fades Away

some money if he doesn't have to stay in a hotel. I'll mention it to him."

"In the meantime, like we discussed on the phone, I'd be happy to pay for Blair to stay here until she and Andrew can come to Chicago."

"That won't be necessary," Henry said.

Andrew's heart was beating faster now—not from fear, but excitement. Finally, he was going to get what he wanted.

"Please," Natalie said. "It's not a problem."

There was more talk about the logistics of what Blair would require to move into their home.

"I'll be calling my sister first thing tomorrow morning. See what we can get out of the house."

"Please be safe," Lily said.

"I don't plan to speak to her ever again after this," Natalie said matter-of-factly. "I'll make sure we have police present, just in case. I wouldn't put anything past her, especially at this point."

There was a tense silence.

"She's done a lot of damage to our whole family through the years. I've always hung on and come back around for Blair, but this... If I didn't think it would stress Blair out even more, I'd be taking her down to file a police report right away to press charges against her mother. But then again, Angela's got that attorney she works for up her sleeve—the same one who helped her win custody against my parents when Blair was a baby."

Wait—what?

"That must have been very difficult for them," Lily offered.

"Angela was so young at the time. She and Blair's father left Blair alone when she was six months old, and the neighbors heard her crying for hours and eventually called the police. However, John Turner helped her get an excellent defense attorney, and she won. I was going to college in Chicago at the time, so I couldn't be around as much as I should have been, but it devastated my parents. Angela and I didn't speak to each other for almost a year."

"Oh," Lily said, sounding truly sympathetic.

"Andrew?" Blair asked, standing at the door.

Andrew startled and turned back to look at her immediately. He brought his finger to his lips, then stood quietly. He picked up the can of Sprite and glass of ice.

"Hey," he said to Blair, kissing her forehead.

"Eavesdropping?" Blair asked with a sheepish grin, stepping back inside the room.

"Yeah." Andrew laughed. "Sorry, I'm not normally nosy like that, but I wanted to hear the game plan."

Blair crawled back into the bed. "And?"

Andrew sat at the edge of the bed. "It sounds like your aunt will try to have you stay here until we can go to Chicago."

Blair didn't seem as happy as Andrew at that news.

"I can't afford to pay rent," she said grimly.

"My mom and dad told Natalie no when she offered to pay for you to stay here, but she seemed insistent. I'm sure they'll work that out somehow."

Blair stared off, her arms on top of the blanket. Andrew placed the glass of ice on the nightstand, then opened the can of Sprite, emptying it inside.

"Gotta stay hydrated," he said, handing her the glass.

Blair took it, her mind clearly off someplace else, then slowly drank.

"Holy shit." She closed her eyes after the first gulp. "I didn't realize how thirsty I was!" She took another drink.

"Are you hungry at all?"

If It All Fades Away

Blair shook her head furiously. "No. God, no. Don't even mention food right now."

"Sorry," Andrew said. "If you do get hungry, just let me know."

Blair nodded. "Will you be able to sleep in here tonight?"

Andrew glanced at the door, as if an invisible Henry or Lily were standing there. "No, I can't," he said.

Blair's eyes lowered to her glass.

"But that's not to say I can't sneak in and out of here to visit you for a bit."

Blair smiled, and Andrew leaned forward to plan a flat kiss against her lips.

"Sorry, I don't want you to taste my mouth right now." Blair laughed.

Andrew brushed her hair behind her ear. After Blair's thirst seemed to be satiated, she placed the glass on the nightstand.

"Scoot over," Andrew said playfully. Blair lifted the blanket and let him slide in next to her. She slipped into his arms easily, and the two lay together, warm and comfortable.

Andrew pulled Blair in a little tighter and closer, and she made a small, breathy noise against him. He looked down, while she looked up at him. She looked relaxed, with a small smile that was beginning to show color again.

Blair wasn't as enthusiastic as Andrew; she was too worried about being a burden, something Andrew knew was deeply ingrained into her psyche from her parents, especially Angela. But eventually, Blair would see and understand that she wasn't a burden. In time, with the right help, love, care, and kindness—and all that Andrew had to give and would continue to give—Blair would one day see that she was worth the world.

***

It was very late when Natalie jostled Andrew's shoulder. Lily was at the door. Andrew groggily pried himself from Blair's embrace and reached the threshold.

"If you need anything," Lily said quietly, "just let us know."

"I will," Natalie said.

Andrew stood with Lily as she closed the door, leaving it ajar.

"You going to bed?" Andrew asked.

Lily looked completely and utterly spent. "I was just going to sit in front of the fireplace for a bit. Your father went to bed about an hour ago."

Andrew wordlessly followed his mother downstairs to the living room. The two sat in silence as they watched the fire burn. Andrew moved to put another log in it.

After the flames' hypnosis finally waned, he spoke to Lily, who was sitting nearby with a blanket over her legs.

"I'm sorry," Andrew began.

Lily turned to look at him, a soft, closed-mouth smile on her face. "For what, dear?"

"For being so mad at you and Dad. For not being more sensitive to everything you've been going through."

"You're not insensitive, Andrew," Lily said. "Quite the opposite, actually."

Andrew readjusted in his recliner, watching the flames dance on his mother's face. She managed another small smile. "You feel things so intensely sometimes—just like all the men in our family. It just worries me, is all."

Andrew said nothing as he turned to regard the flames once more. "What's going to happen now?" he asked, even though he already knew—or hoped he knew—the answer.

If It All Fades Away

"Natalie plans to call her sister tomorrow. See if she can get her to agree to let her and Blair go to the house to get her things."

Andrew looked at Lily, waiting for the next part.

"I don't want you to get too excited—because I want you to remember to stay focused for this last semester—but we've agreed with Natalie to let Blair stay here for the rest of the school year and the summer, until she can move to Chicago with her."

It was music to Andrew's ears.

"Thank you," he said quietly.

Lily managed a weary smile. "You're welcome, dear."

She closed her eyes briefly, as if to rest them to fight off the need to sleep.

"Mom?"

"Yes?" she said, snapping back awake instantly.

"It's okay," Andrew said. "You can go to bed now."

"Oh," Lily said, realizing she had dozed off. "Yes, I suppose I should."

Andrew stood up as she did. She came over and placed a hand on his face.

"Someday, all of this will be a memory." She let her hand brush down his face. "Now you two can move forward—together or apart. Blair's safe now."

Andrew's throat caught, his eyes glassy. He and his mother embraced.

Shortly after, Andrew went to sleep with Blair, staying with her all night and all morning, never leaving her side.

Chapter 55

Epilogue

"*Blair.*"

When Blair opened her eyes, it was nighttime. They'd been driving for a while, and she must have fallen asleep.

"Look," Andrew said with a nod.

Blair turned to her right to look out the window. She gasped.

Chicago.

Lit up brilliantly in the night sky. Consuming all that she could see. The buildings were spectacular in blue, yellow, and black hues. One was even lit up in red and blue. There was a diamond-shaped one, and others fading in and out as they drove closer. Blair recognized the Willis Tower from movies.

"Oh, Andrew!" she cried.

She looked over at him to see him smiling, his eyes glimmering. The water of Lake Michigan reflected the lights in rippling darkness. The sight was better than anything Blair could have ever imagined. It was mid-August, and the summer heat was upon them. Blair rolled down the window and stuck her head out like a dog. For once, feeling like an animal wasn't such a bad thing. She let the wind whip the tears from her face as she smiled and cried.

As Blair continued to take in the buildings, larger than anything she had ever seen, she smelled the air and listened to the sound of the tires and the other cars roaring around them as they approached the city. Blair had only ever seen places like New York, LA, and Chicago on a small television her whole life. Now she was here.

They were going to Natalie's. They were both going to start college in less than two weeks. Blair couldn't wrap her head around any of it. It was happening—*it was really happening*.

Blair felt Andrew's hand reach over to hers. She turned to look at him, bringing her head back in slightly, her hair still thrashing about from the summer night. Andrew threaded his large fingers between Blair's, and she held him there, squeezing tightly. As the lights and buildings continued to come closer and closer into view, Andrew gave her a gentle shake.

"We did it, Blair."

"Yeah." Her voice cracked. She looked at Andrew, tears of joy streaming down her face. They weren't into the thickest part of traffic yet; they wouldn't die if Andrew looked away for a moment, which made Blair laugh.

"Look at me," she said.

Blair leaned in and planted a kiss on his lips.

"We did it, Andrew."

He pulled away, tears in his eyes, matching hers.

"We did it," he repeated, and Blair said it once more with him.

We made it.

* * *

It was hot, but not unbearable.

Rachel was buzzing about, as was Natalie, helping Blair. Rachel's sister, Rebecca, was spraying hairspray into her hair, complaining about the heat making it frizzy. Blair's hair was in an updo, not unlike how it was for the Winter Wonderland Dance and prom. She mused that once again, at the end of the night, she'd have a mountain's worth of bobby pins to remove.

Lily knocked lightly at the door, then stepped into the room, informing Blair that Andrew was a nervous wreck. Andrew had always suffered from anxiety, but today at least, he had a legitimate reason to be nervous.

"It's almost time, dear," she said.

Blair exhaled shakily.

Natalie helped Blair into her heels. Rachel continued to fuss about how her boobs looked in her dress. Natalie remarked that they looked fantastic. Rebecca cracked a joke about Julian motorboating them at the night's end.

As everyone left the room, a final knock came at the door.

"Come in," Blair said meekly.

It was Henry. He smiled. "You ready, kid?"

Blair exhaled one last time. "As ready as I'll ever be."

Arm in arm, Henry walked Blair down the aisle. The cathedral was beautiful, with stained-glass windows, polished oak pews, and tile flooring that made Blair's heels click. Andrew was waiting for her at the altar with the priest, a white rose corsage on his lapel. When Blair saw Andrew crying, she started crying. He looked incredible in a suit, as always.

Blair looked around. She saw Ms. Holland with her wife. She hadn't seen her since high school graduation, but they'd stayed in touch. She had left St. Michael's after Blair's graduating class, noting she had had "enough shit." Father

If It All Fades Away

Donovan couldn't make it, but he'd sent a lovely card. He also noted that Sister Eugene would have been proud of her and Andrew. (She had passed away two years after they left for Chicago.)

As Blair got closer to the altar, she thought about her parents. She'd never thought it would happen, but she felt sorry for both of them. They were missing out on something special. She had grieved them for a long time, and maybe she would never stop grieving them, but the pain became less as time went on. Instead, Blair decided to be thankful to everyone who had helped her over the years.

As Blair and Andrew spoke their vows to each other, Blair thought about everything they were leaving behind and all that they were welcoming ahead. They kissed and embraced to thunderous applause.

* * *

Blair had several significant breakthroughs in therapy, and one particular milestone when she wrote a letter to her parents. She had been no-contact for three years at that point, and intended to remain that way for the rest of her life. Sometimes, she wondered if she had made the right choice. But then Blair remembered what Natalie had told her about baby Blair, crying for hours and hours, all alone, helpless. She remembered child Blair being spanked, pinched, and yelled at, forced to stay in her room for days on end sometimes. And then she remembered seventeen-year-old Blair—her father hurting her, and her mother's hand at her throat, scissors at the ready. It was enough to assure her that she had made the right choice.

As Blair read the letter she would never send her parents to her therapist, she cried all over the paper and smudged the ink. She blubbered and sobbed, and started yelling at one point, then started whimpering, until finally, she was quiet.

I just wish I could understand what I did wrong to make you hate me. But then, I realized over time, what you guys did—and didn't do, to or for me—ultimately had nothing to do with me at all in the first place. And I can't decide what's more painful: that I was never considered, or that you two were children who never grew up.

Were the pictures of you smiling with me as a child all a lie?

Mom, you loved smiling over me when there was an audience, but as soon as the curtains closed, you'd become a monster. I'll never get the satisfaction of seeing you exposed someday for being the narcissistic demon that you are, but I'm proud to say—I don't wait for that day anymore. Because just being you must be its own special kind of hell. And that, to me, is punishment enough.

Blair said her goodbyes in her letter, which reminded her of when she, Natalie, Andrew, and the police had gone to her home to retrieve her belongings, when she had said her less-than-satisfying goodbye. But maybe that was the point—there were no satisfying goodbyes in such an awful situation.

Blair remembered how Angela had sat on the sofa with her arms crossed like a petulant child, refusing to interact with anyone. She kept her answers short and sweet with the police, trying to act like everything was okay, because she knew them from the courthouse.

Blair's dress was still on the floor from a few days prior. They made a few trips out of the house with her books, movies, clothing, and the box from the basement with Blair's name on it. Natalie communicated with Angela about the whereabouts of all legal documents. She also asked for Blair's phone, which Angela reluctantly handed over.

One police officer was on the porch when Blair stopped to look at her mother. Andrew was behind her, followed by Natalie and the other police officer.

Blair found the words she finally needed to say:

"I'm glad I'll never have to see you again for as long as I live."

Angela gritted her teeth, and Blair knew it was taking all of her not to let the monster show. She still refused to look at Blair, which was fine by her. Andrew gave Blair a reassuring touch on her shoulder, and then they were off.

Natalie was the last one to leave. It was a moment. And Blair and Andrew were out on the porch as it happened.

"You know," Natalie said, looking at her sister. "I've thought of every variation of this conversation in some capacity for the last decade or more, and it always ends the same: there's literally no other words I can think of. And I know I speak for all of us who have ever dared to love you when I say: Go fuck yourself, Angie."

The police officer guided Natalie out the door, and Blair was both proud and horrified, because for once, Angela wasn't going to get the last word. She couldn't—because she didn't want to look unhinged in front of the police officers she knew. Blair would later smile at that, knowing that none of them would have to endure what Blair had lived with her whole life ever again.

Blair never got to say goodbye to her father. He was absent that day, just as he had usually been. Blair thought about sending him a text message or something, and she half hoped and half dreaded that he would eventually send her one, too. But he never did.

For the rest of the school year, Henry and Lily treated Blair as if she were their own child. It was all too much. They took her horseback riding with Andrew for spring break, and camping in the summer. Andrew arranged for a small surprise birthday party for her eighteenth birthday at the restaurant he had taken her to before they went to see *Seven* at the old movie theater. There were pointy hats and heart balloons, Julian and Rachel, Natalie (who came back for a day to celebrate), and Henry and Lily. It was perfect. Andrew even gifted Blair an absolutely *obscene* cushion-cut emerald necklace. She had never been happier, surrounded by the people who loved her—by the people *she* loved.

* * *

When Blair and Andrew were strong enough from their individual therapy—Andrew going for his intense anxiety, perfectionism, and need to be the savior and fixer in his life—they went together, to learn how to communicate better, how to heal from the wild ride of their senior year in high school, and most importantly, how to move forward as a couple.

Andrew shook one day as he told Blair that he couldn't put up with violence in his life. And that, while it was only one incident back in high school, what had happened to him ultimately wasn't okay. He cried, saying he now understood how grabbing her arms was a trigger for her, but should something like that happen again, he couldn't stay with her. It was a new boundary for both of them.

Blair cried as well, apologizing and saying that he didn't deserve any of that or how she'd behaved, and that she'd had no idea about how her trauma manifested itself at

If It All Fades Away

the time. She apologized for trying to hurt him with Hudson, explaining that she hadn't realized how she sometimes acted like her mother, weaponizing silence and manipulation as a means of control over those she was supposed to love.

Blair had plenty of sessions where she agonized over all the ways she had hurt people through the years, including those she bullied and those she stole stuff from. She realized that it wasn't okay, even if they were rich. She also realized that while she had hurt Andrew and others, she was different from her parents—particularly Angela—in that she felt remorse for her actions. She was different in that she was willing to admit something was wrong with her. She was different in that she wanted to heal. Blair finally understood that someone like her mother would never improve, because she refused to see anything wrong with herself.

Ultimately, Blair promised Andrew that she would never do anything like that to him ever again, no matter how upset she was. Together, they agreed that violence had no place or future in their lives, including in how they would raise their children. Blair knew it was going to be hard, but she was committed—with the best person beside her—that she would never subject an innocent child to all the things she had been subjected to.

* * *

It was sunny, summertime. Blair was drinking coffee and going over her latest script.

Andrew roused.

"Hey," she said, turning from her desk to look at him.

"Hey," he said.

"You going to want some coffee?"

Andrew stretched out in the bed. "I need a kiss before I need coffee."

Blair groaned playfully, putting the cup down and climbing into bed next to him.

"What do you want to do today?" he asked, pressing his lips to hers.

"It's been a minute since we've done the Shedd Aquarium."

Andrew nodded. "It has, hasn't it?"

"We're not meeting Natalie until six. Could go and come back. Enough time to shower and change." Blair snuggled into his chest.

"Sounds good. How's your script coming?"

"It's almost done—then I'll have you take a look at it before I let the others read it."

"Always good to get a second and third opinion," Andrew said, kissing her forehead, then her lips, slowly working his way down. He pushed her oversized T-shirt up.

"I didn't know tummy kisses were also required before coffee, Dr. Stormant."

"The charts just came in; the patient needs it immediately," he said, blowing a raspberry on her stomach.

Blair laughed. "And what else does the patient need?"

Andrew moved back up to kiss her lips.

"Mrs. Stormant," he said. "Let the good doctor show you."

Blair laid her head back as Andrew kissed her and kissed her.

The sunlight poured in.

And Blair let her husband love her.

Acknowledgments

I want to thank anyone who has taken the time to read this book. This story is near and dear to my heart. For Christine and Kyle, who believed in me no matter what, I love you guys. Thank you to my beta readers: Nichol, Hailey, Betha, and Ericka. Special thank you to my editor, Robin Fuller for making this story shine. Thank you to all my readers on Archive of Our Own who supported this story when it was a Reylo fan fiction. And lastly, thank you to Joanie and Lori for making this book possible by caring for my youngest.

About the Author

A queer, biracial indigenous woman born and raised in Michigan, Myra King spent her youth drawing and crafting stories with her older sister, shaping her personality. She lived in Tokyo, Japan for five years which also influenced her in adulthood. She enjoys spending time with her husband and two boys. *If It All Fades Away* is her debut novel.

instagram.com/myrakingwrites

www.ingramcontent.com/pod-product-compliance
Lightning Source LLC
LaVergne TN
LVHW091701070526
838199LV00050B/2243